POISON ON THE LEVELS

An addictive crime thriller full of twists

DAVID HODGES

Detective Kate Hamblin Mystery Book 7

JOFFE BOOKS

First published 2020
Joffe Books, London
www.joffebooks.com

ISBN 978-1-78931-334-5

*This book is dedicated to my wife, Elizabeth, for her love,
patience and support, and to my late mother and father,
whose faith that I would one day realise my ambition
to be a writer remained steadfast to the end. Their tragic
passing has left a hole in my life that nothing can ever fill.*

BEFORE THE FACT

The girl seated in the corner of the quirky, backstreet café was uneasy, certain that she was being watched. She took another sip of her herbal tea and looked away, but couldn't help her gaze straying back to the man at the table by the door — only to meet a pair of dark, hooded eyes studying her over the top of his mug with unsettling intensity.

She wished now that she had put on the jeans and denim top still folded up inside her rucksack, rather than the very short shorts and skimpy blouse she was wearing, which left her tanned midriff bare. But it had been very hot over the last few days. Furthermore, a lot of the other girls who had headed for the impromptu rave on the Somerset Levels near Mark village after the heady five-day blast at the annual Glastonbury Festival had turned up flashing their navels, so she hadn't thought anything of it. Now, though, in the little café, well away from the rave in-crowd, she felt awkward and vulnerable.

Tammy Logan knew she was attractive to men. She usually enjoyed the admiring glances her glossy, jet black hair and slim, shapely figure received. But the attention she was getting from this particular admirer made her wish, for once, that she was invisible.

Even looking at this chinless creep with the pink baseball cap gave her the shivers.

If only Tony would come. She glanced at her wristwatch. Another fifteen minutes, that's all the time he had left. Then she was off to the railway station and out of his life for good. She had just enough money left for the fare back to Birmingham. No hitching this time. She had made all this perfectly clear in the note she had pinned to the tent before grabbing her haversack and hitching a lift from the rave site, leaving him sleeping off the previous night's skinful. He knew exactly where the café was in Highbridge — they had both had a snack there when the lorry driver dropped them off from the M5 motorway before the main festival nearly a week ago — so he had no excuse for not turning up. "Be there before ten thirty," she had warned in her note, "or you and I are history." In short, it was either her or the cheap little slapper he had shacked up with. His choice.

She wiped a tear away with the back of her hand. She still didn't understand why she had given him another chance at all. She should have simply dumped him and gone. That was what he deserved. But despite everything, she was still besotted with the arsehole — always had been — and they had been together for over a year, longer than any of her previous boyfriends. She sniffed. She was just a born victim, one of those sad creatures who, however badly they are treated, always come back for more. She couldn't help herself. And it wasn't the first time she had been humiliated by him in this way. Tony had done the same sort of thing to her several times before, always promising that this time was the last. Trouble with Tony was that he kept his brains in his crotch and he seemed incapable of turning down anything that was on offer. The bastard!

She took another sip of her tea and found her gaze wandering back to the table by the door. The creep was still there, toying with his mug and staring straight at her. She saw his lips curl into a smirk and tore her eyes away for the second or third time, focusing instead on the street outside.

'Come on, Tony,' she found herself muttering and glanced at her watch again. Ten more minutes, then it was the railway station and the next train to Taunton.

She scanned the street for the familiar figure but there was no sign of him — just groups of other festival-goers making their way homeward along the main Bridgwater Road.

A shadow cut across the sunlight streaming into the café from the end window and she turned quickly. The creep in the pink baseball cap pulled out the chair opposite her, transferred her rucksack to the table and sat down.

'Mind if I joins you, darlin'?' he said in a high-pitched, effeminate voice. 'You looks lonely.'

She felt her skin crawl. 'That — that chair's taken,' she bluffed, putting on a brave front. 'My boyfriend will be here in a few minutes.'

He grinned, exposing discoloured teeth. 'Takin' him long enough, ain't it?' he went on, his gaze fixed hungrily on her cleavage. 'You shouldn't be wanderin' about on your own dressed like that.'

'How I dress is my business,' she snapped, her indignation surfacing in a rush.

He wiped his nose with the back of his hand and sniffed. 'Yeah, but some fellers could get the wrong idea an' that.'

Anger flared inside her. 'Just piss off, will you, you freak!' she blazed.

His smile was replaced by a scowl. 'Rude little bitch, ain't yer?' he said. 'Maybe someone ought to teach you some manners.'

She glanced quickly around the café. There were half a dozen people sitting at the plastic tables — men as well as women — but although several of them looked up, showing mild interest, their attention quickly turned back to their breakfasts and their newspapers and no one chose to intervene. Typical.

She was on the point of getting up to leave when the peroxide-blonde middle-aged woman who had served her the tea earlier appeared beside the table, a cleaning cloth in one hand and a couple of dirty mugs in the other.

'You okay, love?' she asked. 'Is he bothering you?'

Tammy nodded. 'I — I just want to be left alone,' she said, her voice faltering.

'And so you shall be, love.' The waitress glared at her uninvited guest and jerked her head towards the door. 'Sling your hook, Mickey,' she snapped.

'Come on, Marfa,' he replied. 'I ain't finished me coffee yet.'

Martha's face hardened. 'Ring the police, Frank,' she called over her shoulder to the thin, balding man behind the counter. 'Tell 'em Mickey Bishop is back causing trouble.'

There was an abrupt change in the "freak's" demeanour and he held up both hands in front of him in a defensive gesture. 'Okay, okay, keep your wig on. I'm goin'.'

Returning to his table he picked up his mug, drained the contents and pushed through the door, back out into the street.

Tammy treated Martha to a smile. 'Thanks. He was becoming a real pain.'

Martha emitted a short laugh. 'Mickey always is. But don't worry, he's harmless.'

Tammy looked out of the window and saw her tormentor leaning against a shopfront on the opposite side of the road, smoking a cigarette and staring in her direction.

'Is — is there another way out of here?' she asked.

Martha nodded. 'Past the toilets,' she said. 'Come on, I'll show you.'

Sunlight flooded the backstreet outside the emergency exit and, to her relief, Tammy saw that it was deserted.

Martha pointed. 'That way will take you back to the main road. Will you be okay now?'

Tammy nodded. 'I should be just in time to catch the twelve thirty-two to Taunton.'

But Tammy Logan would not actually board the Taunton train — or any other train for that matter. Within minutes of her stepping out into the street, she simply vanished into the sun-dappled shadows, to become just another statistic among the multitude of persons recorded in police files as ‘missing’.

CHAPTER 1

Peter Jackson woke late to a normal Sunday morning in the weathered stone cottage on the edge of the Somerset Levels where he had lived for close on twenty years. The sun was shining through the thin, closed curtains, the bells in the village church were ringing and his elderly neighbour was once more mowing his lawn with the old-fashioned cylinder mower he always used.

Throwing back the single sheet, he felt for his slippers. It was going to be a good day, a day for doing stuff, a day when it was great to be alive. He smiled to himself. Maybe he could give the car a good clean — not that it really needed it — or mow the lawns, once he and Helen were back from church.

He was still wondering what to do first when he went downstairs to put the kettle on, whistling *Greensleeves*. But the large envelope lying on the mat inside the front door was to change all that — though he certainly didn't expect it to when he bent down to pick it up. Addressed in typed block capitals to *"Peter Jackson Esq"* and marked *"Private and Confidential,"* it obviously hadn't been delivered by the Royal Mail. It did not carry a stamp. Someone must have pushed it through his letterbox while he and Helen slept. Probably raffle tickets from the golf club or the masonic lodge.

He ripped the envelope open and started to leaf through the contents. He was still standing in the hallway staring at the grinning mouth of the envelope as if transfixed, when he heard the creak of a stair riser behind him.

'Post, Peter?' his wife asked, yawning sleepily. 'On a Sunday?'

Snapping out of his trance, he wheeled round quickly to face her. 'Just — just some bumph from my lodge, dear,' he gulped, clearing his throat. 'John May — Mayhew must have dropped it in on his way to golf.'

She studied him anxiously for a moment. 'Are you feeling okay?' she queried. 'You look ever so pale.'

He forced a smile. 'I'm fine, honestly. Why wouldn't I be?'

'It's just that you seemed so happy when you got up. I could hear you whistling from my room. Have you had another of your turns? Do you want me to get you one of your tablets?'

'I said I'm fine!' he snapped. 'Don't go on!'

She recoiled slightly, evidently taken aback by his sharp tone. 'Okay, okay. Just concerned, that's all.' She turned towards the kitchen, throwing him a puzzled glance over her shoulder. 'I'll get us some breakfast.'

He took the envelope into the study and closed the door to examine the contents of the envelope more thoroughly. The smell of frying bacon wafted into the room from the kitchen and his stomach tightened, though not from hunger.

The message inside the envelope was short, far from sweet, and certainly had nothing to do with his masonic lodge. It was accompanied by half a dozen photographs.

He flicked slowly through them all with trembling fingers, his head swimming and the acid reflux from his duodenal ulcer erupting in a burning spasm in his throat. For a few seconds he was forced to grip the edge of his desk until the agonising pain in his stomach had subsided, gritting his teeth fiercely to stop himself from crying out. The tears now streamed down his face unchecked, not only from the pain, but in contemplation of the loss of everything he held dear. He had been a damned fool, but it was much too late for regret. Much too late for anything.

Regaining some composure in the light of this cold realisation, he carefully tore the photographs and the letter into pieces and dropped them in the wastepaper basket under his desk. Maybe someone would find them later — when it all got out — but by then it wouldn't matter to him anyway.

'Breakfast in five,' his wife called from the kitchen. 'It's hot, so you'd better come.'

He stared at the door, his mouth twisted into a cynical grimace. Breakfast. Oh, what joy that simple word had once evoked. It meant nothing to him now. What was the point? Dead men didn't eat breakfast, did they? And he was as good as dead, even if he was still breathing.

Abruptly, he stood and went to the front door. He made his way slowly down the shingle path at the side of the cottage to the thatched barn, his face a deathly pale and his eyes glazed.

His new BMW X3 was parked in the barn but he walked right past it to the workroom at the back. He opened an unlocked steel cabinet and took out a double-barrelled, side-by-side Purdy shotgun. He loaded it with two cartridges and, settling himself in an old armchair in the corner, rested the shotgun on the floor between his knees. He hesitated for a moment before bending down to insert both barrels into his mouth. Then, closing his eyes, he reached down for the triggers. The last thought that occurred to him before he blew out his brains was what would happen to the Purdy afterwards.

* * *

There was a heated argument in progress when the slender figure of Detective Sergeant Kate Lewis, clad in blue jeans and a sleeveless fawn tunic, pushed through the doors of Highbridge police station to start her morning shift. She frowned. It was the last thing she needed right at that moment. The nauseous throbbing pain in her head from overindulgence at the previous night's CID barbecue was still with her, despite a heavy dose of paracetamol. Her freckled face was noticeably drawn and a lot paler than normal, her blue eyes — usually sparkling with vitality — dull and listless, her auburn, shoulder-length hair not properly combed and lacking its coppery lustre. All she wanted was a dark room and blessed, total oblivion. But it was not to be.

The stocky black man with the dreadlocks was clearly very unhappy with the service he was receiving from the civilian station duty officer on the other side of the polished wooden counter. He was leaning towards him, his head thrust forward aggressively and his face contorted with anger.

'I'm telling you I want this sorted now,' the black man was saying.

The SDO rolled his eyes in exasperation. 'And I'm telling *you* that shouting and banging the counter will get you nowhere. You'll just have to wait until someone is free to see to you.'

The station duty officer lifted his gaze when Kate appeared and gave her a perfunctory nod.

'Morning, Sarge,' he muttered, as she jerked her warrant card from her wallet, ready to insert it into the card reader by the door.

At once the black man wheeled round. 'Sarge?' he queried. 'You a sergeant?'

Kate paused, nodded, wished she hadn't, and winced. 'For my sins, yes,' she said, thrusting her card into the reader.

'Then you're 'is boss, right?'

Kate closed her eyes for a second and gritted her teeth as she tried to hold down a sudden reflux of acid. 'Not exactly. In fact—'

'But you're above him?'

'Technically, I suppose, but what has that—?'

'Well, I wanna make a complaint.'

Kate swallowed the burp developing in her throat and stood for a moment listening to the irritable buzz of the card reader before reluctantly withdrawing her card again and regaining her focus.

'Look, what's all this about?' she asked wearily.

The black man stabbed a forefinger at the station duty officer. 'This guy's a racist.'

'A what?' She swallowed hard again, trying to control her recurring nausea.

'A racist. Won't do noffin' 'cause I'm black.'

Kate groaned inwardly. Not another one pulling the race card to get his own way. She noticed the station duty officer now smirking at her knowingly, and scowled.

'Okay, okay,' she said in just above a whisper. 'You'd better come through.'

Inserting her card into the reader again, she pushed the door open on the familiar buzz and led the way inside.

The waiting room smelled strongly of BO. Resisting the desire to throw up, she opened a window and motioned him to one of several plastic chairs set before a rectangular table.

'Right,' she said again, massaging her left temple with two fingers and squinting against the sunlight streaming into the room. 'What's your name?'

'Tony Samuel.'

'And what's all this about?'

'Me bitch.'

'Your *what*?'

'Me bird. Me girlfriend. She's gone missing.'

'Since when?'

'Yesterday.'

'You mean, she's been missing for just one day? Missing from where exactly?'

'Flat in Birmingham.'

Confused, Kate said, 'Birmingham? So . . . so, why are you reporting it here?'

'We 'itched to Glastonbury for the festival, an' when it packed up, we heard about the rave down the road and went there 'cause it was on the way back to the motorway. We was going to ’itch a lift home. But when I wakes up yesterday morning, she’s upped and scarpered.’

Kate took a deep breath. ‘You mean she walked out on you?’

He shrugged. ‘Yeah, I s’pose . . . We ’ad this row, see, and she left a note pinned to our tent, telling me to be at some bloody caff just down the road — Blue Pixie, that were it — by 11.30 or we was finished and she were catching the train ’ome.’

‘Did you go?’

He shrugged. ‘Nah. I was out of it from the night before, weren’t I? Didn’t get there in time.’

‘So, she’s not actually missing, is she? She’s just walked out on you.’

‘She ain’t gone ’ome. I phoned the flat and the landlady says she ain’t come back, even though all ’er stuff is still there. And as well as that, she ain’t answering ’er mobile.’

‘Well, it sounds to me like she’s simply dumped you, that’s all.’

‘She wouldn’t do that. Been living together for a year now.’

‘So, what was your row about?’

He made a face. ‘She caught me screwing some bird at the rave.’

Kate raised her eyebrows. ‘In which case, I’m not surprised she walked out on you.’

He shook his head. ‘I’ve screwed around before and she never scarpered then.’

Kate took a deep breath, controlling her irritation with an effort.

‘Did you have a physical confrontation?’

‘A what?’

‘Did you hit her?’

He grinned. ‘Not this time.’

‘You’ve hit her before then?’

‘Might have given ’er a slap.’

Nice. 'And how old is this girlfriend of yours?'

'Twenty-four. Guy at the desk said she were old enough and I should leave it a few days before reporting 'er missing. When I said I wanted somefin' done about it right then, 'e said I would have to wait till someone were free to speak to me. Load of bollocks, that. Why couldn't 'e do it? Not like there were a bleedin' queue out there.'

Kate cursed herself for not asking that most important "age" question herself.

'Well, he was quite right in saying that she is regarded as an adult. Going by what you've told me, it doesn't sound as though she's particularly vulnerable or potentially at risk either.'

'So, you lot ain't gonna do noffin' about it then?'

'I didn't say that. Do you *think* she's come to any harm?'

He shrugged. 'Dunno, do I? World's a dodgy place, innit?'

'But you have no specific reason to believe something could have happened to her.'

Another shrug. 'S'pose not, but maybe if I was white, you lot would be more interested.'

Kate bit back the reply that had formed on her tongue.

'Your skin colour has nothing to do with anything,' she said, as evenly as she could manage. 'I will log your report, but you have to understand we have hundreds of reports like this every year and we haven't the resources to treat them all as a priority.'

'And if she's lyin' in a ditch somewhere wiv 'er froat cut?'

Kate hesitated. Even in her hungover state, she felt strangely uneasy. For some inexplicable reason, something was bothering her about this misper, something she couldn't quite put her finger on. A woman's intuition perhaps? Or was it just the colour of this man's skin influencing her actions to avoid later allegations of discrimination? Maybe a bit of both.

He seemed to sense her hesitation and sat there staring at her, waiting for an answer.

'Look,' Kate said eventually, 'I'll take some details off you now and make a few discreet inquiries. In the meantime, I'm relying on you to let us know if she turns up. Okay?'

He nodded and grinned. 'Sounds good to me.'

Kate produced her pocketbook and sat there with her pen poised. 'Right, so first off, let's have your full name and address and the details of your girlfriend. I don't suppose you have a picture of her?'

He slapped a photograph of an attractive, dark-haired girl on the table in front of her. 'That do?'

* * *

The girl was naked and her clothes were nowhere to be seen. The realisation had come as a brain-numbing shock when she had first awakened on the single bed. That had been the day before — at least, she thought so. Time in the little cell-like room with its high window could be deceptive, but she thought daylight had passed into night and back into daylight again just the once.

Tammy Logan had tried to make sense of it all, but had hit a mental block, remembering only walking down the back street from the Blue Pixie café in the sunlight and passing the Land Rover in the gateway. Then the shadow lunging towards her and the powerful arm tightly compressing her neck before she passed out. She remembered briefly coming to, lying on a long car seat, and then the sharp stab in her arm, like from a hypodermic needle, and shortly afterwards total blackness.

The big, middle-aged man, dressed in an anorak and jeans, came in to see her just after she regained consciousness, leaving a tray of doorstep cheese sandwiches and an enamel mug of some sort of cordial on the single wooden chair beside her bed. His dark, hooded eyes had taken in her nudity with a hard, intense stare, ignoring her tears and her entreaties to give her back her clothes and let her go.

'I've binned them all,' he told her. 'They were nothing more than the instruments of the devil — designed to encourage the lustful ways of men.'

'*You* took all my clothes off?' she exclaimed, pulling up the bed sheet to cover herself. 'You had no right.'

'Right?' he echoed. 'As a God-fearing Christian, I had every right. But don't fret, I didn't do anything to you. I won't succumb to your evil charms again. I am immune to your wicked wiles now.'

'Wicked wiles?' she exclaimed. 'What wicked wiles? I was just walking down the street when *you* attacked *me*.'

'Harlot!' he muttered. 'Just like you always have been. Didn't think I'd know if you came back, did you? But I've been looking out for you.'

'I don't understand what you're talking about,' she said. 'Why are you doing this? I've done nothing to you. I don't even know you.'

'Flaunting yourself in that café,' he continued without answering her question. 'Asking for it, you were, with that weirdo. But I was in there watching you and I could see what you were up to. I nipped around the back when you left, see, and you walked right past where I'd parked my car. Providence, you could call it. Well, you won't get away this time.'

Then he just left, slamming the heavy wooden door after him and turning the key in the lock.

She'd spent the rest of that day trying to find a way out, but it had proved pointless. The room was only about ten feet square, with a bathroom attached to it, accessible through an open archway. There was only the one door and one barred window, and the walls appeared to be made of solid stone blocks. Her shouts for help had eventually turned into panic-stricken screams, but these had gone unanswered and not even he had responded to them. In the end, assailed by a burning thirst and desperately hungry, she had been left with no option but to eat the sandwiches and gulp down the mug of cordial. It was only a short time afterwards that she realised the drink must have been drugged and, with the shadows of dusk moving in again, she had finally succumbed to whatever it was he had put in it.

She had wakened to this new dawn what must have been many hours later, with a violent headache. There was a single item of clothing bundled up on the chair beside her bed now — no underclothes and no shoes, just an ankle-length cotton dress — and, although it wasn't hers, she pulled it on and did up the buttons down the front with a sense of relief, finding it an almost perfect fit.

He came in again shortly afterwards, this time dressed in a green, long-sleeved, polo-necked pullover and dark trousers. He studied her approvingly.

'A lot better,' he said. 'Much more decent.'

Placing a heavy, black book on the bed at her feet, he added, 'But the sin is still within you, girl, and needs to be expurgated. Read, and let the Lord cast out your wickedness.'

When he had gone, she picked up the book and read the title: *Holy Bible*. She closed her eyes tightly. God help her, she was in the hands of a madman.

CHAPTER 2

'What was with our ethnic cousin?' Detective Inspector Ted Roscoe was not a man to mince his words. He scowled at Kate across his desk, his boot-button eyes cold and hard.

One of the old school with close on thirty years' service, this short, muscular man with the slab-like face and Stalin moustache was a surviving relic of the old guard, well out of step with the "brave new world" of gender equality and political correctness, and he wasn't about to change any time soon.

She made a grimace at what she saw as his distasteful reference to her complainant's colour.

'He was reporting his girlfriend missing,' she replied.

His eyes narrowed. 'Oh? Bit sus, is it?'

'Not as far as we know.'

'Then why were you taking the report? Mispers are usually a uniform job, unless it's a child or there are suspicious circumstances.'

'He was giving the SDO a hard time so I said I'd have a chat with him to take the heat out of the situation.'

'You mean, because he was black?'

Kate's mouth tightened. She didn't respond.

'So, when did she go missing?' he went on.

'Er — yesterday.'

'Yesterday? One day? She hasn't even qualified as a misper yet. And where is this so-called girlfriend missing from?'

'The rave festival near Mark.'

'That bloody thing.'

'It was just kids having fun.'

'Tell that to the locals who had them pissing in their gardens and keeping them awake all night with the racket they kicked up. Guv'nor should have had the lot cleared out instead of letting them carry on.'

'That could have provoked more trouble.'

'So, we just let these arseholes break the law, is that it? They've just had bloody Glastonbury, haven't they? What more do they want? They're never satisfied.' He snorted. 'Anyway, as a matter of interest, how old was this girlfriend?'

Kate had been dreading that question, knowing full well what his reaction would be. 'Twenty-four,' she replied.

His bushy eyebrows arched. 'Twenty-four?' he ejaculated. 'This gets worse. She's a bloody adult, there are no suspicious circumstances and she's been AWOL for just one day?' He shook his head in disbelief. 'We shouldn't have taken the report in the first place. Wouldn't have done in the old days.'

'We have no choice under the new national policy on mispers, you know that. I did tell him, however, that in view of the circumstances, we would not be treating the report as a priority issue at this stage.'

He emitted a short humourless laugh and inserted a wad of chewing-gum into his mouth. A former smoker, it was his way of trying to cope with the nicotine abstinence, though it appeared that he was finding the challenge something of a mountain to climb and it certainly hadn't improved his temperament.

'Did you now?' he said. 'Well, for your information, Sergeant, I would have thought that going by the size of your in-tray, you had enough to do as it is, without taking on crap like this.'

He stood up, signifying the briefing was over and, grabbing his pork-pie hat from the corner of the desk, headed for the door. 'Going out,' he growled. 'I'll be back in about an hour. In the meantime, hand this misper thing over to uniform to deal with, and that's an order. You've got a lot more important things to take care of than some barely missing hophead. Understood?' Then he added over his shoulder, 'By the way, you look like shit!'

* * *

Detective Constable Hayden Lewis, Kate's oddball other half and member of Highbridge police station's CID team, was sitting in the canteen over a mug of coffee, halfway through an enormous chunk of bread pudding. She pulled up a chair and deposited herself in front of him.

With the bread pudding halfway to his mouth, he glanced up quickly and met the critical stare she directed at his well-padded midriff, which was already threatening to burst through the buttons of his shirt, and responded with a hesitant smile.

'Got a bit peckish,' he explained defensively through a mouthful of bread pudding, heedless of the greasy particles cascading on to the table and into his lap. 'Chap's got to keep his strength up.'

She closed her eyes in resignation.

She had virtually given up trying to reform her untidy, overweight husband, with his tangled, blond hair, shabby, crumpled clothes and penchant for filling his stomach with anything calculated to pump up his cholesterol to record levels. Deep down, she knew she would never be able to change him, however hard she tried — and sometimes she found herself not really wanting to.

Hayden was Hayden and that was all there was to it. Infuriatingly laid back — some would say work-shy — he had a pompous, unworldly air and an old-fashioned, narrow-minded outlook towards modern living that was a legacy of a traditional public-school upbringing. In short, he was an anachronism, a relic of Britain's imperial past that did not fit with the coarse, more down-to-earth attitude of his colleagues in the department, particularly Detective Inspector Ted Roscoe, who regarded him as a total waste of space.

But his bumbling, laissez-faire persona belied the highly intelligent, analytical brain that lurked beneath all his faults. He had put this to good use in more than a few complicated criminal cases in the past, while his measured approach to critical issues had on several occasions acted as an effective brake on Kate's rather more impulsive, headstrong instincts. But it was on the personal front that he scored the biggest hit with her. Kate had found him to be the kindest, most loyal soulmate anyone could wish for. He was absolutely devoted to her. Despite the tongue-in-cheek insults she often hurled at him, she just couldn't imagine life without Hayden.

Now, however, there was no indication of those innermost feelings when she thrust the single sheet of paper across the table at him.

'Misper,' she said, wincing as he set the remains of the bread pudding down on a corner of her handwritten note while he scanned it. 'Tammy Logan, twenty-four years, from Birmingham,' she summarised. 'Walked out on her boyfriend at the Mark rave yesterday and allegedly didn't return home.'

'Suspicious?'

She shook her head. 'Not as far as I know, but I told her boyfriend I would look into it.'

He looked nonplussed. 'Why? She's an adult. Anyway, at this stage, it's a uniform job.'

'Which is exactly what the DI said. But I want you to make just a few quiet, routine inquiries — telephone Birmingham nick and get them to visit her flat, check the café in Highbridge and the railway station, that sort of thing. Nothing too heavy. Just a bit of PR to keep the boyfriend off our backs. All the info you need is there.'

'Roscoe happy about this?'

'Is he ever happy about anything?' she said. 'Just do it, will you?'

She stood up. 'Oh, and wipe your chin. You've got grease all over it.'

* * *

The phone call from the control room was brief, catching Kate just as she returned to her desk in the main CID office.

'We've got a possible suicide out on the Levels,' the operator informed her. 'Uniform have asked for CID.'

'Why?' Kate asked. 'If it's a suicide, they don't need us.'

'Firearm involved,' the operator said, 'and anyway, they want to cover their backs. Just in case. I'll give you the address . . .'

With a groan, Kate called across to Hayden at his desk a few feet away.

'Job out on the Levels,' she said. 'Get your coat, mister.'

Hayden sighed. 'Do you really need me?' he asked, swivelling round in his chair. Only, you asked me to do some checks on this misper.'

'That can wait,' she replied, glancing around the otherwise empty office to make a point. 'And in answer to your question, no I don't need *you*, but, as you appear to be the only one here at the moment, I have no choice unfortunately.'

He feigned a hurt expression, used to such digs and well aware that they were always meant in a good spirit.

'I say,' he said, 'you could really damage a chap's self-esteem, you know.'

She tossed the ignition keys of the CID car onto his desk. 'You drive,' she said, popping two paracetamol tablets into her mouth and downing half a mug of cold coffee. 'I'm not feeling too brilliant.'

He grinned. 'Something to do with red wine, is it?'

'Shut it, fat man,' she said, swallowing two more paracetamol with difficulty. 'And take the curves gently.'

* * *

The cottage overlooked a narrow lane and backed on to one of the many *rhynes* — the man-made drainage ditches that criss-crossed the marshy Somerset Levels.

A marked patrol car was parked directly outside the front door beside an elderly VW Beetle. A thick-set, uniformed police sergeant met Kate and Hayden on the doorstep.

'Tom,' she said in greeting, recognising the skipper from the local neighbourhood policing team.

'Hi, Kate.' Tom Reeves ran a hand over his bald pate, his craggy face wearing a heavy frown. 'Bad business, this — and the last thing I needed just back from leave.'

'Leave? Been anywhere nice?'

He gave a short laugh. '*Chez nous* actually. My mum and dad left me the house in their will. It's mid-Victorian with seven acres of land and needs a lot doing to it. Holidays are for others at present, I'm afraid.'

He motioned her ahead of him down the side of the cottage, towards a thatched barn at the end of the large garden. 'He's in there,' he said, changing the subject.

Sunlight slanting into the barn through two fanlights revealed a silver BMW X3. Kate glimpsed movement in a doorway behind it, which turned out to be a uniformed woman constable.

The dead man, in a tattered, fully upholstered armchair, had slumped sideways, the twin barrels of the Purdy side-by-side shotgun still pointing upwards in his grip. But for the size and apparent stability of the chair, the force of the blast would probably have tipped him over onto his back, but, as it was, he was just sitting there with what remained of his head held in place against the high back of the armchair and one eyeball glaring at them through the gore. He was wearing a pair of pyjama trousers and a silk dressing gown, which had fallen open at the front, suggesting that he had just got out of bed prior to the event. Kate noted the ragged hole in the roof directly above the corpse, where the simultaneous blast had torn its way through the thatch, and saw that one of the cartridges, which had been automatically ejected by the shotgun, lay on the floor a few feet away.

'Peter Jackson, as was,' Reeves said behind her. 'Has lived here with his wife, Helen, for around twenty years. I live in the village too and I've known them for at least half that time. He is — was — a retired headmaster, one of the church wardens at my church and, by all accounts, a senior member of the local masonic lodge. Never thought he'd do something like this.'

'Where's the wife now?' Kate asked.

'Back in the house. Police surgeon has attended and certified death. Not that it needed much certifying. He gave her a sedative and she's well out of it, I understand. Fortunately, there's a close friend living just two doors away and she came to see what all the fuss was about. She's upstairs with Mrs Jackson now.'

Kate made a face. 'So, no chance of a quick word then?'

''Fraid not. That will have to wait until later. At the moment she's in bits.'

'Not as much as he is,' Hayden commented grimly, wincing under Kate's admonitory glance.

'What are the circumstances then?' she continued, turning to face her uniformed counterpart.

Reeves shrugged. 'According to what Helen Jackson told the doctor, deceased apparently got up this morning in quite a happy frame of mind, and went downstairs to make some tea, as per usual. Wife followed him a few minutes later and found him standing in the middle of the hall, white-faced, with an envelope in his hand, which he'd evidently found on the front door mat. When she asked him about it, he got quite shirty and disappeared into his study, so she left him to it and went to make breakfast. While she was doing that, she heard the front door open and close, then not long afterwards, the blast of the shotgun. She found him — er — like this.'

Kate shuddered. 'Poor woman. This definitely *his* gun?'

'I believe so. I used to do a bit of shooting with him.'

‘A Purdy, if I’m not mistaken,’ Hayden put in again, peering closely at the weapon.’

Reeves nodded. ‘Expensive piece. The Jacksons weren’t short of a bob or two.’

‘So, no idea as to why he should decide to kill himself?’

The sergeant shook his head.

‘From what you’ve said, there don’t seem to have been any money worries.’

‘Hardly, I would have thought.’

‘So, what could have prompted this?’

‘Haven’t a clue. We’ll probably never know.’

‘What about that envelope?’ she said. ‘Could be significant. Where is it now?’

‘No idea. We haven’t had a chance to look yet.’

‘Well, I suggest we do that now. In the meantime, we’d better see what the police surgeon has to say. The coroner would expect nothing less of us.’

‘And we wouldn’t want to upset the coroner, would we?’ Hayden put in again with a weak grin.

CHAPTER 3

When they went back to the house, they found Raymond Makepiece, the police surgeon, a thin, sallow man in his fifties, in the living room. Apart from confirming that, in his opinion, there were no suspicious circumstances to the death and that it was a straightforward suicide, he was less than cooperative under Kate's questioning, palpably anxious to be off.

'Look, Sergeant,' Makepiece said irritably, closing his briefcase with a bang. 'I cannot help you anymore than I already have. I've repeated what Mrs Jackson was able to tell me when I got here. There is absolutely nothing else I can add, and the poor woman is in too distressed a state to answer any questions.'

'We will have to speak to her at some stage,' Kate said.

The doctor nodded curtly. 'But not now. Anyway, she is in bed under heavy sedation — fortunately with a neighbour in attendance — and you wouldn't get a lot out of her. It would be a waste of time trying.'

With that, treating Kate to a cold, 'Good day, I'll leave you to sort things out here,' he left, and shortly afterwards his old VW Beetle could be heard starting up outside and driving away with a noisy rattle.

A slim, dark-haired woman in fawn riding jodhpurs and a green top appeared in the doorway of the study as Kate and Hayden, watched somewhat uneasily by Reeves, searched through the drawers of the old oak desk. She seemed more than a little taken aback by their presence.

'Beverley James,' she said in a strained voice, when Reeves introduced Kate and Hayden. 'What exactly are you doing in here?'

Reeves coughed. 'Apparently,' he replied, 'Mr Jackson received some sort of letter this morning just before — er — before—'

'He blew his brains out?' she finished for him bluntly.

Kate hastened to explain. 'We are trying to establish if there was anything in that letter which may have led to what happened afterwards.'

Beverley James hesitated, as if something was on her mind. 'Helen mentioned the letter,' she said, 'but I don't know what was in it or where it went. From what she told me, Peter seemed quite upset by it.'

She turned towards the door, then stopped suddenly. 'A big brown envelope, Helen said it was, a big brown envelope, but she didn't see a stamp.' She shrugged. 'That's all I can tell you. Now, I'd best get back to her in case she wakes up.'

After James had left, Kate began sifting through a pile of papers on the desktop. 'No brown envelope here.'

'Hold on,' Hayden snapped and, bending down, pulled out a very full wastepaper basket from beneath the desk. Unceremoniously, he tipped it out on to the leather desk pad, unconcerned by the pencil sharpener shavings, screwed-up paper and orange peel it disgorged over the laptop computer, printer and the sifted documents Kate had only just stacked up again in a neat pile.

But any concern over the mess he had created dissipated when he inserted his fingers delicately into the pile to withdraw the corner of a brown envelope. A further search produced the rest of the envelope, which seemed to have simply been torn into four pieces. Putting the pieces together on a corner of the desk, he shrugged.

'"*Peter Jackson Esq. Private and Confidential*",' he read. 'Typed and no stamp, so it was obviously hand delivered.'

'If it's just the envelope, it doesn't tell us a lot,' Reeves commented.

Hayden beamed. 'Patience, my dear sergeant.' He began carefully probing the pile of detritus, while Kate and Reeves watched intently from the other side of the desk.

It wasn't long before he found the photographs, also torn into four and sticking out of the pile. He laid them on top of the envelope. There appeared to be three sets of four pictures, clinging together with part of a letter, and they married up exactly with the torn envelope.

'Must have ripped the lot up together,' Kate said, watching as he recovered the rest. 'So, let's take a look at them.'

Sweeping the remaining detritus from the wastepaper basket to one side, heedless of the bits that cascaded onto the carpet, Hayden assembled the jigsaw more neatly on the desk, the letter first and then the three photographs, side by side. He released a soft whistle and his colleagues moved around the desk to join him.

'Gordon Bennett!' he breathed.

Like the envelope, the letter was also typed and, of course, unsigned. It read simply:

'*Who's been a very naughty boy then? An ex-headmaster and a church warden too! I wonder what your former pupils or your congregation would say if they only knew? Well, they will shortly, because I've sent copies of the photos to our nice vicar. I thought it was the least I could do under the circumstances. But I felt you'd like to know in advance anyway — as a courtesy, you understand. Have a nice day, won't you?*'

The photographs spoke for themselves and could not have been more graphic, depicting as they did two completely naked men in what appeared to be an old shed or barn, indulging in different homosexual couplings. Care had been taken to show the faces of both in one or other of the pictures, and Kate could see from the portrait on the corner of the desk that one of them was Peter Jackson.

'Strewth!' Reeves breathed. 'No wonder the poor devil killed himself.'

'So, it *is* definitely him?' Kate said.

'Oh, it's him all right,' Reeves replied, 'and it looks like the pair of them were at it in his own barn. You can see his Beamer in the background with part of the number plate.'

'I wonder who the other chap is?' Hayden commented.

'Not a clue. No one in the village that I know of. Could be someone he met on the net or in a pub somewhere.'

'Bit old-looking for a rent boy,' Hayden commented drily, collecting up his "jigsaw" and putting the pieces in another envelope he found in one of the desk drawers.

'Doesn't matter anyway,' Kate pointed out. 'Sex between two consenting adults is quite legal, whatever their gender, so no criminal offence has been committed. End of.'

'True enough,' Reeves agreed, 'but this is a narrow-minded community and the scandal will destroy Helen if it gets out. She's very strait-laced.'

'Then you'd better get hold of the vicar asap to make sure it doesn't.'

Reeves nodded. 'I know John Salter well — I'm a sidesman at the local church. I'll pop over to see him as soon as we're done here.'

'And in the meantime, we've still got a nasty poison pen on the loose out there,' Kate said. 'Someone so twisted that they are prepared to go to extraordinary lengths to destroy a person without a second's thought.'

Hayden nodded thoughtfully. 'And someone who seems to have chosen a rather antiquated method of communicating their message.'

Kate looked puzzled. 'What are you getting at, Hayd?'

He carefully withdrew one of the torn fragments of the letter from the envelope and held it up in the light streaming in through the window, with the underside towards her. 'Heavy indentations,' he said simply. 'Whoever sent the letter used a typewriter instead of a computer. A computer printer wouldn't leave marks like that.'

Kate nodded approvingly. 'Good observation, Hayd, which should help us with our investigation later. But right this minute, we have to ask ourselves, why Jackson? Who is upset enough with him to do something like this? There's no evidence of a blackmail attempt. The writer clearly says the photos have actually been sent to the local vicar, so gain doesn't appear to have been the motive. It must have been purely malicious.'

'And whoever took those photos must have gone prepared, since they obviously had a camera with them,' Reeves added. 'I just hope they're satisfied when they find out that they're responsible for a man's death.'

'I doubt it.' They turned to see Beverley James standing in the doorway.

'I'm sorry, I wasn't eavesdropping,' she said, stepping further into the room. 'I came back down to see if you wanted a coffee or anything and happened to hear what you just said.'

'Go on,' Kate said, sensing from her hesitation that there was more she wanted to say and recalling her momentary hesitation earlier.

James bit her lip. 'The thing is, I suspected from the way Helen said Peter reacted on receiving the letter that it was something nasty, but I didn't want to mention anything until I was sure.'

'Mention anything about what?' Kate asked.

James took a deep breath. 'The truth is, we've all been receiving nasty letters in the last week or so.'

'We?'

'Well, half the village, it seems. Vicious personal slurs, most of them untrue, just taken from gossip and suchlike. It's causing awful problems in the community, and we've no idea who's behind it.'

'How do you know all this?' Kate said gently.

James smiled faintly. 'Friends talk and word gets around.'

'I've not received any such complaints,' Reeves said defensively.

'Well, you wouldn't, would you, Tom? These are private, personal things that people don't want to talk about — even if they are a pack of lies.'

'Have you received such a letter?' Kate continued.

'A week ago.'

'Have you still got it?'

James shook her head. 'I destroyed it immediately.'

'Are you prepared to tell me what was in it?'

'I'm sorry, no. It wasn't true anyway.'

Kate nodded sympathetically. 'Can you say who else has received one of these letters?'

'Not until I ask them first.'

'Would you be prepared to do that and get back to me?'

'I'll think about it.'

Kate frowned. 'Excellent. Now there's something else I need to do. So, can I talk to you again, maybe tomorrow?'

James shrugged. 'I doubt whether I will be going anywhere for a while, except to tend to my horses.'

* * *

Kate headed straight back to the barn after leaving the cottage, walking briskly down the side of it towards a row of trees at the back, but stopping after a few feet. There was a high-level window in the slatted, wooden wall halfway along, which was ajar. She studied it for a moment, then, spotting a square, iron overflow tank underneath, fed by a broken drainpipe, she went closer.

'So,' she murmured to herself. 'Was this your vantage point, I wonder?'

In ordinary circumstances, the overflow tank would have been too high off the ground to have allowed her to climb up onto it, but on the other side, almost buried in the jungle of ferns and bracken that choked the area, was a mound of broken bricks and concrete at least a couple of feet high. Someone had obviously been there recently too. A narrow path had been trampled through the undergrowth right up to the mound.

Moments later, Kate was on top of the tank, peering through the half-open fanlight, which provided an uninterrupted view of the building's interior, including the silver BMW car on the far side. She smiled grimly. An enterprising photographer indeed, and one who must have known that Peter Jackson used the place for his assignations. All they had to do was follow him there, a lamb to the slaughter — well, not exactly a lamb, but certainly an easy victim. The only question still burning in her mind was why?

Jumping down again, she saw Reeves walking towards her.

'Found something?' he asked.

She pointed to the high-level window. 'I think our photographer took the photos from up there.'

He made a face. 'Well, whoever did it will have the poor devil's death on their conscience now.'

She snorted. 'You reckon, Tom? Bastards like that don't have a conscience.'

'You may be right,' he said, 'and if we catch him or her, what can they be done for anyway? They didn't kill anyone and, without wishing to seem heartless, Peter Jackson chose to take his own life. It was his decision, tragic though his death was.'

She nodded grimly. 'There's the rub. I will have to seek advice from the CPS, but, as far as I can see at the moment, all they are guilty of is possibly some sort of nuisance offence.'

'Bit lame when you think about it.'

She shrugged. 'We don't make the laws, Tom. That's someone else's responsibility.'

CHAPTER 4

DI Roscoe was back in his office when Kate returned to Highbridge police station, seemingly in an even more truculent mood than he had been in earlier. Motioning her to join him in his glass-panelled office at the far end of the department, he raised an inquiring eyebrow.

'I gather you were called out to a suicide,' he growled.

She propped herself against the radiator and quickly briefed him on the circumstances.

'Dirty bastard deserved it then,' he said, more as a statement than a question.

Kate's eyes narrowed. 'He deserved nothing of the sort, guv. Someone's sexual orientation is a matter for them. We live in more enlightened times today and we shouldn't seek to judge.'

'More's the pity,' he said. 'And he was still having it off in a bloody barn, regardless of what you say.'

'*His* barn,' she countered, 'on *his* property, which he was legally entitled to do if that was what he wanted. It doesn't alter the fact that someone trespassed on that property, invaded his privacy and drove him to kill himself.'

He scowled. 'Yeah, well, you can get down off your soapbox now and think instead about what we are dealing with here. The press will be on our backs soon, demanding answers, and we need to be clear what kind of offence may have been committed by the perp who took the pics. It's a bit outside my area of expertise.' She raised both eyebrows at his use of the word "expertise," and he coughed and looked down at his desk.

'Obviously it's not what in the old days we would have called a standard list offence, like burglary, robbery or theft, but plainly, there has to be an offence here and the only thing I can think of is some sort of nuisance offence, which is really scraping the barrel.'

She nodded. 'I thought the same thing initially, but I've since had a word with CPS and apparently there's the Malicious Communications Act of 1988, which makes it an offence to send or deliver stuff like this for the purposes of causing distress or anxiety.'

He seemed relieved. 'Sounds good enough to me. What's the penalty?'

'I understand that on conviction it is a fine or up two years inside.' She made a face. 'The worrying thing is that it seems Jackson wasn't the only one to have received a malicious, anonymous letter — several others in the village have as well — which means we have a nasty poison pen at work. Nailing the writer doesn't look like it's going to be easy, though, because so far no one has come forward with a formal complaint.'

He scowled. 'Yeah. Well, maybe I can change all that. It just so happens that one of the recipients you speak of has actually been in touch with the super. That's who I went to see this morning—'

'One of his golfing chums, was it?' Kate suggested mischievously.

He studied her for a moment, and then gave her one of his rare wolfish grins, which seldom boded well for his chosen "victim."

'You'll soon be able to work that one out for yourself,' he retorted, 'because I've arranged for you to drop in and see him after lunch, at 1400 hours — something for you to look forward to as you munch your cheese and pickle sandwiches.'

Kate returned his fixed stare with a wary look in her eyes. 'I take it that he is one of our notables then?'

'You could say that, yes. His name is Colonel Herbert Winston. He lives in Winston House, on the outskirts of the village, and may well be a member of the guv'nor's golf club for all I know. But he is also a multimillionaire, the managing director of a London-based property company, Winston-Morgan Holdings, and has friends in very high places.'

He took a deep breath. 'In addition to that, he is a pompous, blustering prick who this morning subjected me to a comprehensive analysis of the failings of the local constabulary in sorting out the riff-raff plaguing the streets of the community — particularly those with the temerity to send him libellous anonymous letters.'

'Did he say what was in the letter?'

He leaned towards her across his desk. 'No, Lewis, he did not. He stated that what it said was confidential.'

'Then how are we supposed to—?'

The grin returned, but there was no humour in it. 'That's for *you* to determine, Detective Sergeant. You can call on that fabled feminine intuition you women are reputed to possess.'

* * *

Almost dragging a protesting Hayden from his lunch, Kate left the police station just after one thirty for the short drive to Winston House. She spent ten minutes outside the big pseudo-Georgian house, studying the place and its extensive grounds through the iron gates. A steel post box was set in the right-hand pillar and a notice on the opposite pillar directed callers to ring the bell just beneath it.

'Bit like a fortress,' Kate remarked, scanning the seven-foot-high walls.

Hayden simply grunted, still annoyed with her for tearing him away from his lunch and determined to enjoy his sulk whatever happened. But that was before he spotted the red sports car drawn up on the shingle apron by the front door.

'Good lord,' he exclaimed, shooting bolt upright in his seat. 'It's a classic E-Type Jag — a nineteen sixties 3.8 Roadster, would you believe? Isn't she a beauty?'

Kate smiled faintly, despite her still throbbing head. Hayden's love of sports cars was legendary, second only to his love of food and good wine. She remembered his last display of adulation, over an Austin Healey 3000 he had glimpsed on a previous crime case, and she breathed a sigh of relief. At least this had caused him to forget his chagrin over his ruined lunch — one aggravation she could well do without on a visit to a difficult complainant.

'Forget the E-Type, Hayd,' she admonished. 'We're here on business.'

Leaving the police car briefly to approach the double gates, she pressed the buzzer on the pillar and a haughty, male voice inquired who she was and what she wanted.

Staring up into the security camera mounted on top of the pillar, she held up her warrant card and said tersely, 'Police. To see Mr Herbert Winston.'

'What police?' the voice drawled back.

Kate controlled herself with an effort. 'Detective Sergeant Kate Lewis and Detective Constable Hayden Lewis.'

'Both of you are named Lewis?'

'Just forget the third degree, will you, sunshine, and let Mr Winston know we're here.'

There was an irritable tutting sound. 'I will see if *Colonel* Winston is available.'

Seconds later the gates quivered and began to open, but the "voice" did not deign to speak again.

Muttering in annoyance at his arrogance, Kate returned to her car, making sure she churned up the gravel in the driveway as she powered through the gateway.

'Hey, steady on, old girl,' Hayden protested, slamming back in his seat. 'You could run into the E-Type.'

Coming to a halt just inches from it, she threw him a tight smile. 'Don't tempt me,' she said, throwing open her door and climbing out.

A thin, dapper man in his late twenties, with blond, curly hair and a pale, pinched face, wearing a dark suit, was standing in the open doorway of the house. He treated them to a supercilious smirk as he stood to one side to allow them through.

'Colonel Winston is in the drawing room,' he murmured, adding unnecessarily, 'Apparently, you are expected,' his tone suggesting that this had surprised him. Kate resisted the temptation to step on his shiny shoes as he turned to lead the way.

The drawing room turned out to be the second door on the left of the thickly carpeted hallway and it was luxuriously furnished with gilt-framed chairs, a chaise longue and two matching sofas. Gilt-framed portraits of fierce-looking men in military uniforms graced the wood-panelled walls and the moulded, white ceiling resembled the top of a huge wedding cake.

A big, overweight man with a shock of thick, iron-grey hair was standing with his back to them, pouring himself what appeared to be a whisky from a cocktail cabinet in the corner of the room.

"Voice" cleared his throat. 'Colonel Winston, sir, Detective Sergeant Lewis and—'

'Get lost, Elton!' the other rapped, cutting him off in mid-delivery, without even bothering to turn around. 'See we're not disturbed.'

The abrupt, humiliating dismissal caused Kate no small degree of satisfaction and she cast Elton a patronising smile as he withdrew with a scowl. But her pleasure was short-lived, for his employer showed them a similar lack of courtesy.

'You'd better be good,' he growled, still without turning around, and Kate heard the squirt of a soda syphon. 'Know what this is all about, do you?'

Kate glanced at Hayden and made a face.

'We've been fully briefed, sir,' she said.

Winston turned, a half-full tumbler in one hand. Veined, slightly bulbous eyes studied her from a flushed, puffy face.

'Ah, it's a woman, is it? Your superior officer — Driscoll, Roscoff—'

'Roscoe, sir, Detective Inspector Roscoe.'

'Whatever. He didn't say it would be a woman.'

Kate raised an eyebrow. 'Is that a problem, Colonel?'

He shrugged and took a sip of his whisky. 'Not as long as you can do the job as well as Driscoll said you could.'

His tone suggested there could be some doubt about that, and only Hayden's warning cough at her elbow stopped her from biting back. Winston seemed to sense this and there was a sharp gleam — a challenge — in his eyes as he looked at her over the top of his glass. This was a man who got a kick out of demeaning others, she decided, a bully, used to getting his own way, who revelled in the power and influence he could wield and in his ability to destroy people who opposed him. She was grateful to Hayden for his discreet intervention, which had stopped her from taking the bait.

'I understand you have received a poison pen letter, sir?' she said coldly.

He nodded. 'Damned thing was put in the post box outside yesterday morning.'

'Have you got the letter here?'

He shook his head. 'Burned the bloody thing.'

'Can you tell us what it said?'

'That's confidential. Load of lies anyway.'

'Was it signed?'

'No.'

'Handwritten or typed?'

'Don't see what difference that makes. But it was typed.'

'And the envelope?'

'Again, typed. Block capitals.'

'Can you think of anyone who would have an axe to grind where you are concerned?'

'Not as far as I know.'

‘What about locally? Have you upset anyone in the village?’

He shook his head. ‘Don’t know anyone in the village. Never go there. Elton gets anything I want.’

Kate frowned. ‘It would really help if you could give us some idea regarding the contents of the letter. It could give us a lead as to who may have sent it.’

His face twisted into a snarl. ‘Didn’t you hear me the first time? I said it was confidential and was a pack of lies anyway. All you’ve got to do is find the culprit and lock them up. What was in the letter is irrelevant.’

‘What about the security camera you have above the main gates?’ Hayden put in quickly, conscious of the tension building between his other half and this boorish individual. ‘Could that have picked up anything?’

Winston shook his head. ‘Camera only covers the buzzer, so that Elton can see who is visiting. It has no memory or recording facility.’

‘Surprised you don’t have a full security system for the house and grounds, considering who you are,’ Hayden said.

‘And you are?’ Winston snapped belligerently.

‘Detective Constable Hayden Lewis, sir.’

Winston started. ‘You’re both named Lewis?’

‘He’s my husband as well as my partner,’ Kate explained.

Winston shook his head in disbelief. ‘And you’re the sergeant — his superior?’

Kate didn’t answer.

‘I bet that takes the biscuit, eh, Hayden? The wife calling the shots?’ He chuckled. ‘Talk about being tied to the apron strings.’

Before Hayden or Kate could think of a suitable reply — if, indeed, it was even worth bothering to think of one — the drawing room door was flung open.

Winston stiffened, glaring at both the door and the person who had barged through, but almost immediately his demeanour changed and he scowled.

The young woman had to be in her mid-twenties, with raven black hair worn to her shoulders. Her slightly mocking brown eyes studied them with apparent surprise over a pair of designer sunglasses. Her nut-brown skin, plenty of which was on show, was due either to long exposure to the sun or from a bottle. She was barefoot and wearing red micro shorts and a skimpy cropped top that exposed her navel and just about covered her small breasts.

'Visitors, Daddy?' She pouted. 'You never told me.'

Winston grunted, but instead of castigating her for bursting in like she had, he simply waved his free arm towards Kate and Hayden with a gruff, 'My daughter, Gabriella,' adding, 'Police officers, Gabby.'

The young woman's eyes widened appreciably, but Kate suspected that this was contrived. She knew who they were, probably from Elton, and it was all part of an act.

'Police?' she murmured, and smiled engagingly at Hayden who, to Kate's sardonic amusement, had become transfixed. 'What on earth have you been up to, Daddy?'

Winston started. 'Me? Don't be so damned impertinent. And — and get some clothes on.'

Gabriella laughed, a husky, sexy sound. 'Oh, Daddy, don't be such a prude.' She stared directly at Hayden. 'You don't mind, Mister Policeman, do you?'

For once, Hayden seemed lost for words.

'Close your mouth, Hayd,' Kate breathed into his ear. She turned for the door and nudged him to follow her.

'We'll leave you with your daughter, Colonel,' she threw back over her shoulder. 'We'll be in touch in due course.'

Winston seemed taken aback by her abrupt departure, obviously unused to someone else deciding when to end a meeting with his august self, but the presence of his daughter seemed to have unsettled him and he merely grunted an acknowledgement. 'Er — keep me informed,' he called after her in a vain attempt to reassert his authority. But Kate had already closed the door behind them.

Elton was similarly caught off guard and while he hurried after them down the hallway, they were already through the front door and climbing back into the CID car. Kate gave him a little wave before turning the car in a flurry of shingle and heading back down the driveway at speed, grinning as she imagined him running to get to the electronic switch to open the gates in time. He only just made it, and the CID car flashed through before they had fully parted, missing them by inches.

'Was that really necessary?' Hayden said with a frown.

'No,' she replied, 'but didn't it feel good?'

CHAPTER 5

'How did you get on?' Roscoe growled from beside the coffee machine when Kate and Hayden returned to the CID office.

Kate made a face. 'Not a very nice man. What do we know about him?'

Roscoe handed her the plastic cup he had just filled and poured himself another coffee, watching Hayden return to his desk with narrowed eyes.

'What *do* you see in that useless prat?' he muttered instead of answering her question.

Kate bristled, well aware of Roscoe's dislike of her husband, whom he did his best to demean at every opportunity. She suspected it was because of Hayden's polished accent and privileged public-school background — not much of an asset in the coarse environment of a CID office. But she chose not to jump to his defence, knowing full well it wouldn't change anything and would only make life more difficult for Hayden later on.

'Why I asked,' she said, ignoring his remark completely, 'is because Winston adamantly refused to tell me what was in the letter he received, which suggests that whoever sent it has something on him that is quite damaging — more than just malicious gossip.'

The DI settled on the corner of her desk and studied her for a moment over his coffee cup.

'Maybe there is something,' he agreed. 'He's into property, after all, so it's possible he could be carrying baggage of some sort. But that isn't of any concern to us. Our — your — job is to find the culprit and put a stop to what's going on, nothing more.'

'Bit difficult trying to get to the bottom of something when we have no idea what is behind it.'

He shrugged. 'It may be nothing specific — just some scandal someone has turned up and is having fun with. Like they did with the antics of the queer boy who just topped himself.'

She made a face. 'Come on, guv. That is totally out of order. A man is dead because of those letters. Heaven knows how many more people will have their lives wrecked because of them.'

He was unapologetic, treating her to one of his wolfish grins. 'Not my problem.' Dumping his coffee cup on her desk and slopping some of the contents over the paperwork neatly stacked beside her in-tray, he stood up and glanced at his watch. 'Anyway, I've got a meeting with the CPS brief at three — some bloody appeal case — so, I'd best be off. I'll be down the Black Cock later if you fancy a swift half when you're finished here.' He glanced across at Hayden, who was chatting to another colleague, DC Jamie Foster, on the other side of the back-to-back desks. 'Bring that wally with you, if you must.'

Kate watched him collect his pork-pie hat and coat from his glass-panelled office at the far end of the department before striding back past her and disappearing through the exit doors. Then she took some paper tissues and began trying to mop up the pool of coffee soaking through the report file on her desk.

'Arsehole,' she muttered, ignoring the chuckle from Ronnie Crouch, the department's new civilian office manager, who was sitting within earshot at his own desk a short distance away.

She jumped involuntarily as the telephone on her desk rang. 'Lewis,' she snapped.

There was a slight pause, then a soft, hesitant voice said, 'This is Beverley James.'

Kate dumped her soiled tissues into the wastepaper bin beside her desk, suddenly interested. 'Yes, Mrs James?'

Another pause. Then her caller continued almost in a rush. 'You said you wanted to come and see me tomorrow about the letters.'

'That's right — when it's convenient, of course.'

'Well, I was wondering if you could pop over this afternoon. There is something I should have told you this morning and I'd like to get it out of the way.'

'Excellent. But what about Mrs Jackson?'

'Oh, Helen's sister has arrived from Wedmore and is with her now, so I've no need to stay any longer. I'm — I'm at home. I'll give you my address . . .' Another pause, and then she added, 'Would you mind if I asked you to come alone, please? I would rather talk to just you.'

Kate glanced across at Hayden, still locked in loud conversation with Jamie Foster — this time about the merits of the E-Type Jaguar over other sports cars — as he dipped a biscuit into his coffee. 'Absolutely no problem,' she said drily. 'Give me fifteen minutes.'

Hayden glanced up as she stood and reached for her police radio. 'Going out?' he called.

'If that's okay with you?' she retorted sarcastically.

'Do you want me to come too?'

'No thanks, I think I can just about manage.'

She headed for the exit, and then turned briefly in midstride, snapping her fingers at a sudden thought. 'Oh, by the way, while I'm out, if it's not *too* much trouble for you, maybe you could tear yourself away from the subject of sports cars to follow up on those misper inquiries I left with you? File's in your tray. Only if you have the time, of course.'

* * *

Kate found the slate-roofed cottage set well back behind a tall hedge a short distance beyond the Jacksons' house. The front garden was laid chiefly to lawn and a new Range Rover was parked outside the stable adjoining the cottage. As she climbed out of the CID car, Kate saw a horse's head poking out of one of the three stable doors and a golden Labrador trotted to meet her from a sideway, wagging its tail in greeting.

'Off you go, Rufus,' Beverley James called firmly, emerging from the stable block still wearing her fawn jodhpurs and green top.

'Sorry about that,' James went on with a smile, watching the Labrador obediently wander off towards the Land Rover. 'Good of you to come at such short notice. Please come inside.'

The sitting room was cool and smelled strongly of old wood and the damp of ages. It was furnished with deep chintzy armchairs and a large sofa. The stone fireplace still held the blackened remains of several logs, despite the fact that it was midsummer.

Waving her visitor to an armchair and offering her a cup of tea, which Kate politely declined, James sat for a moment with her hands in her lap, as if trying to find the right words for what she was about to say. Kate waited patiently until finally the young woman cleared her throat.

'You asked me earlier today what was in the letter I received,' she said. 'I refused to say but told you it was untrue anyway. That was a lie.' She faltered, took a deep trembling breath and continued in a rush.

'The fact of the matter is that I have been married now for just three years and Dan, my husband, desperately wants us to start a family. He is a lot older than me, you see, and feels time is running out for him. But a baby is the last thing I need at present. Later, maybe, but I set up the tack shop business here six months ago and it's only just starting to get off the ground properly, and I am frequently away from home on promotional and buying activities. A baby would put the lid on everything. So, you can imagine my horror when I fell pregnant. At first, I didn't know what to do, but, following some research, I located a private clinic in Surrey and—'

'You went there to have an abortion.'

James nodded, seeming to search Kate's face for a sign of shock or disapprobation. 'I know what I did sounds awful and very selfish, but—'

Kate shook her head. 'I'm not here to judge, Beverley — may I call you that? What people do in their private lives is a matter for them. My focus is solely on catching this poison pen writer, nothing more.'

James released her breath in a deep, grateful sigh. 'Thank you,' she said, and continued with more confidence. 'I told Dan I would be away on a business trip for a couple of weeks, knowing that he would go ballistic if he found out what I was really up to. It could have meant the end of our marriage, which is already in a pretty fractious state. We have had lots of flaming rows over the issue, which ended a couple of weeks ago with him walking out on me in a foul mood. He is currently staying at his late parents' old house on the other side of the village while he renovates the place, ready to sell. As a result, I haven't been seeing him lately, which at least has meant that the issue of babies hasn't come up again.' Her face tightened. 'I thought I was in the clear over the abortion thing, but then this dreadful letter arrived and I am now terrified that Dan will get one too. It could mean the end of everything—'

Kate made an involuntary grimace. 'A letter which you have since burned?'

James shook her head. 'That was also a lie, I'm afraid.'

She stood up briefly, reached into her pocket and withdrew a small crumpled envelope, which she handed to Kate.

'I don't know why I kept it really,' she said with a shrug.

The envelope was addressed to '*Mrs Beverley James*' in typed block capitals and marked "*Private and Confidential*" in the same way as the one that had been retrieved from Peter Jackson's wastepaper basket. The letter inside was also typed, on the same sort of paper.

'Who's got a very guilty secret then?' it read. *'I wonder if Hubby Dan knows about that abortion you recently had at the clinic in Surrey? I reckon he would be pretty upset to hear that you've had his firstborn destroyed, especially as you haven't produced any children for him since you were married. Should I tell him, do you reckon? I will have to think about that. Oh, by the way, you should watch what you throw away in your dustbin. You never know who might be rummaging through it!'*

'Your dustbin?' Kate said, raising an eyebrow.

James made a rueful grimace. 'A couple of days ago, the clinic contacted me as a follow-up to the procedure and to ensure there were no complications. I rang them to say all was okay, then tore the letter up and dropped it in the dustbin.' She shook her head again. 'I never dreamed that anyone would decide to go through my rubbish.'

Kate pursed her lips but made no comment. Instead, carefully slipping the letter back inside the envelope, she folded it up. 'Can I hang on to this?'

James nodded. 'Will you be able to fingerprint it or something?'

Kate gave her a faint smile. 'People always assume fingerprints can be lifted off any surface, but sadly, that is not always a feasible proposition. Because of the rough texture of the paper here, lifting prints off it might be a very tall order and require more sophisticated forensic techniques, which only the main labs can provide. The problem is that an examination at the forensic lab would likely be a very time-consuming, expensive process — with no guaranteed success at the end of it. Due to the possible cost involved and the resource constraints on our labs at present, I doubt whether authority would be given for this to be carried out for something which is, forgive me, quite minor in the scheme of things.'

'What about this DNA evidence we keep hearing about?'

Kate nodded. 'DNA could be present on the material, yes, especially from saliva traces if the sender licked the flap of the envelope to stick it down, or from a hair they left behind, but again, I can't see that line of investigation being pursued in these circumstances, for the reasons I have already given. We are not dealing with a major crime here and we would have to justify sending such stuff off when the labs are already heavily committed to dealing with material from the scenes of serious crimes, like murder and rape.'

'So, you're not going to do anything about it?'

'That's not it at all. Determined inquiries will continue in an effort to nail this character — that I promise you. But you have to remember that even were we able to obtain fingerprints or DNA, if the person is not known to us and we have no suspects in mind, those wouldn't lead us to them anyway.'

'So, exactly what *will* you be doing?'

Kate smiled again. 'Good old-fashioned detective work, Beverley. Asking around. Talking to people, that sort of thing. And you can help us a lot there.'

'How?'

'By telling us who else you know to have received one of these letters. They may come up with some new information which could give us a lead.'

James bit her lip. 'As I told you before, I can't do that, not until I've spoken to them. But there is something that perhaps I should tell you.'

'Go on.'

Another long pause. Kate waited patiently.

'This is a small community where everyone knows everyone else,' James went on finally. 'I'm not sure I should say this, but there is an elderly lady living here who is known as the local gossip. She can have quite a vicious tongue, actually. She once said to me that it was about time I produced a baby for my husband. I just wondered whether — well, you know.'

Kate nodded. 'Thanks for the information. Can you give me her name and address?'

'You won't tell her I said, will you?'

'Mum's the word.'

'Her name is Maisie Taylor and she lives to the right of the local post office and shop. If she's not at home, you can usually find her at the church. She cleans there regularly and plays the organ.'

'A dedicated member of the congregation then?'

'Oh yes, but people like that usually are, aren't they?'

Kate raised her eyebrows. *And they call me a cynic*, she mused.

CHAPTER 6

After leaving Beverley James's cottage, Kate called at the Jackson house again, to check on Helen Jackson's condition. She didn't get far. She was met on the doorstep by a gaunt, grey-haired woman, dressed in a grey two-piece suit and sensible shoes who fixed her with a hostile stare. Kate guessed she was the sister Beverley James had mentioned.

'DS Lewis,' she began, producing her warrant card. 'I thought I would pop over to see how Mrs Jackson is.'

'What do you expect?' the other retorted sharply. 'Her husband has just killed himself. And she can do without the police harassing her at this time.'

Kate winced. 'I have no intention of harassing her, though in due course, I will have to talk to her about what happened.'

'What happened?' the other woman repeated incredulously. 'I would have thought that was pretty clear, wouldn't you? Peter blew his head off with a shotgun.'

Kate nodded. 'I'll call back to see her when she is able to talk to me.'

'Heaven knows when that will be,' the dragon said, only to be interrupted by another woman speaking from behind her.

'Let the police officer in, Wanda. I am quite willing to talk to her.'

The dragon stiffened. 'You'd better come in then. But make it short.'

Kate was shown into the living room where she had earlier spoken to Doctor Makepiece. A slight, dark-haired woman in a knee-length patterned dress was sitting on the sofa waiting for her.

'I'm Mrs Jackson,' she said. 'Please, do sit down.'

Her face was pale and pinched and Kate noticed a slight quiver in her voice, but otherwise she seemed surprisingly composed.

'I am very sorry for—' Kate began, but the woman shook her head with a faint, nervous smile.

'Thank you, Officer, but I am quite resigned to it now and would just like to get this interview out of the way. Does that surprise you?'

'Not really,' Kate lied. 'Each of us deals with grief in our own way.'

'Ah, grief,' Jackson echoed. 'Yes, I suppose I should be grieving, and I am in a way — for all that was lost years ago. But now,' she shrugged, 'I just feel empty.'

'You found your husband, I gather?'

Jackson shuddered. 'Yes, and that was awful. We had only just come down for breakfast, you see, when he got this letter. He took it into his study, and a few minutes later I heard him go out. Then, this awful bang. Finding him like that, well—'

Kate nodded sympathetically. 'Do you know what was in the letter?'

'No, and I don't want to just at this moment, if you don't mind.'

Kate was trying to think of a tactful way of asking her next question, when Jackson answered it for her.

'I know my husband was gay, Officer. In fact, I've known for some time, though he was unaware that I knew. I also know he was meeting with another man late at night in our barn, but I suppose I simply closed my mind to it all. You see, Peter and I haven't slept together for a long time now. We were happy in a way, but we had long since drifted apart emotionally and lived our separate lives. Intimacy was very much a thing of the past.' She hesitated. 'I am, of course, shocked and horrified that he chose to kill himself, but I have to be honest and say that I am not heartbroken about it. Does that sound awful?'

It did, but Kate didn't say so. Instead, she said, 'Have you ever seen anyone lurking about near your barn, apart from the man you said your husband met there?'

She shook her head. 'I never went out there to check, so I wouldn't have seen anyone anyway. What happens now?'

Kate had a fervent desire to leave that she had difficulty concealing. 'There will be an inquest, of course, but not for a while. She stood up. 'Our coroner's officer will be round to see you very soon and she will explain everything to you.'

'And that's it, is it? Job done. So you can leave now.' The dragon stood behind her.

Kate forced a smile. 'Again, I'm very sorry for your loss, Mrs Jackson. I'll see myself out.'

Kate could not have felt more relieved when the dragon slammed the front door behind her. She stood for a moment, taking in the clean, fresh air. She wasn't aware of the figure standing in the shadows by the front gate until it stepped into the driveway and walked towards her. Kate found herself confronted by a woman with spiky hair dyed a bright pink, dressed in skinny blue jeans and a brown leather jacket. She glimpsed the notebook the woman was holding and alarm bells jangled in her head. Press. That was all she needed.

'Hi, Kate,' the woman said with a brief smile. 'It is Kate Lewis, isn't it? We've spoken before at crime scenes. Debbie Moreton from the local tabloid.'

'This isn't a crime scene,' Kate replied drily.

'No, but I gather that there has been a shooting here. Is that right?'

'You're quick off the mark,' Kate retorted, now recalling the pushy youngster from a number of previous incidents.

'I try to be. So, what's the story?'

Kate threw open the door of the CID car. 'There isn't one.'

'A source has told me that a man blew his head off with a shotgun in the barn. Is that correct?'

Kate frowned. The press and their bloody so-called sources. She snapped, 'I have no comment to make.'

'I could always knock and ask.'

Kate smiled, thinking of the dragon lurking behind the door. 'You could, but I certainly wouldn't advise it.'

Then she turned the car and drove off, leaving the young reporter staring after her, scowling.

* * *

Kate's reception at the vicarage next to the ancient Norman church was a lot more welcoming.

'Ah, come in, Sergeant.' The vicar was a large, overweight man in a loosened clerical collar. 'Sergeant Reeves has just been to see me.' Shaking his head, he ushered her down the hallway. 'Dreadful business, just dreadful.'

Showing her into a small study at the end of the hallway, he swept a wad of papers off a chair beside his desk and dumped them on a floor already littered with screwed-up balls of paper and dozens of books. There were books everywhere. Big, leather-bound volumes, crammed into the shelves of a bookcase occupying one entire wall, piled up on the desk and even on the windowsill in front of it. There was also an object that somehow seemed totally out of place in a rectory study. Perched somewhat incongruously on the mantelshelf of the open fireplace, between two photographs of what appeared to be the Rev Salter in his younger days dressed in shorts and a striped T-shirt, was a leather rugby ball.

Salter smiled when he saw Kate stare at it. 'Used to play for the regiment when I was an army chaplain. Sadly, a lifetime ago now.'

Kate smiled back, feeling a little embarrassed to be caught out. 'A rather rough game, by all accounts. Did your team usually win?'

He released a chuckle. 'Only when the lads let us.'

With a nod, he indicated the chair. 'Anyway, do sit down. Sorry about the mess but I was just preparing my sermon for next Sunday.'

Kate perched on the edge of the chair. 'Peter Jackson, Rev Salter,' she began. 'I gather you were sent a letter about him?'

He frowned. 'Yes. Wicked thing to do. As I told Sergeant Reeves, I shredded it immediately.'

'Ah, then you've answered the question I was about to ask. Were there photographs enclosed?'

He nodded. 'Shredded with the letter. Best place for such filth.' He hesitated a moment, removed his spectacles and gave them a vigorous rub with his handkerchief. 'I — I must be honest, Sergeant, I was quite shocked by those pictures. I certainly don't hold with the modern attitude towards such behaviour but, as a Christian, one should never judge others and I try to keep as open a mind as possible. Peter is — er, was — a good church warden and very supportive of this church, as was Helen, his wife, and, as far as I am concerned, what he did in his private life was his own affair.'

'Others in your congregation might not see it that way.'

'They are not going to know about it from me.'

'Perhaps someone already knew of his secret and decided to punish him with the pictures?'

He shook his head. 'Personally, I don't think that is the case. I don't know whether you are aware, but several people in this parish have received anonymous letters—'

'So I believe. Have you any suspicions as to who might be responsible for sending them?'

'No idea, I'm afraid, and I have to say that if I did know, I wouldn't feel it appropriate to inform the police. God knows what wickedness lurks in all our hearts, but we will all be accountable to Him on Judgement Day.'

'Maybe we will, but in the meantime, people's lives are being ruined by this nasty individual, and he or she has to be stopped.'

'I'm sorry, I can't help you.'

Kate studied the clergyman with a level gaze. 'You have a lady in your congregation, a Mrs Maisie Taylor—'

Now he looked truly annoyed. He interrupted her sharply. '*Miss* Taylor, actually. I hope you're not suggesting our Maisie could be responsible?'

'I suggest nothing, but I understand that she is known in the village as something of a gossip and has a bit of a sharp tongue.'

He sighed. 'Maisie is her own worst enemy, Sergeant. Yes, she likes to gossip. Most of my elderly parishioners do. Passes the time, you see. But she has a heart of gold and would do anything for anyone. She is a loyal supporter of the church. Plays the organ, in fact. And she never misses a service. The idea that she could somehow be behind this business is preposterous.'

The atmosphere in the room had suddenly developed a chill. Kate stood up.

'One last question, Reverend. Have you any idea who the man in the photographs with Peter Jackson is?'

He also stood up and shook his head. 'Not a clue, Sergeant — not that I dwelled long on those vile pictures in any case. Now, if there is nothing else . . .'

He glanced at the pile of papers he had removed from Kate's chair.

Kate smiled. 'Of course, the sermon,' and she turned for the door.

'I will be going over to see Helen Jackson later,' Salter said as he showed her out. 'Hopefully, with God's help, I will be able to give her some spiritual comfort at this terrible time.'

Kate thought yet again of the dragon at the Jackson house and forced another smile. 'I'm sure she would be very pleased to see you,' she lied.

* * *

Kate considered visiting Maisie Taylor for a preliminary chat before returning to the police station, but thought better of it. Since Taylor had been put forward as a likely suspect, it would be necessary to tread warily in any interview and it was more sensible to have someone with her as a kind of insurance against future allegations of harassment — particularly in view of the fact that the woman was evidently elderly.

So, acting on a hunch, she decided to drop into the local post office and shop instead, giving the once-over to the stone cottage on the right of it where Taylor allegedly lived before pushing through the glass door.

The shop was virtually empty save for a buxom, blonde woman standing behind the counter, an elderly man in tweeds eyeing up the bottles of whisky on the high shelf at her back and a couple of small children with their mother in tow, arguing shrilly over what sweets they should be allowed to choose from a row of plastic trays at the far end by the post office.

The woman behind the shop counter turned at the loud "ding" of the bell. 'Help you?' she asked with a friendly smile.

Kate returned the smile, automatically reached for the warrant card in her pocket, then stopped herself. She was only there to check on her hunch, so it was probably best not to disclose who she was at this early stage.

'Yes,' she said. 'You don't sell typing paper, do you?'

'At the back, my lovely,' the woman replied. 'Section marked stationery.'

Feeling slightly foolish for asking, Kate strolled past the harassed mother to another, narrower room at the far end of the shop, where two shelf units stood opposite each other. The right-hand unit and a spinner beside it contained displays of greeting cards, while the left was made up of three shelves packed with a variety of stationery items, from envelopes to plastic file sleeves. The packs of paper occupied one half of the middle shelf and Kate went through them carefully, only to face disappointment. There were three different packs in total, but, surreptitiously peeling back one corner of each, she found that they were all of the white, glossy variety and nothing like the kind of paper used in the letters sent to Peter Jackson and Beverley James.

'What you looking for, my lovely?' The voice came from immediately behind her, making her almost jump out of her skin.

The blonde assistant was standing there, giving her a suspicious look.

'Oh,' Kate blurted, hoping the woman hadn't seen her peel back the corners of the packs, 'I was looking for some paper, but I wanted it for my little nephew to use for drawing. I think these packs are a bit too expensive for that and the paper might be too thin. I was looking for something cheaper and coarser. Still, never mind.'

To her surprise, the woman's suspicious frown vanished. 'Your nephew is it, my lovely? Bless him. No, none of that paper will be any good. I did have pads of cheaper, coarser stuff, which would be ideal. The lady next door orders them on a regular basis but she bought all the stock I had about a week ago. However, I do have one more pad at the back, which was soiled on delivery. You're welcome to that if you like — at a discount, of course.'

Kate nodded eagerly. 'That would be great, thank you.' Her heart missed a beat when the woman finally produced the pad, opening up a corner for her to look at. The colour and texture of the paper was unmistakable. She was no authority on paper, but it looked like her hunch had paid off.

'So, you just get the paper in for that one lady, do you?' she asked as casually as she could. 'No one else buys it then?'

The assistant laughed. 'No, my lovely. Quality's not there. She uses it at her Sunday school apparently. Kids don't care what they're scribbling on, do they?' She frowned. 'Having second thoughts on it, are we?'

Kate gave a hasty smile. 'No, honestly, it's exactly what I want.'

Paying for the pad, she nodded towards the wall of the shop. 'Lovely cottage next door.'

The woman nodded. 'Maisie Taylor's place. Needs a bit doing to it, they tell me, but yes, it is a nice little cottage. About a hundred years old, they say.' She chuckled. 'I reckon Maisie has been there about the same length of time.'

'Oh, how sweet. A nice, little cottage occupied by a nice, little old lady.'

There was a loud guffaw behind her. 'Nice, little old bitch, more like,' growled a deep voice.

She turned to see the elderly man she had spotted on entering the shop pulling his wallet out of his pocket. Having obviously decided against the whisky, he was holding a wrapped cut loaf in one hand.

'Now then, Ned Mason, that's not kind,' the woman said reprovingly. 'You shouldn't say things like that.'

He snorted. 'True, though, ain't it? Got the devil's tongue, that one. And her in the church too.'

The assistant frowned and shook her head. 'You pay him no heed, my lovely,' she said to Kate. 'He's just an ignorant old man. Live round here, do you?'

The question nearly caught Kate out and she hesitated before replying. 'No, no. In Burtle. Just down the road.'

The woman smiled again. 'Well, you make sure that little nephew of yours does some good pictures.'

Kate left the shop feeling guilty. Deceit had never been her forte but she had certainly managed it this time. She only hoped she would never have to meet the helpful shop assistant again.

The information she had gleaned was very relevant, however. It seemed that Maisie Taylor might have some questions to answer, but not today. Kate glanced at her watch. It was nearly time to knock off duty, and there was a nice bottle of wine waiting for her and Hayden at home.

* * *

Kate never got her red wine. The moment she walked back into the general CID office she was waylaid by Ted Roscoe. Jamie Foster and another colleague, DC Danny Ferris, were at their desks, Foster studying the screen of his computer, while Ferris was on the phone, but there was no sign of Hayden.

'Where've you been all afternoon?' Roscoe demanded, chewing on a wad of gum. He looked at his watch. 'It's gone six.'

'Making further inquiries into our poison pen writer,' she replied and placed the pad she had purchased from the village shop on her desk in front of him.

'So?' he said, eyeing the garish design on the cover of the pad. 'Don't tell me, you're taking up colouring as a hobby.'

She smiled, stripping off the cellophane wrapping and opening the cardboard cover to expose the coarse, greyish sheets of paper. 'Hardly, guv. I found it in the village shop. Look.'

Producing the envelope Beverley James had given her, she removed the letter and placed it on the desk alongside the pad. 'Matches, see?'

He peered at it, frowned, and then bent down to read the message.

'Another bloody poison pen letter?'

'I got it from a Beverley James, one of the Jacksons' neighbours in the village. She was sent this a week ago.'

He grunted.

'And, as far as I can see, the paper used matches the paper in the pad I have just purchased from the shop.'

He shrugged and straightened up. 'Doesn't mean anything. You can probably buy a pad like that in shops all over the country.'

She nodded. 'I agree, but the interesting thing is, the village gossip, a Miss Maisie Taylor, who lives next door to the shop, regularly orders these pads and a week ago bought up the shop's entire stock, apart from this soiled one.'

He made a disagreeable face, obviously not wholly convinced. 'Okay, it's plausible, I'll give you that, but it wouldn't stand up in a court of law.'

'I realise that, but I'm going to have a word with Miss Taylor tomorrow. See what transpires.'

He nodded, still patently unimpressed. 'You do that and let me know the result. Oh—' and he turned back to the desk and pointed to another envelope leaning against her in-tray. 'That was dropped in by hand for you at the desk this afternoon. Our ethnic cousin from earlier, I gather. I hope you're not still wasting time on that bloody misper?'

'No, guv,' she replied truthfully. 'I've done nothing on it since.'

'Good.' He looked up as two detectives, followed by a disconsolate-looking Hayden, strolled into the office. 'Right, you lot,' he shouted. 'Down the Black Cock in an hour. Kate Lewis is buying. And that's an order.'

CHAPTER 7

Another day, another head! Kate could hardly believe her stupidity when she turned up at the police station the following morning with a hangover nearly as bad as that of the previous day. At least Roscoe was not in the office to mock. She hoped he was flat on his back somewhere with an even worse headache.

Hayden was in almost the same condition this time, and he groaned as he dropped into the chair at his desk. 'I'm never going to touch a drop again,' he moaned, the cup of black coffee in his hand tipping dangerously.

Kate didn't answer, squinting at the note the DI had given her the evening before.

'Been to caff, where me and Tam was s'posed to meet,' it read. *'Old girl there says some weird guy were giving her grief before she left. Dunno who he was, but you better find him before I do!*

'Tony.'

Kate groaned. That was all she needed. A vigilante on the street. 'How are we with that misper?' she called across to Hayden.

He raised his head, frowning, as if he hadn't the faintest idea what she was talking about.

She swore under her breath and straightened up. 'Misper, Hayd? You were going to follow it up?'

Enlightenment dawned with a noticeable jolt and he took a hurried gulp of his coffee. 'Yes, yes,' he responded. 'All in hand. Asked Birmingham nick to go around to her address to see if they could find out anything,'

'And?'

He turned reluctantly to face his computer screen and half-heartedly tapped on the keyboard for a few moments, studied his messages on the screen, then swung back to face her. 'Been around to the address apparently and checked her room out. No sign of Logan or any indication where she might be. Room is apparently in boyfriend's name and she's just been living with him there. Landlady hasn't seen hide nor hair of her since she and Tony Samuel left for the Glastonbury Festival a few days ago. Works as a receptionist at local freight firm and she didn't turn up for work yesterday morning when she was due back. Done it before, apparently. Not very reliable. Boss has no idea where she could be. No known family or associates, apart from boyfriend, so, bit of a brick wall.'

Kate made a grimace. 'Beginning to look a bit dodgy, this one. That's it, is it?'

He pulled a couple of sheets of paper from his in-tray, hauled himself out of his seat and stomped over to her. 'Only that,' he said, dropping both sheets onto the desk in front of her.

'Did some PNC checks and a few follow-up inquiries,' he continued while she scanned them. 'Logan is known to us. Picked up several times as a juvenile for vagrancy after being found sleeping rough. Parents killed in RTA when she was thirteen and she ended up in care. Absconded three times. Has had a couple of minor busts since adulthood for possession of weed, and a caution for shoplifting, so obviously no angel, but nothing too serious. Known to be a bit of a nomad and has tended to move around quite a lot. No known friends or associates, as far as is known. As you can see, the boyfriend is a bit more interesting.'

Eyebrows raised, Kate read Tony Samuel's descriptive sheet aloud. 'GBH, Driving while Disqualified, Burglary and two counts of Supplying Class A drugs (heroin). A total of five years inside, eh? Good work.'

He managed a weak smile. 'One does one's best.'

'But, as well as doing this sitting on your arse, did you manage any legwork in the time I was gone?'

He manufactured a hurt expression. 'What did your last slave die of? Exhaustion?'

She was unrepentant. 'I doubt that would ever happen to you, Hayd. Well?'

He sighed. 'I visited the railway station, but that was a waste of time. It's only a halt manned by ticket machines. No one there to see anything. Had a scout around, but—' He shrugged.

'What about the café her boyfriend mentioned? The Blue Pixie?'

In spite of his hangover, he managed a triumphant grin.

'Waitress there remembers the girl. Showed her out the back way after she was harassed by one of the other customers. Never saw her again'

Kate was alert now and thinking of Samuel's note. 'Any idea who this customer was?'

Like the showman he was, Hayden produced his pocketbook and flipped it open at the right page. 'One of our regulars, I believe.'

Kate snatched the book off him and read the name. 'Mickey Bishop? That little turd?'

'Do you have to be so coarse?' he said. 'It's such bad form for a lady.'

She was already climbing to her feet, shaking off the drumming pain in her head to cross the room and grab the ignition keys for one of the CID cars from the hook beside the door. 'And I'm no lady, Hayd,' she threw back at him. 'Now get your arse in gear. We've got a "Bishop" to see before Tony Samuel does.'

'What? Now?' Hayden protested, looking back at his coffee. 'We don't even know where he's living.'

'Well, just maybe I do,' she said. 'It pays to keep a snout on a very short leash.'

* * *

The old caravan stood on a patch of scrubby waste ground at the back of a derelict warehouse. It was almost buried in a jungle of thorn bushes and sycamore trees and would easily have escaped the notice of a casual observer, but Kate knew exactly where it was and, turning her personal radio off and telling Hayden to do the same to avoid alerting Bishop to their presence, she led the way around the edge of the scrub at a cautious snail's pace.

A narrow, partially concealed path provided access to the caravan on the far side of the scrub, but, quiet as they were, they were detected almost immediately and there was a flurry of activity inside. Not bothering to knock, Kate sprang forward and yanked the door open.

The smell of body odour and stale takeaways rushed out of the van to meet them, and in the gloomy curtained interior, a figure was already halfway through the end window.

Kate grabbed him by the belt of his trousers and hauled him back into the caravan. 'Got an appointment somewhere, Mickey?' she snapped, as the thin, scruffy man sank to his haunches in a corner.

'I've done noffin', Sergeant Lewis,' he whined. 'You can't just burst in 'ere wivout a warrant.'

She crouched down in front of him, while Hayden pulled back the tattered curtains. 'Can't I, Mickey? Well, then, you'd better get hold of your QC, hadn't you? Would you like me to give him a call?'

'Always taking the piss, ain't yer?' Mickey snarled. 'Bloody comedian, you are.'

Kate pulled the photograph of Tammy Logan from her pocket and held it up in front of him. She saw him blanch.

‘Know her, Mickey?’ she demanded.

‘Never seen ’er before,’ he replied sullenly.

‘That’s funny,’ Hayden commented, ‘because Mrs Lister at the Blue Pixie told me you were harassing her a couple of days ago.’

‘Yes, Mickey,’ Kate added, ‘and now she’s gone missing.’

There was genuine panic in Bishop’s eyes now and he moistened dry lips. ‘No, no, I ain’t done noffin’ to ’er. Just chatted ’er up, that’s all. She — she went out the back door. Never saw ’er again.’

Kate nodded slowly. ‘Now, let me see, Mickey. What’s your present form, eh? Two cases of theft from washing lines, three of flashing and then there was that indecent assault three years ago. Hand up a lady’s knickers, wasn’t it? You did eighteen months for that, didn’t you?’

He shook his head repeatedly. ‘I been clean ever since I come out, honest, Sergeant.’ He gulped several times. ‘I admit I chatted the bird up, but I got frown out and as I said, I never saw ’er again after that.’

‘Then how did you know she left by the back door?’

There was a trapped look in his eyes now. ‘You — you’re twisting fings, like you bastards always do. I watched ’er frough the winder and saw ’er go towards the toilets with old Lister. I knew there was a door out back, so I guessed she’d gone that way.’

‘Follow her, did you, Mickey?’ Hayden asked sternly. ‘Nip round the back, did you, and grab her in the alleyway there?’

‘No, no, no!’ he almost screamed. ‘I never touched ’er. On me muvver’s life, I never touched ’er.’

Kate raised her eyebrows and stood up. ‘Your mother’s been dead for at least six years, Mickey.’

She glanced around the caravan. ‘Any women’s undies in here, are there, Mickey? We know you like to raid washing lines. Better tell us before we find them.’

‘In the top drawer of the chest,’ he said with an air of resignation. ‘But I didn’t nick ’em. I found ’em at the tip.

Ask the foreman. Caught me nickin' the bleedin' things from one of the skips.'

Hayden moved towards the chest, but Kate stopped him with a nod.

'Okay, Mickey, we'll leave it at that for now. But we'll be back if we turn up anything else. You know that, don't you?'

He nodded, his eyes like those of a frightened hare caught in a car's headlights. 'I ain't done noffin', Sergeant,' he whimpered. 'Honest.'

Kate gave a tight smile and nodded towards the door to indicate to Hayden that they were leaving.

On the threshold, she paused again and looked back at the shivering wretch. 'If you hear anything, you know where to find me. But don't leave it too late or we'll have to come after you.'

'You're just going to walk away without even searching the van?' Hayden commented on their way back along the path to the car.

'He hasn't done anything to that girl,' Kate replied. 'He hasn't got the guts — it's not his thing — and we wouldn't have found anything in there either, except some soiled underwear.'

'So, what was the purpose of the visit?' he said, throwing open his car door.

She slid behind the wheel. 'To put the frighteners on him,' she replied, starting the engine. 'There's not much that goes on around here that Mickey isn't privy to, and if he does know something about Logan, my guess is it won't be long before he decides to tell me about it — for a little pocket money, of course.'

Hayden slammed the door shut as she pulled away. 'Then you *do* think something may have happened to Tammy Logan?'

She pursed her lips reflectively. 'Not necessarily. I feel there's something funny about it, I'll admit that. But so far there's no real suggestion she may have come to any harm, and the background you have dug up suggests she is more than a bit flaky. She may have simply disappeared to spite her boyfriend. You know as well as I do that most misper reports end up being false alarms. She'll very likely turn up again in a few days after licking her wounds.'

'And if she doesn't?'

She grimaced. 'Then we'll have a real problem on our hands. But we can only cross that bridge if and when we come to it. In the meantime, we have other, more pressing issues to deal with.'

* * *

Kate was certainly right about the "other pressing issues." One of them was already waiting for them when they arrived back at the police station, in the person of a very irate Detective Inspector Ted Roscoe.

'Where the hell have you been?' he rasped when they walked into the general CID office. 'Control room have been calling you up for half an hour.'

Kate glanced at Hayden and winced, suddenly realising that they had forgotten to turn their radios back on again after their visit to Bishop's caravan.

'Sorry, guv,' she said without offering an explanation, crossing her fingers that he didn't pursue the point further. 'Something come up?'

He scowled. 'You could say that. Colonel Winston has been on to the super again. He's received another damned letter. You'd better get over there. He's already thrown most of his toys out of the pram.'

'Who, the superintendent?' Kate queried innocently.

Roscoe's boot-button eyes drilled into her. 'Don't push your luck, Lewis. Just get over there. Like now.'

Winston was in his study when the smirking Elton admitted Kate and Hayden to the house.

'Bloody impertinence,' Winston almost choked the moment they walked into the room.

He waved the familiar-looking piece of paper in front of Kate's nose while Elton hurriedly withdrew. 'Damned thing must have been dropped into the post box in broad daylight. Elton only cleared the box this morning and it wasn't there then.'

'Can I see the letter, Colonel?' Kate ventured.

For a moment it looked as though Winston was going to refuse, but then, abruptly, he threw both arms up in the air before dropping the sheet of paper onto a nearby coffee table.

Kate picked it up and studied the message with interest.

'Further to my previous letter,' it read, *'I thought you might like to hear that I have decided to share what we both know about the Talisman Farm development with the rest of the village. After all, it's only right that the local community should know what sort of a greedy, ruthless parasite is living in their midst. So, I have sent a nice little piece to the parish magazine. I do hope they have the courage to print it. Hope you approve . . .'*

Stapled to the sheet was another typewritten article.

'You may like to know that our multimillionaire near neighbour, Colonel Herbert Winston of Winston House, is managing director of Winston-Morgan Holdings, a London-based property company which has a reputation for buying up rural land sites at a knock-down price and building substandard homes on them for subsequent high-cost rental through its subsidiary company, Cardin Developments. In the past, Cardin have been accused of employing pressure and intimidation on prospective sellers to secure a sale. Remember poor old Bob Dale, who died in a local care home last month? Well, he was actually one of Cardin's victims. After losing his wife a few years ago and then suffering a stroke himself so he couldn't work Talisman Farm, he was ripe for the picking by Cardin, and he was tricked into selling his fifty acres to them for a song at a time when he was at his most vulnerable. Still, maybe that nice Colonel Winston will send him a wreath at his funeral — who knows?'

'Pack of blasted lies,' Winston raved. 'Libel, that's what it is.'

Kate acknowledged his outburst with a curt nod. 'Whether it is or isn't, Colonel, is of no interest to me. My job is simply to identify the person behind these letters.'

He glared at her. 'And what the hell are you doing to catch the swine?' he said. 'Nothing, by the look of it.'

Kate's mouth tightened. It took some effort to control herself.

'Exhaustive inquiries are being made, I assure you, sir, but without more information, it is proving very difficult. Presumably, the contents of the first letter you said you burned were in a similar vein?'

He grunted an affirmative. 'Said I should look forward to some interesting publicity shortly — damned scum.'

Kate thought for a moment. 'Well, if it's any consolation to you, Colonel, I would be very surprised if the parish magazine publishes these allegations. As you observed, they could be construed as being libellous.'

'Word will still get around. Whole damned village will know about it soon. And I'm a JP, don't forget. Could ruin me.'

'Sadly, I can't do anything about that, but one thing that does puzzle me is how the writer knew so much about the Talisman Farm deal and about the link between your company and Cardin — if there is a link, of course?'

He shuffled his feet and glanced out of the window. 'Er, Cardin *is* one of our subsidiary companies, yes,' he mumbled, 'and they *have* acquired Talisman Farm, but the allegations are hogwash. Perfectly legitimate purchase. Good price paid for the land too. Not our fault the old chap died.'

Kate met his embarrassed gaze, aware of a nasty taste in her mouth and trying to ignore it. 'So, where did the writer get all this information from?'

He frowned. 'Good point. The business link between Winston-Latham and Cardin is not public knowledge. There were some spiteful comments in the property press about Cardin a few years back, but they were scotched. As for Talisman, the farm was purchased through a local estate agent on the understanding that the buyer's identity would remain confidential — quite usual in these circumstances — but somehow there must have been a leak.' His frown deepened into a vindictive scowl. 'I'll find out, I can tell you that for nothing.'

'Any chance you left correspondence lying about or put it in the rubbish bin?'

'No way. All confidential stuff is shredded.'

'By yourself?'

'Or Elton, yes.'

Kate thought about that for a second, then smiled. 'Can we keep this letter? It will remain completely confidential.'

He shook his head and snapped his fingers to take it back. 'Absolutely not. I'll keep it here — just so I know where it is.'

She shrugged. 'Your prerogative, Colonel. We'll see ourselves out, thank you.'

For some reason he didn't argue, and neither did Elton materialise to chase after them down the hallway, but to Kate's annoyance, someone else did.

Gabriella Winston had apparently been for a swim. She was wearing a fluffy white, knee-length bathrobe and flip-flops and dripping water all over the flagstones at the foot of the short flight of steps.

'Oh, Sergeant,' she exclaimed, smiling coyly at Hayden. 'Whatever has Daddy done now?'

'Nothing, as far as I know, Miss Winston,' Kate replied stiffly. 'Enjoy your swim?'

The young woman allowed the bathrobe to slip open so as to reveal that she wasn't wearing anything underneath. 'I like to keep fit,' she replied with a husky giggle, pulling the robe about her again. 'And we have our own pool. Do you keep fit, Sergeant?'

'I try,' Kate said, trying to hustle Hayden towards the car.

'Then you must come over one day and use our pool. I'm sure Daddy wouldn't mind.'

'Too busy, I'm afraid,' Kate replied tersely. 'Good afternoon, Miss Winston.'

'Did you see that?' Hayden exclaimed as they drove away. 'She had nothing on under that robe.'

Kate nodded. 'And she made sure you noticed. Why else would she come around to the front of the house just as we were leaving, when the pool must be at the back?'

He shrugged. 'Just coincidence, that's all.'

'Yeah, right. Well, I wouldn't let you within a hundred yards of Miss Gabriella Winston without a chaperone, I'll tell you that'

He grinned. 'Why, jealous?'

She sighed. 'No, Hayd, I just don't want you to make a fool of yourself.'

His grin disappeared. 'I am quite capable of resisting her charms.'

She cast him an old-fashioned look. 'She'd eat you alive, fat man.' She smiled. 'But let's see how you fare with the lady we're going to see now. From what I hear, she has all the charm of a rattlesnake.'

'Er — what about lunch?'

'Try tightening your belt — if that's possible.'

CHAPTER 8

It took three rings on the bell before Maisie Taylor answered the door. She was a thin, raw-boned woman with mousey hair tied up in a bun and pale, angular features that gave her a severe, unforgiving appearance. She looked to be in her late sixties, but there was not a hint of vulnerability in her demeanour, just hostility and suspicion. She was dressed in an ankle-length grey dress and sandals and carried a pair of secateurs in one gloved hand.

'Yes?' she said irritably without any pretence of a welcome, her sharp brown eyes boring into each of them in turn over her black-rimmed spectacles.

Kate introduced Hayden and herself and flashed her warrant card.

'So?' Taylor said. 'What do you want?'

'Can we come in for a moment?' Kate asked, with what she hoped was an engaging smile, remembering her experience with Helen Jackson's sister and wondering wryly if all the elderly women in this village were cast from the same formidable mould.

Taylor tutted irritably. 'I was dead-heading my petunias, but come in if you must.'

The hallway was dark and smelled of damp. A black cat emerged from a room to one side, studied them with liquid green eyes, and then raced ahead, to disappear through another open doorway. Maisie Taylor's "familiar"? Kate thought uncharitably. Probably rode on her broomstick with her.

They were shown into a dark sitting room with semi-drawn curtains, furnished with two shabby armchairs and a sofa. A picture of Christ as "The Light of the World" hung over the fireplace and a variety of religious texts adorned the other walls. Kate shivered. The place gave her the creeps.

Waved to the sofa, she and Hayden perched on the edge in a less than comfortable position.

'Well? What is all this about?' Taylor snapped.

Kate glanced quickly at Hayden. 'Just routine, Miss Taylor. I don't know whether you are aware, but several people in the village have been receiving malicious letters from someone—'

To Kate's surprise, the hard face softened into a tight smile and the elderly woman released an unexpected chuckle. 'And you think I've been sending them?'

Kate was completely taken aback. It was the last thing she had expected Taylor to come out with, and for a moment she was thrown.

'Why . . . why would you say that?' she went on after a brief pause.

Taylor shrugged. 'The village is full of vicious gossips and I know I'm not popular here. But as long as the Lord is content with me, that is all that matters. Ned Mason been spouting again, has he?'

Kate remembered the man in the shop and frowned. 'Ned Mason?'

'Local nuisance. Drinks too much and has a particular dislike of me for reporting him to what used to be the local constable a few years ago for poaching. He has nothing to occupy him since his poor wife walked out on him and he retired from farming. Spends far too much time brooding over his misfortunes in that great, big empty house of his. It's not healthy. The saying that the devil makes work for idle hands could never be more true than in his case.'

Kate tried to recover the initiative. 'No one is accusing you of anything, Miss Taylor, but we have to make inquiries. This is a serious business and it is causing a lot of trouble locally—'

Taylor nodded. 'Peter Jackson get one of the letters, did he?' she interjected. 'Is that why he shot himself?'

'And how do you know about that?' Hayden put in.

She treated him to a contemptuous smile. 'The whole village knows about it, young man. This is a very small community and word gets around rather quickly. His death is obviously a tragedy, but it was to be expected under the circumstances.'

'Why do you say that?' Kate resumed.

Taylor sighed. 'The wages of sin is death, Sergeant. If you scorn the Lord by indulging in perversion, you must expect to be punished for it.'

'What perversion is that?'

Another chuckle. 'Sergeant, the whole village knew Peter was having an unnatural affair with another man. The only one who didn't seem to know was poor Helen. I have heard that he received an anonymous letter, so I must assume that that was the reason he took his own life — out of shame that he had been found out.'

Kate studied her for a moment, all at once acutely conscious of the fact that she had underestimated the calibre of the woman she would be dealing with. She hadn't expected a shrewd cookie like this. Clearing her throat, she said, 'I understand you recently bought several pads of this kind of paper from the shop next door?' She held out the soiled pad for her to see.

Taylor smiled again. 'That's quite correct.'

'Unusual kind of paper to buy.'

The elderly woman stood up and went to the door. 'Let me show you something,' she said, and disappeared into the hall.

Almost immediately she was back, carrying a wad of the same kind of paper. 'Take a look, Sergeant,' she said, tossing the bundle of sheets into Kate's lap, and she chuckled again at the expression on Kate's face when she flicked through them quickly. All were pictures, drawn in what looked like charcoal, depicting crude images of angels, camels, donkeys and five-pointed stars, each one plainly drawn by a juvenile hand.

'I teach at the village Sunday school,' Taylor explained with evident satisfaction. 'This cheap paper is ideal for charcoal and the youngsters love it, plus the fact that I am very much committed to ecology and the reduction in global warming. This particular paper is made from recycled material, you see, and, as I support ecological initiatives like this, I had the local shop put in a regular order for me.'

'How does using charcoal fit in with your support for ecological initiatives?' Hayden murmured, but she ignored the comment, treating him instead to a frosty stare.

'Have you ever used the paper to type anything?' Kate went on. 'Say, a letter for church, for instance?'

'From your questions, Sergeant, I assume that the anonymous letters being sent are typed on identical paper. Well, the answer is no. I have never used the paper in that way, not even for a note, and on the very rare occasion that I have found it necessary to send a letter, I have written it by hand on proper writing paper. Old habits die hard, I suppose.'

'*Can* you type?'

'Maybe with one finger, but I've never had to. Unlike most people nowadays, I've never been tempted to buy a computer or a printer. In fact, I'm rather behind the times on a lot of things. I don't own a mobile phone or a television and I don't drive either. I suppose I haven't really joined the twentieth century yet, never mind the twenty-first.'

'What about a typewriter?'

She laughed again. 'Is it possible to buy them nowadays? But no, not even one of those. I do have an old thing — an Imperial, I think it's called — up in the spare bedroom, which belonged to my late sister who used to live with me, but I have never used it and it's broken anyway. I dropped it on the floor while cleaning the room a few weeks ago and just left it to gather dust.'

'May we see it?'

'If you must. Check the whole house while you're about it. I have nothing to hide.'

The rest of the cottage was as gloomy as the room they had just left, and also smelled strongly of damp. Ancient black beams supported the ceilings and the plastered walls were badly cracked in places. They disturbed the cat again, this time curled up on a single bed in what they took to be the spare bedroom off the landing, and it once more fled when they pushed the door open. They found the typewriter — it *was* an old Imperial — dumped on a desk in the corner, with a pile of psalm books and Bibles stacked beside it. But it wasn't very "imperial" anymore. The casing was split and closer examination revealed that there were no ribbon spools fitted. Furthermore, the "a" and "f" keys were missing, and a large black spider inhabited the space between them. It was obvious that the machine had not been used for a very long time.

A check of what was plainly the main bedroom and, shortly afterwards, the other downstairs rooms in the cottage, together with several cupboards, produced a similarly negative result. It seemed that Maisie Taylor was speaking the truth, and they both returned to the sitting room feeling more than a little embarrassed.

'Satisfied now, Sergeant?' Taylor asked with another frosty smile. 'Am I now in the clear, or are you still going to cart me off in the Black Maria?'

Kate gave a short, awkward laugh. 'Oh, I don't think there'll be any need for that, Miss Taylor,' she said, perching once more on the sofa beside Hayden. 'I'm just sorry we have had to bother you in the first place.'

Taylor shrugged. 'No harm done, but I do have one question to ask.'

'Go on?'

'Have you ever considered *why* this poison pen person has chosen to use the same paper as myself for their mischievous shenanigans? It is obviously less than ideal for letters, so it seems very likely to me that they have done this precisely because they happen to know I use it regularly at the Sunday school and keep some spare pads there in case I run out. Obviously, as the alleged village gossip, I make an ideal suspect.'

Kate nodded. 'The thought had already occurred to us. And it is an avenue we will be pursuing. But one last question before we leave you in peace. Do you own a camera?'

'A camera?' Taylor exclaimed. 'What on earth do you want to know that for?'

'I'm sorry, but I can't tell you.'

'Well, it so happens that I do.'

Rising to her feet, the elderly woman crossed to an antiquated corner cupboard and bent down to open the single door. She rummaged inside for a moment. Then, turning as she straightened up, she pulled out a tan coloured canvas bag.

'I haven't used it for years,' she said with a mocking smile and handed it to Kate.

Unzipping the bag, Kate found herself looking at an ancient-looking box camera, bearing the name "Brownie."

'I'm not sure you can even get film for it now,' Taylor said innocently, returning to her chair. 'It belonged to my grandfather and must be about seventy years old by now. It used to produce sepia pictures, I believe.'

Kate handed the bag and camera back, almost tempted to acknowledge Taylor's obvious mickey-take with a wry, '*Touché*.'

'I don't think it's quite what I was thinking of,' she said drily and climbed to her feet, nudging Hayden to do the same. 'Anyway, we will now leave you in peace. Thank you for your cooperation. I trust you have not been offended by any of our questions?'

'Far from it, Sergeant,' Taylor replied, a sparkle in her eyes now. 'I found it most entertaining, a bit like being a suspect in an Agatha Christie novel.'

‘Bugger it!’ Kate muttered as she and Hayden returned to the car. ‘She was laughing at us.’

‘Can you blame her?’ Hayden retorted. ‘I mean, our inquiry was a bit flimsy, wasn’t it? But she did raise an interesting point. It seems very likely, going by the facts, that whoever is sending these letters deliberately set her up as a likely suspect. This indicates that not only do they know about the sort of special paper she uses and the fact that there are spare sheets readily available at the Sunday school, but that she has a typewriter in her cottage rather than a computer—’

‘Which would explain why they are using a typewriter for the letters.’

‘Precisely.’

‘And it also indicates that they must be someone who knows Miss Taylor very well, has actually been in her cottage and seen the typewriter there,’ Kate added.

Hayden nodded. ‘But what they didn’t appreciate was that the machine was broken, so Taylor could not possibly have used it.’

Kate paused with her hand on the half-open car door. ‘Unless, of course, our Miss Taylor *is* the poison pen after all and she is a lot cleverer than we thought. Maybe she has another typewriter — *and* a modern camera — stashed away somewhere? Offenders like this can sometimes resort to the strategy of hiding things in plain sight.’

‘Very possibly, *Miss Marple*.’ He grinned, remembering what Taylor had said about Agatha Christie.

‘Quite the comedian, aren’t you?’ Kate retorted. ‘But I wouldn’t give up your day job if I were you.’

* * *

The police canteen was packed when Kate and Hayden returned to Highbridge for a late “lunch” — a National Crime Squad team passing through on their way somewhere had swelled the usual numbers to near capacity — and they had to queue for quite a while before they got their meal and found seats. Kate had hardly dipped her fork into her potato salad when the tannoy system activated. 'Detective Sergeant Lewis to ring the CID office asap.'

Stabbing a piece of potato angrily with her fork, she grabbed a couple of mouthfuls and climbed to her feet.'

'Are you going to come back for that?' Hayden said innocently.

She gave his barely started steak and kidney pie dinner a scathing look. 'It's all yours, Hayd,' she retorted. 'I'd hate to see you starve.'

Kate dialled the office extension on the telephone outside the canteen. Ronnie Crouch, the civilian office manager, answered and, obviously sensing from her snapped response that she wasn't entirely happy, chose to adopt a tactful approach. 'Sorry if you were at break, Sarge,' he said, 'but the station duty officer downstairs says he has a feller at the front desk who needs to see you about the death of a Peter Jackson.'

At once forgetting her meal, she marched quickly along the corridor to the open door of the SDO's office and glanced through the wide glass partition opposite. A tall, balding man in blue jeans and an open-necked pink shirt was pacing the floor of the waiting area a few feet away.

'Who is he?' she said to the uniformed civilian standing just inside the doorway.

The station duty officer consulted a pad lying on the counter. 'Julian Brookes. Lives at a Bridgwater address. Bit of a fruit, I think.'

'What has that got to do with anything?' she snapped at the plump officer angrily. 'Bring him through. I'll see him in the waiting room.'

Brookes was still plainly very agitated when he was shown in. Kate invited him to sit down and studied him as he pulled up a chair. His pale, clean-shaven face twitched and one freckled hand constantly rubbed the negligible fringe of ginger hair circling his otherwise bald pate. In the sunlight streaming through the window, the fringe seemed to resemble a fallen halo. In any other circumstance, Kate would have found this amusing, but there was nothing remotely amusing about the man's appearance. He looked utterly distraught.

'Would you like a coffee or tea?' Kate asked him quietly and he nodded briefly. 'Tea, please,' he whispered in a soft, trembling voice.

Kate went to the door and called for a mug of tea to be brought. She had barely closed the door and returned to her seat when tears began flooding down the man's cheeks. She guessed at once who her visitor was.

'It — it's about Peter Jackson,' he said. 'I've just heard what happened and I can't . . . just can't . . .'

She placed her hand gently on his other wrist, which rested on the table between them. 'You and Peter were seeing each other?'

He nodded. 'For six months. We used to meet secretly in his barn. Thought we were safe there. I don't think his wife ever suspected he was gay, and she and Peter had grown apart anyway. He . . . he was going to tell her when the time was right.'

He produced a handkerchief, dried his eyes and blew his nose. Kate waited patiently, saying nothing.

'We — we were in love. We were going to get — get married,' he blurted out and collapsed into more tears. Then, abruptly, he stared straight at her and whispered, 'Did — did he suffer?'

She shook her head. 'Death would have been instantaneous.'

'But why? Why would he do such a thing?'

She hesitated, not wishing to add to his anguish but knowing it had to be done. 'You don't know about the letters then?'

His mouth twisted. 'That horrible person sent me a copy, together with those awful photographs. I shredded them all. But I still can't understand why Peter would — would kill himself over it. We were going to tell everyone eventually anyway.'

'Maybe he wasn't strong enough to cope with it. Maybe he needed more time and couldn't deal with the brutal way your intimacy had been revealed.'

His tea arrived, and he swallowed a couple of tablets with the first gulp. 'Why would someone do that?' he almost pleaded. 'We were hurting no one. It was in private.'

Kate's face was grim. 'I don't know, Julian, but I intend to find out, I promise you. But tell me, how could this person have known where you lived?'

He shook his head. 'I just don't know. No one else knew who I was.'

Kate made a guess. 'You didn't write to each other, did you?'

His eyes widened. 'But — but yes, we did. Oh lordy — I sent Peter a little love letter on my headed paper just before—' He swallowed hard. 'He rang and told me not to write again in case Helen stumbled across my letter. That got me worried and I told him to make sure he had got rid of it, and he said he'd—'

'Thrown it in the bin,' Kate finished for him, in a resigned voice.

He buried his face in his hands. 'How could we have been so stupid?'

Kate decided they had to move on and adopted a more business-like tone. 'Okay, forget about that for now. Tell me, did you see anyone when you met in the barn that last night?'

To her surprise, he nodded. 'We didn't think anything of it at first. It was like something blowing in the wind — a loud knock. Then we realised there was no wind. We ran to the double doors and saw a figure race off down the drive and vanish into the dark. Peter was very worried about it, but I told him it was probably someone who had been thinking of stealing the car and had fled when they realised the barn was occupied. We — we didn't think for one momen—'

Kate cut in impatiently, 'What did this figure look like?'

He thought a second. 'It was dark with only a faint moon so it's difficult to say, but I thought it was dressed in black and wearing some sort of hooded coat and high boots.'

'Male or female?'

'I couldn't tell from that distance, sorry.'

'Nothing else you can tell me? No one you can think of who would have done this out of personal spite?'

'No one.'

'And you haven't been aware of anyone following you, or any feeling of being watched during your previous meetings with Peter?'

He shook his head miserably. 'I just wish—' he began and broke off.

'If wishes were horses,' Kate said grimly, 'beggars would ride.'

'So, what happens now?' he asked.

She shrugged. 'We keep looking and making inquiries.' She stood up. 'And I'm sorry, but I must get on. Will you be okay?'

He got to his feet and nodded weakly. 'Have to be, won't I? Thanks for your time — and for the tea.'

CHAPTER 9

It is often said that problems come in bundles, and Kate had cause to remember these words when she got back to the CID office.

She hadn't returned to the canteen as it was now approaching four o'clock, which meant that the staff would be clearing up ready to close. The bar of fruit and nut chocolate she kept in her desk drawer would have to do instead.

But even that wasn't to be.

Hayden was sitting at his desk when she walked in. She sat down, throwing him a baleful look, thinking about the lunch she had sacrificed, which he had undoubtedly scoffed after his pie. To her surprise, he got up and came over to her, an unusually serious frown on his face.

'What's up?' she snapped. 'Indigestion bothering you?'

He shook his head. 'Mickey Bishop. He's in hospital.'

'What?'

'Got one hell of a beating, it seems, and uniform have got Tony Samuel in custody for it. Looks like he followed us to Bishop's caravan and worked him over after we left.'

'Shit, shit, shit!' Kate breathed, closing her eyes tightly for a second. For once Hayden didn't pull her up on the language.

'We'd better get over there,' she said, getting to her feet. 'On the way, I'll tell you all about an interview I've just had concerning Peter Jackson.'

Mickey Bishop looked as though he had been hit by a truck. His face was a multi-coloured mess, his nose appeared to have been broken and he stared at them from the bottom of two purple pits.

'He'll live,' the nurse said cheerfully, plumping up his pillows. 'We're just keeping him in overnight for observation, in case he suffered some concussion. Don't be too long with him.'

'Bloody hell, Mickey,' Kate exclaimed, relieved that his condition was not more serious. 'You look like a mugged banana.'

'Fanks lot,' he murmured thickly through swollen lips, framing his words slowly and with difficulty. 'Wanna see rest? Doc reckons couple cracked ribs.'

Hayden winced. 'Poor old feller. Tony Samuel do this to you, did he?'

Bishop made a weak snorting noise. 'No, bleedin' Tooth Fairy did it.' He turned his head to stare directly at Kate. 'All your fault. Bastard follered you to me.'

Kate's mouth tightened. 'I'm sorry, Mickey, really I am. But he's in custody now, so he won't be back.'

'Until 'e gets bail,' Bishop said. 'Next time 'e might kill me.'

'There won't be a next time with his form,' Kate reassured him. 'He'll be remanded in custody. But we do need to find this girlfriend of his. Is there anything else you haven't told us that might help?'

There was a very long pause. 'Only some motor I see,' Bishop said finally.

'What about it?'

He squirmed with sudden pain. 'Come out street behind caff real fast as I stood on corner,' he said through gritted teeth. 'But bird never come out after. Went an' 'ad a dekko, but street was empty. No sign of 'er nor no one else.'

‘Perhaps she’d already left the street before you got to the corner.’

‘No way. Went there soon as I seen ’er go out back of caff. Couldn’t have got there before me.’

‘Then perhaps she went the other way.’

‘Couldn’t ’ave. Street ends at caff. Dead end.’

‘But why were you standing on the corner in the first place? Fancied her and thought you’d try your luck again?’

He scowled. ‘Wanted to apologise for what I done in caff, an’ that’s all. Fought I might get reported for bovverin’ her. Didn’t want to go back inside.’

Kate grunted. ‘Well, that figures. So, what sort of motor was this you saw?’

‘Old Land Rover. Red, I fink. Grey soft top.’

‘Hmm. Did you get the number?’

‘Yeah, an’ when it were last serviced too. What do *you* fink?’

Kate smiled faintly in spite of the situation. ‘So, no number then. But what about the driver?’

‘Never clocked ’im, just motor.’

‘Anything unusual about it?’ Hayden put in.

There was another long pause as Bishop gingerly adjusted his position in the bed. ‘Mickey Mouse sticker on back winder,’ he said, wincing.

‘Mickey Mouse?’

‘Like in movies.’

Kate sighed. ‘Well, that’s something anyway. Why didn’t you tell us all this before?’

Another snort. ‘Then you *would* ’ave fought I’d done ’er, wouldn’t you? Reckoned it were best to keep schtum.’

Kate nodded. ‘We might still think you did her, Mickey,’ she said mischievously. ‘But thanks for your help anyway. Want us to get you some grapes?’

‘No, I bloody don’t,’ he snarled. ‘Just piss off, will you! Don’t want noffin’ to do wiv you lot no more.’

‘So rude,’ Hayden commented airily. ‘So rude.’

Kate chuckled. 'Okay, Mickey, we'll leave you to it. Get well soon, and no flashing at the nurses. The doc might cut your little show-piece off.'

The expletives followed them out through the double doors of the ward.

* * *

'Right, what now?' Hayden said as they sat in the CID car outside the hospital. 'This misper thing is beginning to look more than a little sus.'

Kate nodded. 'I agree. Might be nothing in this sighting of the Land Rover, but strange that Tammy Logan vanished so quickly after leaving the café. I think we should gear things up for a full-blown misper inquiry.'

'Roscoe won't like it.'

'Roscoe will have no choice. If Logan still hasn't returned to her lodgings by now — and I'll leave you to check that out again when we get back — I think we can rightly fear for her safety after all that has come out.'

'What about Tony Samuel? If there is anything dodgy about Tammy Logan's disappearance, he should be our chief suspect and be properly interviewed. After all, reporting her missing could have simply been a ploy to allay suspicion in the first place. You know, the old adage — best form of defence is attack. Plenty of others have done that sort of thing before.'

Kate shrugged. 'True, but talking to Samuel can wait. He's not going anywhere for a while and, as I said to Mickey Bishop just now, with his form he's unlikely to get bail.'

'So, what about this Land Rover Mickey told us about? If the story is kosher, could it be connected to Logan's disappearance, do you think? If it is, maybe Samuel was the driver and he carted Logan off in the thing?'

Kate shook her head. 'Why would he suddenly shell out for wheels? He and Tammy Logan apparently hitched a lift to get here. If he'd wanted wheels, he'd have had them to start with. I can hardly see Samuel suddenly going out and buying or hiring a vehicle for the express purpose of bumping his girlfriend off. There would have been much simpler ways of doing it.'

'Maybe the Land Rover has nothing to do with it at all then?'

'Could have nothing to do with anything, but we daren't simply discount it from our inquiries.'

'That's if Mickey's story is actually legit in the first place. It's possible he made the whole thing up.'

She shook her head firmly. 'I don't buy that. Mickey is thick. He hasn't the imagination to come up with something like this, and why would he mention it anyway unless it was kosher? Especially as he's had to admit he went looking for Tammy Logan after he was thrown out of the café, which could put him in the frame as a suspect.'

Hayden sighed. So, our next move is . . . ?'

Kate started the engine. 'To trace the Land Rover,' she said. 'And the Blue Pixie café seems a good place to start looking. If we turn up nothing there, then it might be an idea to see if we can find anything on VODS — the Vehicle Online Descriptive Search—'

'I do know what VODS is.'

She gave a thin smile. 'Then you're just the man to do the search. I'll leave it with you.'

'Thanks a bunch.'

As it turned out, the Blue Pixie was open and the proprietor, a man called Frank, was on the premises when they arrived. But they were out of luck with their inquiry. Both Frank and the waitress with the dyed blonde hair — a Mrs Lister — remembered the incident involving Mickey Bishop, as they'd told Hayden before, but they still had no idea where the girl could have gone and they had never seen a Land Rover of the description Kate gave. In fact, about all Kate and Hayden got from their visit to the café was the offer of a complimentary tea or coffee, which Kate refused on their behalf, and a large apple turnover, which Hayden spotted in the glass cabinet on the counter and bought without hesitation, practically drooling as the waitress slipped it into a paper bag for him.

Leaving the café by the back door, as Tammy Logan had allegedly done, and ignoring Hayden's protests at the enforced exercise, Kate led the way along the narrow street to the point where it curved round to join the main road. They saw nothing of interest and ten minutes later were back at the car.

'Satisfied now?' Hayden grumbled, dropping into the front passenger seat beside her, panting with the exertion and reaching for the apple turnover in his pocket.

'Not entirely,' Kate replied, 'but one thing's clear. If Mickey Bishop was telling the truth, it is unlikely Tammy Logan could have walked the length of that back street and out on to the main road before he got to the corner. It's only about a hundred yards from the café. That means something must have happened to her in between the café's back door and the main road.'

'The Land Rover.'

'Exactly. Now all we've got to do is find it.'

Hayden used his finger to remove the cream that had squirted out of the apple turnover and attached itself to the corners of his mouth. 'Nothing too difficult then,' he commented sarcastically, unperturbed by Kate's horrified gaze. 'But what about this poison pen business? Roscoe will be looking for results, especially with Winston on his back.'

'Tomorrow,' Kate said wearily, looking at her watch. 'It can all wait until tomorrow.'

Hayden brightened. 'Then it's home for dinner, is it? I must admit, I am quite peckish.'

'You're disgusting,' she said severely.

He licked his fingers with a flourish. 'But indispensable.'

* * *

Tammy Logan sat bolt upright. The sound of the key turning in the lock of the heavy wooden door was like a whiplash in the confined space. When he came into the room, he was dressed in the same green, polo-necked, long-sleeved pullover and dark trousers, and carrying a bowl of what looked like thick stew and a mug of coffee on a tray. He placed it on the small table beside her bed and stood there for a moment, staring at the Bible lying on the floor where she had dropped it. He drew in a breath with a sharp hiss, and bent down to pick it up.

'I see you haven't yet sought to redeem yourself through the word of God, Janice?' he said. 'That disappoints me.'

'My name isn't Janice, I don't believe in any damned god, and I don't care whether you are disappointed or not, you perverted creep,' she snarled in a sudden burst of anger.

She was completely unprepared for the blow, which struck her so hard across the face that her head slammed back against the wall. The room swayed in front of her for several seconds and she felt blood oozing from a split lip.

He pulled a handkerchief from his pocket, sat on a corner of the bed and tenderly dabbed at her lip before she could draw away. 'Now you've made me angry, Janice,' he said softly, 'and that's not good. You know what happens when I get angry. I lose control and then I do things I later regret. So, it's best not to make me angry in the first place. You do see that, don't you?'

She was shivering now, in a mixture of shock, pain and a deep, nameless dread.

He frowned and ran a large palm over his forehead. 'Janice got me angry,' he went on, staring past her at nothing, a strange distant look in his eyes. 'And she kept making me angry. That was a mistake.'

'J — Janice?' she whispered, confused by the sudden change of manner and the fact that he had earlier called her by the same name. 'Who's Janice?'

His gaze refocused on her and he smiled vacantly. 'Oh, she's not here anymore. Went away, you see. Didn't make the grade.'

Tammy gripped the edge of the bed tightly. 'Please,' she whispered, 'I don't know what this is all about, but please let me go. My name is Tammy Logan. People will be looking for me.'

He shook his head and screwed up his face, as if trying to get his thoughts in order. Then with equal suddenness, the coldness returned to his expression and in a *Jekyll and Hyde* transformation, the harder side of his personality reasserted itself.

'You'll not deceive me again, Janice,' he said, getting to his feet. 'This time it will be different. I'm just glad your poor mother is no longer here to see you like this. It would break her heart.'

'I am not Janice,' she sobbed. 'I don't even know you.'

He simply ignored her. 'Now, I want you to read *Genesis*, Chapters one and two, and when I come back, I will expect you to be able to tell me what it says.' He sighed again. 'Otherwise, there will have to be a punishment, I'm afraid.'

Then once more he was gone, the key turning in the lock on the other side of the door, and she was left with the silence.

CHAPTER 10

Kate rarely bought a newspaper. She'd had enough of the constant talk about Brexit and the succession of celebrity stories that seemed to fill the headlines lately. But, visiting a local takeaway for a nice greasy fish and chips to share with Hayden on their way home, the headline in one of several copies of the local rag left out for waiting customers caught her eye. She scooped it up on her way out.

The layby out on the moor seemed the perfect place to stop and, leaving Hayden to pillage the polystyrene takeaway box, she spread the newspaper out on the steering wheel and went through the story in the last rays of the dying sun.

It was written by Debbie Moreton, the pink-haired reporter of earlier acquaintance, and the headline that had drawn her attention now shouted at her: *"Bin Raider At Work."* She read the first few paragraphs aloud for Hayden's benefit.

'Police are investigating the theft of confidential information stolen from dustbins, which has provided a ruthless poison pen writer with the opportunity to torment local residents in a picturesque village near Highbridge. Just such a letter has already led to the death of one resident, Peter Jackson, who was found in a barn at his home with fatal shotgun wounds two days ago. It is not known what was in the letter,

but it is believed to have prompted him to take his own life. There is concern that if this poison pen writer is not caught soon, more tragedies may follow. Local detectives, led by Detective Sergeant Kate Lewis of Highbridge CID, have been making inquiries in the village and have already interviewed some local residents in an effort to unmask the person responsible, but so far this has not led to any arrest. Detective Sergeant Lewis refused to comment on the case, but one long-term resident police interviewed, a Miss Maisie Taylor, was unsurprised by the situation and told me that the village was, and I quote, "a den of iniquity," and that "God's punishment came in many guises."'

The piece went on to describe the village in detail, with a map showing its location and a photograph of the local church.

Kate released her breath in a loud exhalation. 'The cow! Where the hell did she get all that information? I told her absolutely nothing.'

'That's where you went wrong,' Hayden commented through a mouthful of fish, waving his wooden fork at her. 'You know the press. They'll find out anyway, and what they don't know they'll make up.'

He burped, apologised, and added, 'But the quote from Maisie Taylor is a bit silly. Saying something like that might suggest to some people that she is condoning the letters and, with her reputation as it is, that could lead to problems for her in the local community.'

'Saying we interviewed her could also lead people to assume we think she's behind the letters,' Kate added sourly, tossing the newspaper over her shoulder onto the back seat in frustration, 'and it still doesn't explain how that little shit of a reporter found out about the poison pen and the fact that Peter Jackson had received one of the letters.'

With a shrug, Hayden offered her the polystyrene box containing the remains of the fish and chips. She shook her head irritably and he dumped it on the floor at his feet.

'Enough people knew about it,' he said and counted the names off on his fingers. 'There's Helen Jackson and the dragon sister you told me about—'

'She wouldn't give you the time of day.'

'Then there's Beverley James who may have told her husband, not to mention the undertakers who took away the body — and, of course, the police surgeon—'

'Who wouldn't have told anyone anything. He's too much of a professional, you know that.'

He nodded. 'Yes, but the point I am making is that people talk, and in a small village word soon gets around.'

She stiffened suddenly. 'You're exactly right. So, how about a night out?'

He gaped at her, having difficulty putting both remarks together. 'A night out? Where?'

She beamed. 'The Soldier's Arms.'

'Where on earth is that?'

She grinned at him and he groaned, covering his eyes briefly with the palm of his hand. 'Not in that blessed village?'

She clapped him on the arm and started the engine. 'You're a genius, Hayd, you know that, don't you? As you say, things soon get around in a small village — and where is the best place for a bit of gossip? The village pub, of course. All we have to do is sit quietly in a corner and listen.'

'But I thought we were going home!' He sounded plaintive.

She engaged gear and pulled out onto the road. 'We are, Hayd — eventually.'

* * *

The public bar of the Soldier's Arms was crowded, despite the fact that it was quite early in the evening. Kate got Hayden to buy a couple of drinks while she retreated to an alcove in the corner.

Service was slow and it was a good ten minutes before Hayden reappeared from the press of bodies, carrying a pint of beer and a large glass of red wine. Placing both drinks on the little round table in front of her, he took a chair and reached for his pint.

‘Full house tonight, eh?’ she said, taking a sip of her wine. ‘If the devil could cast his net.’

Frowning, he looked around him, splashing some beer down his trousers in the process. ‘What do you mean?’

She nodded towards the bar counter. ‘The big chap in the checked shirt at the bar is one Ned Mason. He was the guy I told you about who was mouthing off about Maisie Taylor in the shop. Next to him with the pink hair is our very own newshound, Debbie Moreton, and, if I’m not mistaken, next to her is Beverley James’s husband. I’ve not actually met him, but I recognise him from a photo in her living room.’

She cast a mischievous glance at Hayden. ‘Quite a good-looking chap actually, with that blond hair and muscular build. Pretty fit by the look of him, even though he must be well into his fifties, wouldn’t you agree?’

He ignored the obvious wind-up and raised his glass to his lips. But he only managed a single gulp. She tapped his arm before he could take another, nodding towards the door. ‘And look who’s just walked in — your girlfriend, no less.’

Gabriella Winston was dressed casually in blue jeans and a matching denim top and she joined the others at the bar with an air of familiarity.

‘Well, well, well,’ Kate observed. ‘Now we know how local scandal gets around.’

Hayden deliberately avoided looking at Gabriella Winston, concentrating instead on her E-Type, which he could see through the side window, drawn up in the car park outside.

‘Feel a faint stirring when you see her, do you, Hayd?’ Kate mocked gently. ‘But there again, I suppose not. I mean, she’s got her clothes on now.’

Before she could wind him up any further, the long-haired man behind the bar tapped a glass with a spoon, silencing all conversation.

‘Quiz teams to the room at the back, ladies and gents,’ he announced. ‘Fred would like you all to go through now, please.’

There was a gradual movement towards another door and within a few minutes the room had emptied of most of its customers, leaving just the four Kate had named and a couple of other men standing at the bar.

Suddenly Kate felt a lot more conspicuous. She shrank back further into the alcove, motioning to Hayden to bring his chair round, so that his back was to the bar and his not insubstantial body provided a measure of cover for her.

'Not taking part in the quiz then, Ned?' Beverley James's husband joked. 'I thought you would be one of the key participants.'

Mason snorted. 'Enough to quiz about round here at the moment without that, Graham,' he said. 'You heard what happened to poor old Peter Jackson?'

'Suicide, I believe,' Debbie Moreton said casually, taking a sip from her glass. 'Don't know why he would do something like that, though.'

'Shame probably,' one of the other men at the bar suggested. 'Everyone knows he was havin' it off with another bloke. Queer as a five-bob note, that one,'

'His business.' Mason spoke up again. 'Feller can do what he wants in his own place. No reason to hound him, is there?'

'So, who was hounding him?' Gabriella Winston put in, her eyes shining at the prospect of a bit of local scandal.

Mason snorted. 'Only one person you can blame for that,' he said. 'The old bitch living next door to the shop. I reckon she's the one who's been sending out all them letters. Plain as a pikestaff, isn't it?'

'Letters?' Winston said, feigning puzzlement.

'Poison pens, they calls 'em. Everyone's been getting 'em.'

'It doesn't make her the one responsible, Ned. Be fair,' the long-haired barman interjected. 'I know she's a bit of a gossip but I can't see Maisie Taylor doing a thing like that.'

Mason set his beer glass down on the counter and leant towards him conspiratorially. 'Then why was Old Bill there this morning, eh? Had a long chat with our Maisie, they did. CID too. A woman and a fat bloke.'

'How did you know they were police if they were in plain clothes?' Graham James asked. 'They could have been Jehovah's Witnesses.'

Mason grinned and tapped his nose with one finger. ''Cause I seen one of 'em, the woman, in the shop before. Come out with some cock and bull story about buying special colouring paper for her grandson. She was snooping, you can count on it.'

'What has colouring paper got to do with poison pen letters?' Graham James said.

'Nothing probably', Mason said, ''less she was looking for the sort of paper the letters was writ on.'

'Whatever,' the barman interjected again. 'There's still nothing to say the pair at Maisie's place were police.'

Mason chuckled. 'No? Well then, listen to this. When they was at Maisie's, I had a quick look in their car, didn't I? One of them fancy radios was in there and a clipboard on the back seat with papers on it, saying "*Avon and Somerset Police.*" So, what you got to say about that then?' He drew himself up. 'No, Maisie's the one doing them letters, ain't no one else.'

'Then, knowing how you and Maisie Taylor get on so well, you should have got one too,' James said.

Mason scowled. 'Maybe I have and maybe I ain't. That's my business.'

'You ought to have been a detective yourself, Ned,' Gabriella Winston put in with a laugh.

He picked up his beer glass and puffed out his chest. 'I don't miss nothing. Maisie Taylor is behind them letters, you mark my words.' He drained his glass and held it up in front of Graham James. 'Your round, I think, Graham.'

In the alcove, Kate shrank back in her seat. 'Sussed by a country yokel. That's a bit embarrassing.'

'He called me a fat bloke,' Hayden said irritably. 'Darned cheek. He's no spindling himself.'

'Drink up, Hayd,' Kate muttered, glancing around the room for another way out and spotting the "Exit & Toilets" sign. 'Time we were gone, I think.'

But she was already too late. At the exact moment Kate and Hayden got up to leave, Debbie Moreton happened to look round.

'Well, I do believe it's Sergeant Lewis,' she exclaimed. 'Ears burning, Kate?'

All the eyes in the room turned in their direction, and Gabriella Winston emitted a rich, husky chuckle. 'Doing a bit of extra-curricular snooping, Sergeant? Naughty. Naughty.'

'Having a quiet drink actually,' Kate replied stiffly, nudging Hayden towards the exit door. 'We happen to be off duty.'

'But we did enjoy your conversation,' Hayden added. 'It was very illuminating.'

Unbeknown to either Kate or Hayden, they weren't the only ones who had found the discussion at the bar "illuminating." Sitting well back in a snug on the other side of the bar, the middle-aged man supping a glass of beer behind a raised copy of the local newspaper had been less interested in Debbie Moreton's front-page story than the inflammatory comments of Ned Mason. Shortly after the departure of the police officers, when the discussion had moved on to sport, he finished his beer and quietly left the hostelry, giving a nod to the barman on his way out. There was a strange glint in his eyes as he climbed into the Land Rover he had left in the car park. He pulled a crumpled piece of paper from his jacket pocket and sat for several minutes re-reading the anonymous letter he himself had received that morning.

'Who's been a naughty boy then? And in your position too? You shouldn't have dumped that ladies' underwear in your dustbin, you know. You may have hidden it under the rest of the rubbish, but it wasn't difficult to find. Now, whose washing lines have you been raiding, I wonder? Do you like to dress up in those skimpy things when you're alone in your room? Does it give you a hot flush? And how much more of it have you got stashed away? Ah well, it takes all types, doesn't

it? I can't wait to tell the rest of the village what you've been up to, maybe with a little piece in the parish magazine. I'll let you know what I finally decide to do. In the meantime, I have to say I do admire your taste in underwear.'

Crushing the letter in his hand and dropping it on the floor, he hammered the steering wheel with both hands in a fit of anger, before taking several deep breaths and leaning back against his seat in an effort to regain control. Then he started the engine, driving slowly past Gabriella Winston's distinctive red E-Type and on to the road, disappearing in the direction of the moor with a painful grinding of gears. It was a pity Kate and Hayden had parked outside the pub instead of in the car park, because they would then have spotted the Land Rover. It was an old red Defender with a Mickey Mouse sticker on the back window.

CHAPTER 11

Maisie Taylor awoke with a jolt and stared into the darkness. She was quite a deep sleeper, so the sound she had heard must have been pretty loud to have awoken her. She had lived in the old cottage for so long now that she knew every one of the noises it made — the crack of rafters as they eased their position like the limbs of old men suffering from cramp, the rattle of the letterbox, the creak of the sitting room door that had never fitted properly . . . No, this was something different, something to be concerned about.

She glanced at the bedside clock. Its luminous dial told her that it was just before two am. She climbed out of bed and pushed her feet into her slippers. Then she felt her way across the bedroom, opened the door and stood there, listening for a repeat of the sound that had disturbed her. Nothing.

The moonlight, which heavy curtains had denied access to her bedroom, flooded the landing through the tiny window over the vault of the staircase and she shuffled out of her room to peer over the bannister. Nothing moved in the gloom below. Maybe she had imagined the sound, whatever it was, and the best thing to do was to go back to bed. But something stopped her. She had to check downstairs, if only to satisfy herself that all was as it should be. As she made her decision, she couldn't help thinking about the article she had read somewhere claiming that women were more likely to be the victims of assaults by nocturnal intruders in their own homes than men, simply because on hearing a noise men would invariably turn over and go back to sleep, whereas a woman's natural curiosity drove her to investigate. She didn't know if this was true or whether it was just another of those tongue-in-cheek statistics, but it didn't deter her, and she crept across the landing to the head of the stairs.

Again, she stood very still to listen before beginning her descent. Again, she heard nothing but the familiar noises she always heard.

But then suddenly there was a new sound directly behind her, one that she hadn't heard before. It was the definite creak of a floorboard under the pressure of a footfall.

Too late, she remembered the spare bedroom opposite her own, where her intruder must have been hiding, and as she whirled round, the dark figure lunged at her across the intervening space. Then the tiles at the bottom of the stairs were rushing up to meet her.

* * *

At first, Kate thought it was the alarm clock shrilly cutting through her dreams and she reached out to turn it off — only to succeed in knocking it from the bedside cabinet onto the floor. Then she heard Hayden's distorted voice booming in her head and, as she surfaced from the fug that was clogging her brain, she saw that he was sitting on the bed beside her with the telephone receiver in one hand, apparently talking to someone on the other end. For Hayden to be woken up by anything less than a nuclear explosion was a phenomenon she had never before been privy to and she gaped at him as she hauled herself up into a sitting position.

'What's the time?' she queried in a slurred voice as he put the telephone receiver down again.

'Just after three,' he muttered, plainly unimpressed by her failure to answer the call. 'And, as the phone is on your side of the bed, I would have thought you'd have got to it first.'

She swept the hair out of her eyes and frowned. 'So, who the hell was it?'

He grunted. 'Control room at the nick. Sus death on the moor.'

She was wide awake now. 'Sus death? Where?'

He switched on the bedside light. 'Our favourite village.'

Her eyes narrowed. 'Go on. Who's the stiff?'

'Maisie Taylor,' he replied. 'Found dead at the bottom of the stairs.'

'Bloody shit!' she exclaimed.

'Or words to that effect,' he added drily.

* * *

Two marked police patrol cars were parked outside Maisie Taylor's cottage, with a familiar VW Beetle up behind them. The cottage blazed with light and Kate saw that there were several lights on in the adjacent houses too, and a knot of people, wearing coats over their night attire, were gathered outside on the opposite pavement.

A young ginger-haired constable was waiting on the doorstep. 'Deceased woman is in the hall, skipper,' he said respectfully. 'The police surgeon is examining her body now.'

Kate didn't have to go much beyond the front door to have his information confirmed. Maisie Taylor, in a long cotton nightdress, was lying in a contorted position on her back at the foot of the stairs, the lower part of her body draped over the final three stairs and the upper part resting on the tiled floor of the hallway. Her head was bent back at an impossible angle, her eyes wide and staring and her mouth gaping open in an obscene rictus grin, while one arm was flung outwards, the other twisted under her body. A large pool of blood, which had crept out from under the halo of grey hair, stopped just short of a long raffia mat covering part of the tiled floor to the front door.

Doctor Raymond Makepiece didn't even look up when they appeared, he appeared to be too engrossed in his examination of the body, but Tom Reeves materialised from the back of the house and beckoned to them. He led the way into a dining room crammed with dark wood furniture.

'I thought you were on days?' Kate said to him.

'Short staffed,' he replied. 'Asked to do a split instead — you know, four hours in the morning from ten, then another four at night from ten, covering two shifts.' He shrugged. 'At least it gives me most of the day off and I'm on a couple of rest days after this anyway — which is a bit of a dirty trick after finishing at two in the morning — but there you are.'

Kate made a face. As she knew from her own time in uniform, splits were never a popular choice. It still meant working eight hours, but taking your meal break in your own time, so the force ended up gaining an hour for nothing.

'What does your inspector have to say about one of his neighbourhood policing team being pinched for shift duty like this — particularly as I wouldn't have thought Police Regs would allow staff to be given a rest day after finishing at after two in the morning?'

'He's on leave himself until tomorrow,' he said, 'and I couldn't really have objected under the circumstances. Anyway, I was just about to go home when this shout came in.' He made a rueful grimace. 'That'll teach me to clear off when I should and not stand around gassing.'

'You might as well get off home now then. Hayd and I can handle things from here.'

He shook his head. 'No, I'll stay on for a bit longer. Not much at home for me now Judith has gone, so I might as well be at work.'

She nodded sympathetically, knowing that he'd lost his wife to a brain haemorrhage a few years before and conscious of how lonely he obviously felt. 'Fine, Tom, I can understand that, but go whenever you're ready, okay? First, though, what have we got?'

'Not a lot really. Looks like Maisie Taylor got up for some reason in the middle of the night, went to go downstairs, slipped and tumbled down the lot.' He shrugged. 'Stair carpet looks old and could be loose in places, so it's feasible that an old woman like her could have tripped on that — or the cat, which ran out when I forced the front door.'

'How was this reported?'

'Control room was alerted by a local security firm, it seems. The old girl was wearing one of those personal alarm pendants around her neck — you know, you press a button and the central station rings you to see if you're all right. In her case, the device was activated around two am. They called her and when she didn't respond, they contacted us.'

'And I suppose there's no way of telling whether she pressed the button before or after her fall?'

Reeves shook his head. 'If she pressed it at all, that is. The thing could have been activated when it struck something during her fall. From what I could see without a physical examination, the pendant appears to be busted. No way of knowing for sure how or when it was triggered.'

'But equally, it's possible she could have disturbed an intruder and fell or was pushed when she confronted him at the top of the stairs.'

Reeves looked dubious. 'Nothing to suggest that, though, is there?'

'Well, it's still possible, isn't it?' she persisted. 'She was pretty well known as a malicious gossip. If someone in the village received one of the poison pen letters and thought she was responsible, they might have decided to shut her up for good.'

Kate thought of the conversation she had overheard at the Soldier's Inn the previous evening and added, 'Any sign of a break-in?'

He shook his head. 'Haven't checked upstairs, of course, but I've been all over the ground floor and couldn't find any broken or forced windows, but,' he shrugged, 'security was plainly not her thing. Several fanlights are ajar on their stays, probably because it's quite a warm night, and the back door was not locked, so anyone could have walked in.'

Kate sighed. 'Okay, Tom, point taken. We'll take a look around a bit later, but in the absence of anything to suggest foul play, we can only go by the doctor's assessment.'

'Which in crude terms is a broken neck, occasioned by a fall,' Makepiece commented gruffly from the doorway. 'Time of death probably within the last two hours.'

Kate looked at her watch. 'So, round about two am, the same time as the alert went off?'

'If you say so.'

'An accident then?' Reeves suggested hopefully.

Makepiece shook his head. 'Can't say that. All I can say is that her injuries are consistent with a tumble down the stairs. No defensive marks, as far as I can see, and, being an old lady, she wouldn't have bounced too well.'

'And the pendant alarm device around her neck?' Kate went on.

'Broken by the look of it.'

'Could she have pressed that *after* her fall and before she actually passed away?'

'Highly improbable, unless she pressed it as she fell. Normally in such cases death would be instantaneous, but you can never be certain about anything like that. Stranger things have happened in my experience.'

'Which doesn't help us much.'

'Sorry about that, but there it is. Death can sometimes be quirky. We may know more after the PM, but at this stage, I can only say I've found nothing to suggest that the lady's death was in any way suspicious.'

Then he was gone, and a few minutes later Kate heard his car pull away and fade into the gathering dawn.

'Accident then?' Hayden said, repeating Reeves's suggestion as he watched him also head off with a brief wave.

Kate thought for a moment, grimaced, and then nodded reluctantly. 'Well, it certainly looks like it, I have to admit, but I'm still uneasy about the alert from the monitoring device. It all seems a bit off to me. So, let's get the police photographer out here anyway. At the very least we will need to have the body photographed in situ.' She smiled at her husband. 'In the meantime, we can have a chat with our curious onlookers.'

The knot of locals gathered on the other side of the road had grown by the time Kate and Hayden went out, and a few general questions soon revealed that the majority were only there because of the arrival of the marked police car responding to the call, its flashing blue roof strobe waking them up and arousing their curiosity. None had seen anything unusual, which was hardly surprising as they had been fast asleep, and they drifted away almost as soon as Kate started asking questions. It was only as she and Hayden turned back towards Maisie Taylor's house that the woman called out after them.

'There was a car.'

Kate turned quickly to see that the speaker was the middle-aged woman who had served her in the shop next door.

'A car, you say?' Kate asked.

The woman nodded. 'Must have been well after one in the morning. I was up getting a drink when I heard it pull up over there.' She pointed further down the road. 'I noticed it because of the noisy engine. Sounded pretty rough, like an old diesel.'

'Go on.'

'It sat there a while with the engine switched off, then I heard a door slam and some footsteps. I looked out again, but didn't see anyone so I went back to bed.'

'Can you remember what sort of vehicle it was?' Hayden asked.

She thought for a second. 'Well, there was a moon, but it was parked in shadow so I didn't get a close look at it.

My eyes aren't too good now and I'm not much use on cars anyway.'

'You said it sounded like a diesel. Any idea of the shape? Was it a saloon or an estate do you think?'

She hesitated. 'It was sort of square, like a van. Yes, I think it was a van or something like that.'

'And did you see it drive away again?'

'No, but I heard it just as I was drifting off again, quite some time before the police car arrived.'

The woman peered at Kate. 'Aren't you the lady who came into the shop about that special paper?'

Kate winced. 'Yes, I was,' she admitted, waiting for the inevitable follow-up question.

'Did your grandson like the paper?'

Kate was relieved that she was not being asked about the real purpose of her shopping trip. 'Yes,' she lied, the darkness hiding her guilty expression, 'he loved it.'

CHAPTER 12

When the new day fully dawned, it was as grey as Kate and Hayden's faces. Insufficient sleep, coupled with a lack of any sustenance, had had a significant debilitating effect on them. Hayden was even having difficulty keeping his eyes open. Detective Inspector Ted Roscoe was his usual "cheerful" self as he faced her across the desk in his own office, either oblivious to or unconcerned about how she looked.

'So, no evidence of foul play — a fact actually confirmed by the police surgeon. No evidence of a forced entry, yet you still want to make a murder out of it?' he grated, staring at Kate with that familiar baleful stare.

'It was necessary to call out a SOCO photographer, guv,' Kate replied firmly. 'The reason for Maisie Taylor's fall was not one hundred percent conclusive in my opinion and, under the circumstances I have just outlined to you, I decided it was better to be safe than sorry, particularly in relation to securing photographs of the scene.'

'Elderly women fall down the stairs all the time,' he snapped back. 'It's been said that dodgy, ill-fitting carpet slippers are frequently the cause of accidents like this. Probably that's what happened here. She tripped in her slippers on a loose stair carpet and pitched down the stairs.'

'We don't know that for certain, guv, and you must admit it's funny that the very person the locals seem to suspect of being the poison pen writer should suddenly end up having an accident—'

'Yet you didn't find anything in her place to suggest she *was* the perp, did you? No computer or printer — only the old broken typewriter you say you'd already examined — nothing at all to indicate that she could have been behind the letters.'

Kate shook her head. 'No, just packs of the same paper that was used for the poison pen letters, plus a number of used sheets of charcoal drawings depicting angels, donkeys, stars and crucifixion scenes — which must have frightened her Sunday school pupils half to death — suggesting she was telling the truth about what she was using the paper for.'

'There you are then.'

'But if someone did push her down the stairs, they weren't to know they were targeting the wrong person, were they? As for the slippers she was wearing, they did not look particularly dodgy to me and, though the stair carpet was loose in places, it must have been like that for some time. Why should she trip now?'

He didn't answer, but his expression remained dubious, so she pressed on.

'There's also the curious thing about the personal alarm pendant that alerted the central monitoring station. Did she press it before she fell — and if so, why — or was it pressed by her afterwards — in which case how, if she was already dead?'

'But, as you yourself admitted to me just now,' he countered, 'it could have been triggered during the fall. After all, the bloody thing was broken, so that's a definite possibility.'

'And what about the motor Denise Merchant from the shop saw pull up in the street nearby at after one in the morning, a short time before Taylor's pendant alert was activated.'

'Anything to actually connect it to the scene?'

'No, but it was mighty strange at that time of the morning.'

He shrugged. 'Someone coming home after a late night out or dropping someone off? Happens all the time where I live.'

Kate said nothing. She was too tired to try and press her point.

Roscoe chewed rhythmically on his gum for several seconds, his little boot-button eyes studying her fixedly.

'Okay,' he grudgingly agreed, 'I'll accept that there are some unanswered questions that need to be resolved, but there's not enough here to justify initiating a major crime inquiry. It's the last thing we need right now anyway, with our resources already stretched to breaking point. We'll put it down to an unfortunate accident, unless something further comes to light, and in the meantime await the result of the PM.'

He bent over to spit his gum into his wastepaper basket and sat back in his swivel chair, his elbows on the arms and his stubby fingertips together under his chin, his gaze fixed on her again.

'Now, about this misper inquiry you were dealing with. DCI isn't happy about the circumstances and wants more done to try and trace this girl. How are we with it?'

'You told us to shelve it, guv,' she replied innocently.

He scowled. 'Don't give me that, Lewis,' he retorted. 'I know what a disobedient maverick you are and I'm fully aware of the fact that her boyfriend has been nicked for doing over that low life, Mickey Bishop. So, what's the current situation?'

She smiled, ignoring his insulting reference, and passed on what information she had.

He grunted. 'And no trace of the motor Bishop says he saw?'

'No joy at the café where she was last seen, but Hayden should be doing a check on VODS today. That might have something.'

He glanced through the internal window at the detective nodding over his desk. 'When he wakes up, you mean. Well, you can forget that job now anyway. I'm handing it over to DS Percival. He's back from leave later today and is just the man to deal with it. I want you to concentrate on this poison pen business and get the super off my back. Bloody Winston has been on to him again today, shouting the odds. So, brief Des on everything you have on the Logan woman and leave it to him. And, for frig's sake, call in on Winston again to keep him sweet.'

Kate frowned. Her colleague, Detective Sergeant Des Percival, had only recently joined the department on transfer from the National Crime Squad but was already Roscoe's blue-eyed boy. It stung her ego to have the inquiry taken from her in such an abrupt way, but she was too tired to argue the point. .

She shrugged. 'You're the boss.'

He flashed one of his wolfish grins. 'You'd better believe it!'

* * *

Des Percival was a tall, athletic, thirty-something-year-old, with blond, shoulder-length hair, a matching, military-style moustache and the charm of the devil. An unashamed ladies' man, he exuded the sort of natural charisma that had won him privileged status in the hierarchy's popularity stakes. Tipped for eventual ACPO rank, he was due for promotion to Inspector imminently and saw his posting to Highbridge CID as merely a brief stepping stone to greater things. Lucky beggar, Kate mused.

He walked into the CID office half an hour later, winking at Kate as he dumped his briefcase on his desk and skimmed through the contents of his in-tray. Roscoe spotted him almost immediately and called him into his office, closing the door after him.

The ensuing conflab lasted a full half hour. Kate was certain her ears should have been burning during the course of this secret briefing, especially as Percival turned to glance back at her through the glass partition several times and Roscoe nodded in her direction. She had the updated misper file on Tammy Logan neatly assembled inside a buff coloured folder and placed on the corner of Percival's desk well before he returned to the general office. He picked it up, smiled and wandered over to her.

'Mr Roscoe tells me I have to take this over from you, Kate,' he said. 'Apparently you have another job on your hands he wants you to concentrate on?'

Kate stood up, slipping her personal radio into her pocket. 'More like a poisoned chalice, Des. Anyway, everything you need is in the file. There's a sus vehicle that might be connected to the girl's disappearance, so a check on VODS, which we had intended doing, might be worthwhile, but that's up to you. Okay?'

'Any other thoughts?'

'Plenty, Des, most of them unrepeatable.'

His smile froze and the blue eyes narrowed. 'Nothing else to tell me then?'

She smiled back at him. 'Probably "the Best of British" might be the most appropriate thing to say.'

* * *

Tammy Logan struggled to breathe. The ice-cold water forced its way into her lungs, rapidly shutting down her senses. Powerful arms held her pinned to the bottom of the big bath, the white blob of a face looming over her, distorted and unreal. She could do nothing. Her frantic struggles were to no avail. Then, for the fifth time, he was hauling her to the surface again, watching dispassionately as she gasped, choked and hyperventilated, vomiting much of the water she had ingested back into the bath.

He had arrived in her room just ten minutes earlier and, apparently incensed at the sight of the Bible lying on the floor by her bed, had ripped off her dress and dragged her screaming into the bathroom, where he had dumped her roughly into the bath and held her down while filling it with cold water.

He gripped her by the shoulders and forced her head under the surface. 'Confess, harlot! Confess your sins before the eyes of the Lord.'

She remembered reading stories of the so-called water-boarding torture techniques the US forces used in Guantanamo Bay. In her first moments of terror, before her brain had begun to freeze along with her body, her panic-stricken thoughts had centred on the question of how many of them had survived.

'Do you confess then?' her own torturer demanded as she surfaced for the umpteenth time. 'Or do we carry on?'

She held up one hand, desperately gasping her answer through the water still spurting from her mouth. 'No, no! I confess. I have sinned! Please, I confess.'

His gaze roved over her body and as it lingered she felt the cold stab of another sort of fear. So far he had not attempted to force himself on her sexually, seemingly disinterested in her nakedness, but she didn't like the way he was looking at her now. She shuddered — from more than just the cold.

The next instant she saw that his expression had softened and, to her astonishment, he took her hand and helped her out of the bath before draping a towel around her and beginning to dry her hair with a tenderness that was in utter contrast to his previous aggression.

'Do you remember when you were little, Janice?' he said in a strangely soothing voice. 'How I dried you like this after you went swimming at the local pool?'

He chuckled. 'You used to chatter away to me all the time and say how much you loved your old dad. Remember that?'

Tammy swallowed hard, not sure how to react to this sudden change in behaviour. It was obvious to her now that her captor was a dangerous schizophrenic, who for some reason had latched on to her as a substitute for his absent daughter. She realised it would be as well not to antagonise him. Then, inadvertently, she did just that by cringing away when he rubbed the towel delicately over her breasts and she felt him tense and saw the shadow of a frown pass over his face.

'But they were good days, weren't they?' he said almost defensively. 'You won the first prize at Sunday school too, remember that? I was so proud of my little girl. You do know that, don't you, Janice? You do know I was proud of you?'

'Of course,' she whispered, trying to play along with him, while at the same time carefully drawing away from him as the hand inside the towel moved downward. 'But' — she coughed — 'but I'm dry now, thank you.'

Despite her caution, she felt him freeze and at once the hardness was back in his tone.

'Get dressed,' he said, snatching the towel off her and pushing her roughly through the archway back into her room. 'Don't try your harlot wiles on me!'

The badly torn cotton dress was on the floor by her bed and she snatched it up and quickly pulled it on, shrinking away from him again as he strode towards her, his face set into a cold mask.

Picking up the Bible, he dusted the front cover with his hand and placed it on the bedside table. '*Genesis*, Chapters one and two,' he said harshly. 'Read it and, if you defy me again, your punishment will be even more severe.'

Then he left, his footsteps fading away along a gritty stone floor, leaving her sobbing desperately into her pillow.

* * *

'I've been thinking,' Hayden said, pushing his empty plate away from him and sitting back in the plastic canteen chair. Breakfast had merged into lunch after their late return to the station, but at least the meal had put some colour back into their cheeks.

Kate drained her coffee cup and dabbed the corners of her mouth with her paper serviette, throwing him a curious glance. 'I've told you never to do that, Hayd,' she said gravely. 'It could be injurious to your brain.'

He shook his head impatiently. 'I'm being serious, old girl. We've already agreed that whoever tried to set Maisie Taylor up must either have been fully conversant with what sort of paper she used for her Sunday school classes, enabling them to purchase the same brand and quality, or have known where she stored the spare pads at the church, which would have allowed them to help themselves as and when they required a few sheets.'

'So?'

'So, it follows that they must have had a close connection with the Sunday school — an assistant teacher, a supportive parent or someone like that.'

'Maybe even the vicar?'

He shrugged. 'Never met the chap myself, but, yes, it's possible. And there's something else.'

'Go on.'

'We've already accepted that the perp must have been in Taylor's cottage at some stage to know she didn't own a computer, only an old manual typewriter. That typewriter is upstairs in the spare bedroom, so they must have known the old girl well enough to have been able to nose around the house and see it in the bedroom. What they didn't appreciate was that the thing was unusable, of course.'

'Good so far, but you forget that when Maisie Taylor died, Reeves found that her back door was unlocked. If you remember, he said anyone could have walked in. It's a typical country thing. I bet you'd find half the village don't lock their doors. So, our perp could have reconnoitred the house on a day when she was out.'

He waggled a finger. 'True, but if they had done that, they would have seen that the typewriter was broken, and remember, the old girl herself said she had dropped it a few weeks ago — obviously before the first of the letters we know about were sent. This suggests to me that our perp only managed a quick look round — perhaps had asked to use the toilet, which is upstairs — and didn't have time to examine the typewriter properly. They had seen no sign of a computer in the house and probably knew already that Taylor didn't use one. But clocking the typewriter standing on a table, they assumed that was what she used instead.'

Kate pursed her lips reflectively. 'Okay, so where does all this take us?'

'Well, Maisie Taylor didn't strike me as being the gregarious type — not one of those pensioners who like to socialise at afternoon tea parties. Anyone invited into her house would have had to have been there for a precise purpose—'

'Like attending a Sunday school leaders or church council meeting, for example?'

He beamed. 'Exactly. Which narrows down our field of suspects considerably. And the person most likely to know who Miss Taylor associated with and when would be the good old vicar himself.'

Kate pushed her chair back. 'Okay,' she said without too much enthusiasm, 'so, let's go visit the vicar, though I don't see that getting us very far. And before we do that, we have a more pressing call to make on behalf of our esteemed DI — one which I just know you will really enjoy.'

CHAPTER 13

Colonel Winston was not at home, though Gabriella Winston obviously was, as her E-Type Jaguar was drawn up outside the house and the gates were open. When they rang the bell, Elton informed Kate and Hayden in his usual condescending manner that the colonel was "away on business". But he didn't get to close the door again.

'Who is it, Elton?' a familiar voice called, and Gabriella Winston pushed past him.

She was barefoot and dressed, as on their first meeting, in very short shorts and a cropped top.

'Well, well, well, if it isn't the strong arms of the Law,' she mocked gently. 'Do come in. Unfortunately, Daddy is out of the country for a couple of days. Sudden decision. Didn't Elton tell you?'

She glanced back at him with a pout. 'Naughty boy, Elton. What you need is a good spanking.'

'It's fine, Miss,' Kate said hurriedly. 'We'll come back when he returns.'

The young woman shook her head and stepped to one side. 'But I insist, Sergeant. And anyway, I have something to tell you.'

Mystified, Kate shrugged and led the way inside, just catching a glimpse of Winston deliberately brushing against Hayden as he made to follow her.

'Can I get you a drink or something?' Winston offered. They had joined her in the same luxuriously appointed drawing room as before.

Kate shook her head. 'No thank you, Miss Winston,' she said. 'We're on duty.'

'Oh, you stuffy old thing,' the other replied, crossing to the cocktail cabinet and pouring a decanter of something into two glasses.

'I'm sure *you* would like a little snifter,' she said, holding one of the glasses out to Hayden.

He swallowed hard, trying to avoid staring at her. 'No thank you.'

She froze for a second, studying him fixedly, then emitted a husky chuckle, draining one of the glasses and setting it down on a coffee table.

'So, what did you want to tell us?' Kate said tersely.

Winston did a little pirouette and deposited herself on the chaise longue, crossing her legs and meeting Kate's gaze defiantly over her second glass as she slowly sipped whatever was in it.

'Have a seat, both of you,' she said. 'You look so awkward standing there.'

Kate sighed. She had a good idea that Winston was just playing with them. 'If you haven't got anything to tell us, then we will be on our way.' She turned for the door.

Winston jumped to her feet, exclaiming in a shrill voice, 'No, no, please. I do have something, really I do. It's about this poison pen person.'

Kate turned back towards her and waited.

Winston sighed and sat down again. 'The thing is, I know Daddy got one of those awful letters, though he isn't aware that I know yet. I overheard him talking to your detective inspector when he originally reported it—'

'You mean you eavesdropped,' Kate interjected drily.

'Guilty as charged, Sergeant,' she said without a hint of shame. 'I had no idea what was in it, but it was obviously something nasty because he went up the wall. I must admit, at first it made me chuckle. He's such a pompous, self-righteous prune and I rather thought he deserved being shaken out of his tree. That was until I received a letter myself this morning.'

'*You* received one?' Hayden exclaimed.

Winston nodded. ''Fraid so. Bit of a shock actually.'

'What did it say?' Kate asked, without a hint of sympathy.

'Look for yourself.'

Winston slipped a hand into the pocket of her shorts and tugged out a crumpled piece of paper. Kate took it from her, musing in a bitchy sort of way that it was surprising there was any room for a pocket in such a minuscule item of clothing.

The letter was typed in block capitals on the same sort of paper, with no signature, as per the others.

'Oh dear,' it read, *'you really have been a bad girl, haven't you? I mean, having it off with your daddy's faithful retainer, Elton. I wonder what Daddy would say if he knew? Shall I tell him, do you think? It would be curtains for Elton then, wouldn't it? And what about you? How would you cope on your own if Daddy threw you out? Watch this space and I'll let you know what I've decided to do.'*

Kate sighed and handed the note to Hayden to read. 'Well, did you have it off with Elton?'

Completely unabashed, the young woman gave her a smirk. 'It was just a moment of madness,' she said and looked straight at Hayden. 'You see, we have a private pool and I always swim in it naked. Elton brought some clean towels and a drink to the hut we use as a changing room while I was drying myself,' she shrugged, 'and one thing led to another.'

'And, as the letter suggests, the colonel wouldn't be too amused if he found out?' Kate summarised, taking the note back off Hayden, whose face was now glowing a bright red.

Another husky laugh. 'He would blow a gasket.' Her eyes sparkled with amusement at Hayden's embarrassment. 'And I would be grateful if you would keep this matter between us. You see, Daddy and I don't get along too well. Haven't ever since Mummy died. He thinks I am too forward and he doesn't like the way I dress. He regards it as too revealing and decadent.'

She crossed and uncrossed her long, tanned legs and inspected her toes. 'You don't think I look decadent, do you, Constable?' she said with feigned innocence, once more staring directly at Hayden from beneath lowered lashes.

He coughed and looked away, and before he could construct a suitable reply, Kate cut in again, snapping, 'How did you receive the letter?'

Winston frowned at the intervention. 'It was in our mailbox. Poor old Elton brought it in to me. Ironic, isn't it, that he was the unwitting messenger?'

'And you haven't told him what was in it?'

'Lord, no! He would have kittens.'

'And the envelope?'

'Chucked. I tore it up and dumped it in the bin.'

'Could we see it?'

'Not possible, I'm afraid. Bin collection this morning.'

'And you received just the letter? There were no photographs enclosed?' Hayden put in, finally recovering his composure.

'Constable!' Winston chortled. 'You cheeky thing. I didn't realise you were into voyeurism. Sorry to disappoint you but no, just the letter.'

Growing increasingly annoyed, Kate tutted. 'Just show us the pool, will you, Miss Winston?'

Winston smirked again. 'But of course. You could always go for a dip while you're there.'

She stood up and wiggled her way to the door, brazenly winking at Hayden as she passed him.

The pool was in the centre of an expansive lawn at the back of the house, close to a small hut and bordered by pink paving slabs. About twenty yards beyond, it was fringed by a narrow belt of woodland and Kate glimpsed part of the perimeter wall through the trees.

Crossing the lawn to peer into the woodland, she saw that the wall was about seven feet high and she heard the sound of a car driving past on the other side.

'Pretty private here,' she commented, returning to where Hayden was standing in a markedly defensive position about four feet away from Winston, as if he feared she was about to bite. 'That's obviously where they would have hidden themselves to watch you, but I wonder how they got in?'

'If you'd have gone a bit further along, you would have seen that the wall has collapsed at one point,' Winston said. 'It would have been easy to gain entry through the gap.'

'Our poison pen certainly seems to be pretty determined,' Kate said. 'Whoever it is, they must have been keeping a close eye on you to know when you would be using the pool.'

Winston hesitated for a moment, and Kate raised an inquiring eyebrow. The young woman gave a quick smile and took a deep breath. 'Look, I don't like speaking ill of people,' she said, 'but it seems to me that the most likely suspect in all of this has to be Maisie Taylor. You heard what Ned Mason was saying in the pub and, if you speak to anyone in the village, they will tell you she is quite a nasty gossip. I hardly know the lady, but by all accounts she is very religious and narrow-minded about sexual things. It would explain why poor Peter Jackson and I were picked on.'

Kate nodded. 'There is only one problem with that theory, Miss Winston,' she said grimly. 'Maisie Taylor was found dead in the early hours of this morning at her home, so it's most unlikely she could have been responsible for depositing the letter you received in your post box.'

Winston's hand went to her mouth. 'How terrible,' she breathed. 'What a horrible thing to have happened. Do — do you know how she died?'

'We think it was an accident — she fell down the stairs — but this has yet to be confirmed.'

'But that means—'

‘Precisely. Our poison pen is still out there, distributing their poison.’ Kate smiled mischievously. ‘So, if I were you, Miss Winston, I’d keep my clothes on in future.’

‘Spoilt little hot arse, that one,’ Kate muttered as they returned to their car. ‘Too much money and a dangerously over-active libido’

‘Doesn’t have any effect on me,’ Hayden said loftily, climbing into the front passenger seat beside her.

‘Is that so?’ Kate threw him a quizzical glance. ‘Then your red face must either be due to blood pressure or an early sign of the change, Hayd. You ought to be seeing a doctor.’

* * *

Like Colonel Winston, the Reverend Salter was not at home when Kate and Hayden turned up on the doorstep of the vicarage, but the lady of the house greeted Kate and Hayden with a welcoming smile.

‘Please come in,’ she said. ‘Perhaps I can help you in my husband’s absence.’

Jane Salter was a short, plump woman in her mid-sixties. She wore her greying hair in a bob and there were laughter lines at the corners of her sparkling blue eyes. She was dressed in a rose-patterned dress and sandals and there was a small, silver crucifix suspended on a slender chain around her neck. The epitome of a vicar’s wife.

‘Nice place you have here,’ Kate commented as they followed her a short distance along the hallway into a cosy sitting room.

Salter sighed. ‘Yes, we have been very happy in this house, but sadly, it isn’t ours. It belongs to the church. It is a bit too big for just the two of us too — four bedrooms, three reception rooms, a study. There’s even a quite enormous basement, part of which John has commandeered as his wine cellar. But I never go down there.’ She shivered. ‘It’s crawling with spiders and I hate the things.’

She waved them both to a big three-seater settee. 'Do sit down. I'm sorry, but John won't be back until later tonight. Masonic business, you understand,' she added in a conspiratorial whisper. 'Can I get you some tea or coffee?'

Kate shook her head. 'Thank you, but no. We won't take up much of your time. As you will be aware, we are investigating a spate of poison pen letters that are being sent to a number of your husband's parishioners.'

Her smile vanished. 'Dreadful,' she said, 'truly dreadful. And some people were accusing Maisie Taylor of sending them, I believe?'

Kate nodded. 'Actually, it is about Miss Taylor that we are calling. We believe the real perpetrator deliberately set out to incriminate her.'

Jane Salter made a disapproving noise. 'And my husband tells me the poor woman is now dead?'

'Last night. An unfortunate accident by the look of it. We would like to try and set the record straight by catching the real culprit.'

'I will help in any way I can, Officer,' Salter said. 'What do you want to know?'

'We understand that Maisie Taylor ran the Sunday school at the church?'

'Yes, had done for many years — even before John and I came here. She was a real asset to us and so dedicated too. She also played the church organ at evensong. A very talented lady.'

'Was she the only Sunday school teacher?'

'No, though she was in charge. A couple of the other ladies helped her most Sundays — poor Helen Jackson and also Beverley James. Oh yes, and the Winston girl, Gabriella, when she was in the mood—'

'You're saying Gabriella wasn't that committed then?' Hayden put in.

Jane Salter sighed and made a face. 'It was her father who insisted on her doing it. He felt she should be seen to be supporting the village, but I got the impression her heart wasn't really in it. Sadly, I have my doubts as to whether she was the sort of young lady who was really suited to the role. Does it sound awful for a vicar's wife to be saying that?'

Kate smiled. 'Not at all, Mrs Salter. I sense that you did not approve of her.'

There was a startled look on the other's face. 'No, no,' she said hastily, her thin hands twisting in her lap. 'It isn't for me to pass judgement on anyone. We are all God's children. But—'

'But she was not exactly the ideal role model for little children?' Hayden encouraged gently.

'Well, the — the way she dressed, you know, very short shorts and skimpy tops or low necklines, and I think she attracted the wrong sort of interest from some of the male members of our congregation.'

'A bit of a flirt then?'

'I suppose you could put it like that. She seemed a well-meaning young lady, but I would have expected her to have presented a more, er, conventional image in the House of God.'

'Did you speak to her about her mode of dress?' Kate asked.

A brief shake of the head. 'Not exactly, but hints were dropped by both myself and my husband, as well as some other members of the congregation who felt quite strongly about the matter.'

Kate raised an eyebrow. 'Which members were they?'

Salter flushed and looked down at her feet. 'Oh, I don't think it would be right for me to say. Gossip is the tongue of the devil, Sergeant.'

Kate sighed in irritation. 'I'm not asking you to slander anyone, Mrs Salter, but this is important. People are suffering from these vicious letters and we need to establish who might have a particular axe to grind. We will not be telling anyone that the information came from you.'

There was a long pause while Jane Salter picked at her dress with the fingers of one hand and studied the toes of her sandals, her lips tightening and her brows puckering in a frown. Then, abruptly, she threw Kate an embarrassed glance and blurted out, 'I'm not accusing anyone, you understand, but Denise Merchant — the lady who runs the local shop and post office — was quite indignant about Gabriella Winston and rather demanded that my husband ban her from the church. Of course, John refused and there was a quite unpleasant row over it. That was when I sort of hinted to Gabriella that she might like to cover up a little.'

'And did she?'

'No. She just laughed, I'm afraid.'

'How did that make you feel?'

A shadow seemed to pass over Salter's face and for the first time her eyes seemed to narrow slightly.

'I was a bit put out, I must admit. After all, a church is a sacred place and should be treated with respect. Abuse of the Almighty's beneficence should not be tolerated. But,' and she emitted a self-conscious laugh, 'at the same time, Christians must not seek to judge, only to educate and gently cajole sinners into following the right path.'

'And do you think it might be appropriate to "cajole" those sinners by sending them an admonishing anonymous letter?'

Salter laughed outright, though there was an edge to it. 'Of course not, but I'm sure you realise that licentious behaviour can arouse strong passions among the Christian community and we can all be guilty of overreaction.'

'What do you think your local Christian community would think about homosexuality?'

'You are, of course, referring to poor Peter Jackson?' Salter said.

'How did you know about his sexual proclivities?' Kate asked.

'I think the whole village knew, and John also told me about those horrid photos he received.' She took a deep breath. 'Regardless of the current social attitudes, traditional Christians still regard homosexuality as a sin, Sergeant, and I am quite sure most of the village would consider it abhorrent. That said, I cannot think of anyone in our congregation who would persecute someone because of it.'

'Well, someone seems to have a bee in their bonnet about such things,' Kate said. She stood up. 'But thank you for your time anyway, Mrs Salter, and if anything occurs to you which you feel might be of help to us in our inquiries, you know where to find us.'

'Well, what do you reckon?' Kate said after she and Hayden had taken their leave of the rectory and climbed back into their car.

Hayden shrugged. 'I'd say we've opened a right can of worms with this job. The whole village seems to be awash with poison. There are so many likely suspects it's difficult to know where to start.'

'And Mrs Salter? What about her?'

'I think she knows a lot more than she's saying.'

'She did give us another possible suspect.'

'You mean, after her "gossip is the tongue of the devil" excuse for *not* doing so?' He snorted. 'Strange how just minutes later, she did exactly that.'

'What are you saying?'

'Nothing really. Just that maybe she gave us Denise Merchant's name to send us off on a wild goose chase.'

'But surely she would only have a motive for doing that if she was somehow implicated in the sending of the poison pen letters?'

He shrugged again. 'Or was trying to protect someone she suspected of being responsible.'

'Like her husband, you mean?'

'Like anybody. It's just that she was a little bit too wholesome for me.'

Kate stared at him. 'Hayden Lewis, I do believe you are becoming cynical in your old age.'

'That's working with you for so long,' he retorted with a grin. 'I've become infected.'

‘Well, there’s only one cure for that, isn’t there? Home and—’

‘I’ve got a headache,’ he cut in.

She gave him an old-fashioned look. ‘I was going to say wine.’

CHAPTER 14

The DCI was leaving Roscoe's inner sanctum when Kate and Hayden — this time after a good night's sleep — walked into the CID general office the following morning. He nodded curtly to Kate, opened the door for her and clattered off down the stairs. Kate noted Ronnie Crouch, the office manager's, warning flick of the eyebrows as she headed for her desk and at the same time spotted the DI hovering in the doorway of his office, staring at her.

'Another visit from the boss, guv?' she commented guardedly.

He gave Hayden the once-over, cast a baleful glance at two other detectives sitting at their respective desks opposite, and gestured for her to join him.

Rolling her eyes at Hayden as if to say, "What now?" she left him by the coffee machine and joined the DI in his office, closing the door behind her.

'Your bloody misper,' he growled, dropping heavily into the chair behind his desk. 'You haven't been talking to anyone about it, have you?'

She shook her head. 'Not my case anymore, guv,' she said, taking the chair opposite without invitation.

He popped some gum into his mouth and chewed for a few moments before studying her again.

'It is now.'

'What? But you said Des Percival—?'

'Des got a last minute call to attend the Crown Court in Aylesbury tomorrow morning, so he had to leave sharpish.'

'Aylesbury? But that's Buckinghamshire, isn't it?'

He shrugged. 'Some big drugs bust he dealt with when he was on the NCS apparently. One of the perps has changed his guilty plea to not guilty and the judge wants the case to proceed, so Des is required to give last minute evidence. Likely to be away a couple of days at least.'

'But what about the other job I'm dealing with?'

He blew a bubble and sucked it back in. 'You women are supposed to be good at multitasking, aren't you? So multitask!'

He pulled a folded newspaper out of one of his trays and tossed it across the desk.

'Besides which, as far as the DCI is concerned, the misper inquiry has suddenly become a lot more of a priority.'

She caught it just in time and saw that it was the local tabloid. Opening it out, she found herself staring at page two and a short, innocuous piece about the tragic death of local resident, "Miss Maisie Taylor," from a fall.

She threw Roscoe a puzzled, inquiring glance.

'Front page,' he said, and watched her turn the page back.

At once the headline screamed at her: *'Police Hunt For Kidnapped Girl.'* Her eyes narrowed, her anger mounting as she quickly scanned the story.

'*Highbridge Police searching for a missing girl, suspect she has been kidnapped. Tammy Logan, a twenty-four-year-old from Birmingham, was last seen on Saturday in the Blue Pixie café in Highbridge, when she left by the back door after suffering abuse from a male customer. She then vanished. Police are looking for a red Land Rover, possibly a Defender, with a Mickey Mouse sticker on the back window, and are asking the public to contact Highbridge police station if they have any information on Tammy or the vehicle. Tammy is described as . . .*'

The piece was attributed to one Debbie Moreton.

'The bitch!' Kate said through clenched teeth, dumping the newspaper back on his desk. 'How the hell did she get hold of all this info?'

He shrugged. 'Tony Samuel, it seems.'

'What? But he's locked up and due in court soon.'

'Not now he isn't. Apparently, that little shit, Mickey Bishop, has refused to testify against him. Told the plod who went to see him in hospital that he wouldn't recognise his assailant again. Coupled with which, Samuel was arrested well away from the scene and cannot be placed there.' Another shrug. 'No choice but to kick Samuel out.'

'And like the good, upright citizen he is, he runs straight to the newspaper. I wonder what sort of a bung he got for that?'

Roscoe nodded. 'You might want to read on. There's an interesting bit at the bottom.'

Kate retrieved the paper and, skipping through the description and the alleged circumstances pertaining to Logan's disappearance, found the sting in the tail he was obviously referring to.

'Tammy's partner, Tony Samuel, who was originally arrested for assaulting a suspect interviewed by police and has now been released without charge, has expressed his concern that something serious could have happened to his girlfriend, but that the police have shown little interest in trying to find her. We understand that the officer who took the report was Detective Sergeant Kate Lewis, and Mr Samuel has expressed the concern we must all feel that Tammy Logan's disappearance is not being treated as a priority . . .'

Kate tossed the newspaper back on to the DI's desk. 'The nasty, lying little cow!'

Roscoe gave one of his wolfish grins, patently enjoying Kate's furious reaction. 'She obviously doesn't like you for some reason,' he mocked. Then his face suddenly became serious. 'But what's more important is the fact that she's buggered a key plank in the investigation—'

'The description of the Land Rover,' Kate finished for him. 'Especially the bit about the Mickey Mouse sticker on the back window. Meaning that as well as ourselves, Bishop must have told Samuel about that when he attacked him. No one else — apart from ourselves — could have known about it.'

Roscoe said nothing, and reading the insinuation in his dark eyes, she swore. 'You don't seriously think Hayden or myself passed that info on to Moreton, do you? That's bloody ridiculous. You might just as well suspect Des Percival.'

He said nothing for several moments, and then sat back in his chair with an explosive grunt. 'No, I don't think that, but I suspect the DCI is not quite so charitable in his views. Anyway, he's going to get HQ Press Office to ring the paper's editor to give him a rollicking and to warn him about future releases.'

'Fat lot of good that will do.'

'Maybe you're right, but we can't just let that grubby little rag off the hook. They need to understand that once our perp sees the story, he'll have his scraper and white spirit out pdq, which means that with no sticker, we'll have no way to ID it, even if we see the thing being driven right past us.'

'And worse still,' Kate added grimly, 'if Tammy *has* been snatched, there's every chance our man will now panic and decide to cut his losses by getting rid of her altogether.'

'Good news all the way then, eh?' Roscoe said. 'Which reminds me, did you call on Winston again re the poison pen inquiry, as I instructed?'

Kate nodded. 'He was out, but we saw Gabriella, his trollop of a daughter—'

'And?'

'Turns out she has now received a poison pen letter herself, alleging she's been having it off with the colonel's resident gofer, Elton.'

'So, has she?'

'Apparently. She was quite brazen about it too and didn't seem particularly bothered that she's been targeted — although she insisted that neither her father nor Elton were to be told.'

He scowled. 'The colonel will go ape-shit if he finds out,' he muttered. His face darkened even more as he apparently pondered on the likely consequences for him if that were to happen.

'So, what else are you doing to nail this perp?' he went on without waiting for a reply. 'There must be other avenues of inquiry now Maisie Taylor has been ruled out as a suspect.'

Kate said nothing and he chewed furiously on his gum for a few seconds. 'Well, stop farting about, Lewis, and get me a result, if you don't want to be back on the streets wearing a funny hat! *Capiche*?'

The threat of being returned to uniform had little effect on her. She had heard it too many times before to be overly concerned about what she recognised as simply the same old Roscoe bluster. So, treating him to a tired "whatever" look and muttering a brief, 'Got it in one,' she stood up and left his little office, wondering for the umpteenth time how such an arsehole could ever have managed to gain the "dizzy heights" of Detective Inspector.

* * *

He spotted the headline on the front page of the local tabloid when he called in at the village shop.

'Police Hunt For Kidnapped Girl.'

Taking a copy from the stand, he resisted the temptation to buy the paper and rush out of the place to read it straightaway, instead forcing himself to act normally to avoid attracting attention. He completed his regular weekly selection of basic groceries and included the paper with the rest of his purchases when he came to pay at the counter.

Back behind the wheel of his Land Rover and half a mile down the road, he pulled into a layby and quickly scanned the front-page story. The words immediately jumped out at him: '. . . *red Land Rover Defender . . . Mickey Mouse sticker on the back window . . .'* His stomach juices began to churn and he glanced instinctively in his rear-view mirror. He couldn't actually see the sticker from where he sat, but he knew it was still there. He stared blankly out through the windscreen, his thoughts racing.

He had been a fool. He ought to have removed that sticker when he'd first bought the wagon. Someone had obviously spotted it when he'd snatched the girl in Highbridge, and now every copper in the area would be on the lookout for it. Not only that, but there was every chance some sharp-eyed local would spot it too — maybe already had. And what about the guy he had bought the thing from, Ted Southerby? He would certainly know about the sticker. It had been on the bloody window when he'd sold the Land Rover to him. If Southerby saw the press story and decided to ring the police about it, the inevitable knock on the door and the discovery of his reluctant "guest" would spell ruination for him and the end of all that God had assigned him to do.

At that moment, a sudden wailing bearing down on him from behind shook him out of his reverie, instantly jerking his gaze to his offside wing mirror and causing him to shrink right down in his seat as the pulsing blue light washed over the Land Rover. But though the sight of the ambulance that then went racing by drew a relieved humourless laugh from him, it also served as an effective wake-up call. He needed to get himself into gear *pdq*. There was some urgent tidying up to be done.

The engine chose to stutter, then cut out the moment he turned the key. 'Not now!' he snarled through clenched teeth. '*Not now!*' He tried again, felt the Land Rover shudder as it tried to start, then a loud "clonk" as it died on him again. He was being punished. God was telling him he had failed His Holy purpose with the girl. She had still not repented — just like the others. This starter problem was the sign of the Almighty's displeasure. He closed his eyes and clasped his hands in prayer, rushing the words, promising a renewed effort with her if he could just get home. He tried the key again. The engine coughed, hesitated, and then stammered into life.

He took a deep breath. God had heard him and had given him another chance. This time he would succeed with the girl. But first, he had to consign Mickey Mouse to the shredder, mothball the Defender in his barn and use his other car for a while. An urgent visit to good old Ted Southerby was called for. Praise be to the Lord for His wisdom . . .

* * *

Ted Southerby had farmed on the Somerset Levels all his life, and his father and grandfather before him. Now seventy-five, with arthritis, a troublesome stomach ulcer and a gammy leg from an attack by a bull twenty years earlier, he had had enough and wanted out. His elderly Friesian dairy herd wouldn't last for very much longer and he hadn't the capital to invest in new beasts. That, coupled with the abysmal price he got for his milk, the cost of fodder in the winter months and the curse of flooded fields — when the rivers overflowed and the rhynes were unable to cope with the volume of water, which spread for miles over the flat landscape — meant that he was fighting a losing battle. His wife, Beth, had died of cancer three years before and with no children and just a half-day cowman to help him with the milking, the only option he had was to sell up, lock, stock and barrel. If he could find a buyer.

The notices advertising the auction for the following month had been put up on the adjoining roads only that morning and he felt sad but hopeful as he stomped back into the kitchen for his lunch after doing the rounds of the farm and paying his cowman.

Grunting at the pain in his leg, he crossed to the table to collect the newspaper which had been delivered from the village shop that morning. Then, settling in his battered armchair by the stove and spreading the paper out on his lap, he reached for his tankard and bottle of Somerset Cider — only to set them both back down on the side-table when the headline caught his eye. As he always did, he followed the text with his index finger and muttered each word aloud as he went, until he suddenly straightened in the chair, his sharp exclamation startling the cat.

'. . . *Red Land Rover Defender* . . .' he read incredulously, '. . . *Mickey Mouse sticker* . . .'

'Well, I'll be buggered! That sounds just like Bertha,' he exclaimed, using the pet name he had given to the old Land Rover he had sold three months before. 'This be a right rum do, it be, and no mistake.' He poured himself some cider and sat back in his chair, the liquid sloshing in his trembling hand.

He sat on for at least another half an hour, thinking and sipping his drink, before finally making up his mind. Then he hauled himself to his feet and limped across the kitchen to the hall, where the phone stood on the half-moon telephone table by the stairs. He dialled the number slowly and deliberately. For the first time in ages he felt excited, but when the call was answered, he delivered his message slowly, savouring every word.

In fact, he was so engrossed in the call that he failed to hear the vehicle drawing up outside and he was totally unaware of his cat streaking out of the kitchen door between the legs of the man who was now standing there.

CHAPTER 15

'Message for you, skipper,' Detective Constable Danny Ferris called to Kate as she walked back into the general office. He left his desk to walk over to her with a piece of paper in one hand.

She tutted. 'So, where's Hayden and Jamie Foster?' she said, referring to the other detective constable who had been in the office with Ferris.

Ferris shrugged. 'Jamie was called out to a burglary and Hayden said he'd be in the canteen.' He grinned. 'Elevenses, I think he called it.'

'I'll give him elevenses,' she muttered, taking the note from Ferris and studying the badly scribbled text. 'What's this message about anyway? I can hardly read it.'

Ferris coloured up. 'Some old boy rang regarding that misper, Tammy Logan. Bloke called Ted Southerby, Rhynebank Farm. Says he has some info. Wants you to ring him. Des Percival's away and—'

'I know he is,' Kate cut in irritably. 'Did the caller say what the info was?'

Ferris nodded. 'Something about that vehicle with the Mickey Mouse sticker on it.'

'What?' Kate's irritation was instantly replaced by a surge of excitement as she grabbed the phone and dialled the number on the message, jigging up and down impatiently as she listened to the ringing tone. After what must have been a full minute, there was still no reply.

'You sure you got the right number?' she shouted across at Ferris.

He scowled. ''Course I'm sure. He said he'd wait for your call.'

She dialled again, with the same result. 'Well, he's not answering now. Do you know where Rhynebank Farm is?'

'Never heard of it, but he shouldn't be that difficult to trace. The phone number is a local one.'

She saw him pull a telephone directory from the drawer of his desk and waited while he flicked through it.

'Not here,' he said a moment later. 'Must be ex-directory.'

'So, get on the web and check the electoral roll,' she snapped, then added, 'No, cancel that. Is Tom Reeves on duty today?'

'Dunno.'

She ended the call and rang the control room. 'Tom Reeves — is he on today?'

'Day off, skipper. On again for a twelve-hour shift at 1400 hours tomorrow.'

She cursed inwardly, remembering he had told her this at the scene of Maisie Taylor's death. 'Get me his mobile number, will you?'

To her relief, Reeves answered almost immediately. 'Sorry to bother you on your day off, Tom, but I need your local knowledge. Do you know a guy called Ted Southerby? Rhynebank Farm?'

There was a pause and then Reeves came back to her. 'Yeah, he lives a couple of miles down the road from me.'

'Thing is, he rang here earlier with some info on the misper girl, but he's not answering his phone. Can you give me directions to his place?'

'Do better than that, Kate. I'll pick you up and take you there.'

'Are you sure?'

'Absolutely no problem.'

'Do you want me to get Hayden up here?' Ferris called after her as she left.

'Don't bother,' she snapped back over her shoulder. 'Let him enjoy his bloody lardy cake.'

* * *

Reeves picked Kate up in his old Volvo V70 twenty minutes later. He was dressed in a T-shirt and jeans.

'Thanks for this, Tom,' Kate said again. 'I owe you. But you look very tired.'

He shrugged. 'Lots of DIY to do at home, which I have to squeeze in between these constantly changing shifts. And I'm on a twelve-hour jobbie tomorrow, from two.' He grinned. 'But what is it they say? If you don't like it, you shouldn't have joined.'

She bit her lip. 'Look, I'm so sorry — perhaps I shouldn't have bothered you — but I'm very concerned about Southerby, as he's not answering his phone.'

Reeves nodded and threw her a sympathetic smile. 'No problem, Kate. I don't mind, honestly. Always happy to help *you* out, you know that. What information did Southerby say he had?'

'Something to do with the motor used by the perp who may have snatched Tammy Logan. It is said to be a red Land Rover Defender with a Mickey Mouse sticker on the rear window and I'm hoping he can tell us who it belongs to.'

'Let's hope he's got what you need.' He glanced across at her. 'Any luck with your poison pen job?'

She shook her head. 'Blank wall at the moment. Plenty of possible suspects, but nothing positive yet.'

'So, Maisie Taylor was definitely not the perp?'

She shook her head. 'No, and I still think her death was sus, but we're waiting for the results of the PM.'

'All a bit frustrating then?'

'You could say that.' Kate shot him an inquiring glance. 'One name has come up, though. What do you know about Denise Merchant?'

He thought a second. 'Possible contender. She's sharp and well educated, but on the other hand, what would her motive be? She runs a business and needs loyal customers. She's hardly going to jeopardise that to stir up trouble on her own doorstep, is she? No, I think you've been given bum info there.'

'And Jane Salter?'

He laughed outright now. 'The vicar's wife? Not a chance. I've known her and John ever since they came here, and she's more religious than he is. I can't see her sending out poisonous letters, and I certainly can't see her going through people's dustbins looking for ammunition. But why should the perp be female? Couldn't it be a man?'

Kate snorted. 'Oh, it's a female all right. Trust me. The letters have all the hallmarks of a bitter, twisted woman. No man could aspire to be so persistent and vindictive.'

Another chuckle. 'That's a bit sexist.'

'Maybe it is, though I'd still put money on it.'

But Reeves was no longer listening. He had suddenly thrust his face closer to the windscreen. 'Eh up, I don't like the look of that.'

They had turned off the main road onto a muddy track which headed off between tall hedges, and the fierce red glow was clearly visible ahead of them, lighting up the grey day. By the time they reached the end, their worst fears were realised. Even from where they sat in the car, they could feel the heat given off by the flames, which engulfed the thatched farmhouse and a car parked in front of it. Then, as the burning mass suddenly erupted in a violent explosion, showering their car with debris as the roof timbers and front wall disintegrated in front of them, Kate knew that Ted Southerby would not be helping them with their inquiries — at least, not this side of the hereafter.

* * *

'Gas bottles,' the senior fire officer declared several hours later. 'Pretty devastating things when they go up.'

Kate's face was still pale and drawn as she and Reeves took in the scene of devastation.

The farmhouse was now a blackened ruin, still smouldering and hissing under the jets of the fire-hoses. Just one end wall of the building remained standing, with a few upstairs joists sticking out of it like jagged teeth, and the car that had been parked there, which was definitely not a Land Rover, was just a burned-out skeleton.

'Very old building,' the fireman went on. 'Thatch and wattle mostly. Would have been like a bloody tinderbox.'

Kate glanced towards the plastic sheet lying a few feet away, remembering the horrific sight when the blackened, twisted remains of what had once been a human being had been carried out. Ted Southerby hadn't stood a chance. She could only hope the old man had died from smoke inhalation before the flames got to him.

Reeves's expression was grim. 'Poor devil. Any idea how the fire started, Dick?'

The fire chief shook his head, nodding towards the marked police patrol and fire service cars parked to one side of the hardstanding in front of the burned-out building.

'There'll have to be a full investigation of the scene with our guys and yours before we can say,' he said. He hesitated slightly before adding, 'but my money is on the gas cooker. Maybe a loose connection or a damaged hose. He lit one of the rings and boom!'

Raymond Makepiece, the police surgeon, appeared round the side of one of the fire trucks, dressed in his protective nylon suit. 'Not much left of him for me to look at really,' he said coldly. 'Though I'll do my best with what there is when I get him on the slab.'

Kate shuddered at the vision this conjured up. 'At least the PM is likely to be straightforward.'

He snorted. 'Don't you believe it. You'd be surprised at how difficult partially cremated cadavers can be to examine properly.' He made to walk over to his car drawn up against the hedge behind them, then turned and said, 'Your Maisie Taylor's PM has been done, by the way. My colleague had a spare slot just before lunch. I've told your DI. Nothing sinister, as it turns out. Death occasioned by a fall — snapped vertebrae among other things. No other suspicious injuries or signs of trauma. Sorry to disappoint you.'

'Story of my life,' Kate muttered, then, seeing the chunky figure of Ted Roscoe walking towards them from the lane, she added, 'And things just got a whole lot worse.'

* * *

Kate desperately needed a shower and to wash her hair. The stench of the burning building still clung to her after reconnoitring the scene with the DI. But at least she could take comfort from the fact that he smelled as bad as she did when she returned with him to his office. Reeves had gone home again when Roscoe insisted on driving her back. She had agreed to it only reluctantly, aware of his almost legendary poor driving skills. 'Any last requests?' Reeves had whispered in her ear as she'd climbed into the DI's beaten up Honda Civic. She'd made a face at the big, affable sergeant through the front passenger window, and they'd lurched away, narrowly avoiding a gatepost at the start of the lane leading to the main road.

'You think he was stiffed by our so-called kidnapper, don't you?' Roscoe growled, tossing his car keys onto the desk and slumping into his chair.

Kate shrugged. 'I'm not in any position to say that, since as yet we have no direct evidence that the fire was sus. But it's a mighty big coincidence that he rings me with info on the Land Rover we're looking for and within the hour he ends up cremated.'

The DI grunted. 'Yeah, well, we'll need to wait for the PM report and the findings of the fire service investigation team before we can take this any further. I'm not going to cry wolf and initiate a major crime inquiry now, and look a pillock later if the fire turns out to have been an accident.'

'And if they find it was arson?'

'There will be a full investigation into the fire as a matter of course. If there's anything untoward, the joint investigating team will find it, as you well know.'

Obviously noticing her doubtful expression, he leaned towards her with a sneer on his face. 'I'm not going to dance to your tune, *Miss*. After all, if I'd listened to you over Maisie Taylor, we'd have launched a full-blown murder inquiry by now, wouldn't we? And, as subsequent events have proven, it was a bloody good job I didn't.'

Refusing to let him wind her up, she met his stare. 'And maybe before this business is over, you'll wish you had.' She jumped to her feet and turned for the door. 'Now, unless you have any more pearls of wisdom to impart, guv'nor, I'm going home for a shower and something to eat.'

Then, before he could say anything else, she marched smartly out of his office and went to look for Hayden.

* * *

Escape! Tammy Logan had thought about nothing else since her kidnapping. She had made a futile attempt to force the door lock with a spoon her captor had given her with one of her meals and had also pulled herself up to the high-level window by gripping the protruding sill — only to find the window protected by two iron bars. But now at last she had been presented with the very opportunity she had been waiting for.

He was later than usual when he came to see her with sandwiches and a can of Coca Cola. She had failed once again to satisfy him by correctly answering his questions on the passage from the Bible he had left her to learn — primarily because she did not understand the wording. English had never been her forte and the way it was written made it seem like gibberish to her. His limited patience had snapped again, and he'd flown into one of his rages. Her face was still sore from the back-handed slap he had given her. Then he had abruptly stormed off into the bathroom, obviously with the intention of subjecting her to further "waterboard" torture.

Ordinarily, she would have been paralysed with terror, but not this time. He had made a big mistake. Already in a foul mood when he'd arrived, he had forgotten to lock the door behind him.

Waiting until she heard the squeak of the big, old-fashioned tap and the noise of the water pumping out of it, she sprang from the bed and darted across the room, her bare feet making little sound on the solid floor.

The door opened easily, any faint creak of the hinges drowned by the sound of the water thundering into the bath.

She found herself in what appeared to be a store room, lit by an overhead strip light. The room was cluttered with old furniture, rolls of carpet and wooden tea chests stacked against one wall. At the far end, steep, wooden stairs rose between handrails towards a half-open door. She realised she was in some sort of a basement or cellar.

Halfway up the stairs, she heard his roar of anger coming from the room she had just left. She slammed the door back against the wall in a blind panic. Terrified moans issuing from between her clenched teeth, she gathered up the hem of the long dress and took to her heels.

A long hallway opened up before her, doorways opening off on each side. And there, at the end, a heavy-looking outer door with a brass letterbox and what looked like a spy-hole near the top. It had to be the front door.

She could hear his heavy feet pounding on the cellar stairs behind her, bellowing his threats, and practically threw herself at the door. The handle turned easily, and with an overwhelming feeling of relief, she pulled the door open and sprang through.

A grey, gloomy evening greeted her. There was a broad gravel apron in front of her, enclosed by dense woodland, and a narrow driveway snaking off through the undergrowth to her left.

His feet were pounding along the hallway she had just left. She ran across the apron, heading for the security of the trees, heedless of the sharp gravel cutting into the soles of her feet.

Then she was among the trees and waist deep in a sea of ferns and shrubs, wet leaves slapping across her face, brambles snaring her dress as if they were trying to hold her back. And all the time she could hear him crashing after her through the undergrowth.

There was a pounding in her head, and everything started to spin, as acid burned in her throat and chest. Her lungs were on fire, but she couldn't stop. It was her one and only chance. She had to get away.

Then, abruptly, the woodland came to an end before a broken-down fence, and she glimpsed a strip of road on the other side. She found a gap and ducked through onto a grass verge. The road appeared to be the sort of unclassified back-road that was prevalent on the Levels. It was deserted, striking out on each side of her for a short distance before curving away among the trees and undergrowth. She hesitated for a moment, but spurred on by the sound of her pursuer seemingly just yards away, she chose to turn right, running with renewed energy towards the bend, desperate to get beyond it before he got to the road and saw which way she had gone.

She felt sure she had succeeded when a quick glance over her shoulder as she reached the apex of the bend revealed that he was not yet in sight. She ran on.

CHAPTER 16

Hayden was sitting beside the Local Intelligence Officer in his small, cramped office when Kate found him, and she paused in the doorway to peer over the LIO's shoulder. The computer screen was showing video footage of a building and part of a street.

'So, what are you doing in here?' she said.

Hayden turned and sniffed the air. 'Phew! You smell as if you've been standing too close to a bonfire, old girl.'

She glared at him, still annoyed at his earlier disappearance and angered even more by his use of "old girl."

'Never mind that,' she snapped. 'I asked why you were in here.'

'Before I answer that, as our politicians would say,' he went on, completely unabashed, 'and before I forget to tell you, good old Dave here has already interrogated the VODS database for us re the Land Rover in the misper case and we've found nothing there that's of any use to us. But,' and he waggled a forefinger theatrically, 'what we've got before us now might be of greater value with regard to poor old Maisie Taylor's death.'

Kate peered at the computer screen again. 'So, what have we got?'

‘A surveillance tape, skipper,’ Dave Gort, the LIO replied, glancing back at her over his shoulder.

‘Surveillance tape from where?’

‘The post office and shop in our favourite poison pen village,’ Hayden replied cheerfully.

‘What?’

‘I had this idea, you see,’ Hayden went on. ‘As village post offices are frequently targeted by criminal gangs, perhaps this one might have had a security camera installed outside, like many others have. I thought it might show us who is out and about in the village at night and also reveal who could be foraging in dustbins and the like. So, I rang the shop. One Denise Merchant confirmed the fact and was happy for me to go over and borrow a copy of the most recent tape. Came down here to use Dave’s video, as we only have digital facilities in our department.’

‘So that’s where you went to. When I left the DI’s office, I was told you were having elevenses.’

He fidgeted slightly. ‘Well. I — er — was actually. Seeing as you appeared to be having such a nice conflab with old Roscoe, I thought I’d leave you to it. The — er — idea came later.’

‘The only problem is there is a lot of imagery on the tape,’ Gort put in, freezing the frame, ‘and, as it’s an old videotape system, probably bought off the shelf from somewhere, the picture quality is not the best. The job’s therefore taking a bit of time.’

Kate drew up another chair and sat behind him. ‘Then lead on McDuff. We’re in no hurry,’ she glanced at her watch, ‘unless you are?’

‘I can do with the overtime dosh,’ Gort said with a grin, ‘so I’m here for as long as you want me.’

In fact, checking the tape took even longer than any of them had expected, and Kate was actually nodding off when Hayden shouted, ‘Stop! Take it back a few frames.’

She jerked upright in her chair with a start, for a moment confused as to where she was. But then Hayden added, ‘Stop it there,’ and her gaze focused on the screen.

It was night time. In the yellow pool cast on the road by the shop's security light, they saw a figure in a long, black, hooded coat. It was impossible to identify the person, or to be sure whether it was male or female, though it looked to be a man, and it disappeared again a couple of seconds later when Gort touched "play."

'0120 hours,' he said, studying the electronic counter.

'And the day Taylor died,' Kate breathed, suddenly losing interest in Hayden's search for the poison pen marauder and focusing instead on something that seemed a lot more sinister.

'He must have gone down the alley between the shop and Maisie Taylor's cottage,' Hayden pointed out.

'*And* the unlocked back door,' Kate added.

Three pairs of eyes remained fixed on the screen for several minutes after that, while the tape continued to run. Then, quite suddenly, the figure was back, walking towards the camera, but with its head down so that the face was hidden.

'That's definitely a man,' Kate said. 'You can see by his build and the way he walks.'

Maybe a couple of minutes later, the upper part of a vehicle, with its lights out, suddenly appeared from the direction in which the figure had headed, then disappeared. Gort hit the "pause" button again. 'A Land Rover,' he said. 'Red. And it looks like an old Defender.'

'Can we try for the number?' Kate suggested.

The LIO took the tape backwards and forwards several times, then shook his head. 'As it's a static camera with a very limited range, it will only pick up objects directly in front of it.'

Kate was not satisfied. 'Take the tape back again very slowly.'

Gort nodded and worked with the controls on his machine.

'There!' Kate shouted.

The tape froze again, showing the upper side, rear panel and the top part of the back door and rear window of the Land Rover.

'Can you enhance the pic?' Kate went on.

Gort gave a dry laugh and shook his head. 'Not with this baby. It's almost steam-driven.'

'Hayd, did you see any CCTV units on the other properties in the vicinity?' she said. 'Maybe another camera picked up a better pic?'

He shook his head. 'I checked. There weren't any.'

She thought a second and tapped Gort on the shoulder. 'Do you have a magnifying glass?'

'A magnifying glass?' He threw a startled glance over his shoulder then, to her surprise, nodded and pulled open the top drawer of his desk. 'It just so happens . . .' he began, rummaging through the drawer and producing one with a large black handle. 'I need it sometimes for some of the documents I have to look at.'

He handed it to Kate and she placed it over the right-hand side of the screen where it had paused.

Hayden's sharp gasp close to her ear made her jump. 'Good Lord!' he exclaimed. 'I don't believe it!'

Right in the corner of the magnified section of the rear window, Mickey Mouse was looking straight back at them.

* * *

Kate found Roscoe ensconced behind a bamboo screen in his favourite local, the Black Cock, a pint of beer in front of him. It was late — almost eleven — and Kate should have been off a long time ago at the end of another exhausting tour of duty. But she felt that the information about the Land Rover was too important to save until the following day, so had sent Hayden home while she followed things through.

The DI raised his eyebrows when he saw her, the beer glass stationary in his hairy paw, like a paused lift on its way to an upper floor.

'Nice of you to join me,' he commented drily and took a gulp of his beer, thrusting it in her direction. 'A double scotch chaser with this would do the trick.'

She ignored the invitation. 'Something important has come up, guv,' she said, sitting down on the bench seat across the table from him.

'Don't tell me,' he said, 'you've decided to divorce that prat of a husband, eh? I'm in the market, if you're interested.'

She ignored the jibe. 'Well, first, bad news about the VODS check I said we would be doing on the Land Rover in the misper case. The LIO's interrogation of the database has produced nothing of value.'

'Surprise, surprise,' he retorted, showing little interest.

'But,' she added with more emphasis, 'there does seem to be an actual link between the misper and the poison pen case. We have a security tape to prove it.'

She told him what they had found out, Roscoe listening silently for a change. He took another pull on his beer.

'So, you're suggesting that the bloke you caught on camera is our kidnapper and that he also stiffed Maisie Taylor, despite what the police surgeon said?' he summarised.

'It seems to me that that there is a definite link there, yes,' she said. 'I think it's highly likely he is either holding Tammy Logan or has murdered her and our poison pen somehow found out and sent him a letter — maybe in an effort to extort money. Then, suspecting from local gossip that Maisie Taylor was the culprit, maybe he stiffed her to shut her up. There's a sort of alleyway between Taylor's cottage and the shop leading round to her back door, which we know was unlocked, so it all fits.'

He grunted. 'Bloody load of maybes here, aren't there?' he commented. 'And it would make our perp a local boy, living in or near the village.'

'I think he is.'

'Can we actually put this character in Taylor's cottage?'

She shook her head. 'No, the camera only has a limited range and he was out of sight once he passed the shop doorway.'

'Any other CCTV cameras in the vicinity that could have picked him up?'

Kate had no option but to trust in what Hayden had told her. 'None, as far as we know,' she said.

Another grunt. 'Your man could just have been passing by,' he suggested without any real conviction. 'Could have just stopped for a pee down the alley, or to check one of the notices on the shop window.'

'What, at almost half one in the morning?' she protested. 'Come on, guv, you don't think that any more than I do — and there can't be many Land Rovers driving around with Mickey Mouse stickers on their back windows.'

He scowled, upped his glass and drained the contents.

'Okay, point taken,' he conceded. 'But all this makes things pretty difficult. On the face of it, Taylor's cottage could now be considered a potential crime scene, but we can't prove beyond doubt that your man entered her cottage in the first place and we've got nothing from the police surgeon or anyone else to indicate foul play, so whatever we do could be criticised.'

Kate smiled wanly at his use of the word "we." As usual, he found comfort in sharing a responsibility which in reality could only be his.

'So, what do you think we should do?' she asked, going along with him.

He thrust out his empty beer glass. 'Well, the first thing *you* can do is get me a refill of Best Bitter,' he said, 'and, while you're up, get yourself a drink too.'

That's nice of you, she said to herself, seeing as I'm paying. She snatched his glass and eased herself out of the bench seat.

'Then what?' she said, staring at him.

'Just get me that beer,' he growled.

* * *

The writer studied the front page of the local newspaper draped over the old Imperial typewriter and tapped out a two-fingered rhythm on the edge of the rosewood desk with a thoughtful frown.

It was late in the evening, and the hunched figure had pulled the heavy curtains and turned on the light. But sleep was out of the question after reading Debbie Moreton's lead story.

A red Land Rover Defender with a Mickey Mouse sticker on the back window. She had seen it. It had been parked up in a barn somewhere. But where? So many properties reconnoitred in recent days, so many outhouses and dustbins checked that it was difficult to remember which property was which.

What about Peter Jackson's home? After all, she had caught him at it in a barn, hadn't she? The writer smiled. Brilliant photos too. Just the right elevation and angle to capture the two queers together — *in flagrante delicto*, in fact. Disgusting!

But no, it wasn't the Jackson place. There had only been a flashy BMW in that barn and anyway, snobby Peter Jackson wouldn't have been seen dead in a Land Rover Defender, would he? The word "dead" elicited a humourless chuckle from her. No, maybe not dead in a Land Rover, she mused without a trace of sympathy or guilt, just dead in a barn, eh?

Mickey Mouse? Mickey Mouse? The sticker had been on the rear left-hand side window of the vehicle. The torch had picked it out quite clearly. So, where had that been? She cast a lingering glance at the pad of rough-textured paper lying beside the typewriter. Over a dozen letters sent in and around the village so far after her nocturnal foragings, which meant there were plenty of possible properties to consider. Furthermore, in a farming community like this one, there had to be any number of red Land Rover Defenders about. Yes, but not with Mickey Mouse stickers on the back, that was the point.

And it was then that something suddenly clicked and her subconscious reluctantly gave up what it had been holding back. Clarity dawned in a rush. Of course! It was the "psycho house," and that big, black barn with the peeling, corrugated iron roof at the side. That was where those ladies' fripperies had been found, with the old haversack, and that was where the Land Rover had been parked up.

So, this naughty boy was not just a knicker-snatcher then, but into something a lot more serious. Common sense dictated that the police should be alerted immediately, but, after a moment's deliberation, the writer decided against it. Why let them have all the glory? And this could be a bit of an earner too.

The so-called kidnapper may already have murdered the girl, of course, but if he had, she was dead anyway and it was too late to prevent that happening. But if she was still alive, then maybe there was a chance of getting to her, being the one to set her free and subsequently hailed as a hero. Naturally, questions would be asked as to why the "gallant rescuer" had gone to the property in the first place, but it would be easy enough to come up with the line that the suspect vehicle had been spotted and "bravely" followed there on a spur of the moment decision. After all, following the newspaper story, it was a feasible explanation, so who could say otherwise?

Furthermore, the whole thing would be exciting and a lot more fun than continuing to wind up the dull, stupid village with the anonymous letters. So, when to do it? Well, there was no time like the present, was there?

* * *

Headlights! Tammy Logan had stumbled painfully slowly along the road for what she judged to be about two hours without seeing a soul or another human habitation. The woodland had given way to flat marshland, dotted with scrub and bordered by rhynes, and seemingly populated solely by cattle, which had stared curiously at the ghostly figure in the gathering dusk, before shying away with panicky snorts.

She had finally taken temporary refuge in an open-fronted barn close to the road, which was stacked with bales of hay and currently untenanted by any ruminants. She had intended staying there and resting her sore, bleeding feet and aching muscles until daylight, when there was more chance of help from someone coming along the lonely back road. But, maybe an hour and a half later, the twin white beams cutting through the hedgerows and briefly lighting up the inside of the barn as the approaching vehicle negotiated a bend was just what she had been praying for. Scrambling to her feet, she limped across the small stone bridge spanning the adjoining rhyne and out into the road, waving her arms frantically at the oncoming vehicle.

The vehicle was almost on top of her, though fortunately not travelling at any real speed, when she jumped out. Nevertheless, there was a squeal of tyres and what from the front looked like some kind of van, slewed round slightly on the smooth surface of the road as it slammed to a halt.

'Please,' she gasped, jerking the front passenger door open and hauling herself up on to the seat inside, 'you have to help me!'

The driver, clad in a hooded anorak, turned towards her and, reaching across, pulled the door shut behind her.

'But that's what I'm here for,' said her former captor. 'And I've been looking everywhere for you.'

* * *

'House to house,' Kate said when she got home late that night.

Hayden poured her a glass of wine and set it on the coffee table in front of her. 'House to house?'

She sighed. 'Roscoe is organising it with uniform in the morning. Des Percival will lead it. Guv'nor reckons if we knock on a few doors, it will show the gods at HQ — and the press, of course — that we are doing something positive to trace the misper and we could also pick up some useful info.'

Hayden looked unconvinced. 'Bit hit and miss, that,' he said, sipping his own drink thoughtfully and sitting down opposite. 'Also, the plods can only ask questions — they can't search without a warrant. That makes it rather pointless, coupled with which, it will alert the perp to the fact that we now know he's local to the village, giving him time to get rid of the Land Rover—'

'And spook him into getting rid of the girl too,' Kate finished grimly. 'Bloody ham-fisted, if you ask me, but the truth is, it's all about internal politics and preserving Roscoe's skin.'

Hayden sighed. 'And are we part of these shenanigans?'

She shook her head. 'Apparently not. We're excluded, so we can carry on with our inquiries into the poison pen.'

'But we now know there's every chance both cases are linked.'

She shrugged. 'The DI's theory is that if we tackle things from both ends, it could produce the right result. In short, assuming our kidnapper was responsible for Maisie Taylor's death in the belief that she was the poison pen, it follows that he must have received an anonymous letter too. So, maybe if we can turn up the perp sending the letters, they will have the SP on our kidnapper and where he lives.'

Hayden poured them both another drink. 'Bit of a long shot, isn't it? If a letter *was* sent to him, it may not have had anything to do with our misper but about some other mucky transgression.'

'Ours is not to reason why.' Treating him to a humourless smile, she raised her glass. 'So, my good man, I offer you a toast — to the *Don Quixote* of Highbridge CID and his latest tilt at windmills.'

CHAPTER 17

Tammy Logan struggled with the door handle for several seconds before it dawned on her that it would not open.

'Modified lock,' her captor said with a grin. 'You can do that on an old motor. Only opens with a key from outside.' His grin became a derisory laugh. 'Nowhere to go, sweetheart.' He slipped the car back into gear and swung in a wide U-turn, across the road and up over the verge to go back the way he had come. 'You see, I gave up the chase in the end and got the wagon out instead. Knew you wouldn't have got far. Probably gone back into the woods to hide somewhere until dawn. So, all I had to do was cruise around until you popped up again. You went the wrong way too. Miles of nothing the route you chose. The other way would have got you to the village. Maddening, eh?'

Tammy Logan threw back her head and screamed for all she was worth — only to subside in a bubbling moan when the back of his hand caught her a hard blow across the face, drawing blood and opening up the split lip he had previously given her.

'Do that again,' he said, 'and I'll do a lot worse to you. Savvy?'

Seconds later, he turned off the road into a tunnel-like entrance, the headlights of the vehicle burrowing deep into dense woodland.

She saw the familiar house come into view and sat there, sick and sobbing. Ignoring her distress he parked by a big, black barn and came around to her side of the Land Rover to get her out.

'More punishment on the cards, I'm afraid,' he said, seizing her wrist in a vice-like grip and dragging her to the front door. 'It's your own fault, you know. I won't be defied.'

'Please,' she choked, struggling futilely as he pulled her along the corridor towards the basement. 'Why are you doing this to me? I've done nothing to you. You have no right—'

'Right?' he echoed with a snarl, stopping a moment to press his face close to her. 'I have every right. Yet again, you have mocked the Almighty, and His will must be obeyed.'

'You — you're crazy,' she shrieked. He seemed not to hear. Dragging her into the basement room, he threw her onto the bed. Then, locking the door, he stalked into the bathroom. Seconds later, she heard the tap running . . .

* * *

The figure in the black hooded coat and dark trousers parked the car in a gateway in the same narrow back road that had provided an escape route for Tammy Logan a few hours before. She lowered the window to listen.

The moon had been out, but had since retreated behind scudding clouds, and the night was deathly still, the trees and shrubs choking the verges impenetrable to the naked eye. A ghostly winged shape — a barn owl possibly — flashed by close to the road within feet of the parked vehicle and from somewhere in the depths of the woodland, a vixen shrieked.

The writer studied the ungated entrance a few yards away on the opposite side of the road. The house itself was hidden deep inside the woodland, but even without seeing it she knew that this was the place. This was where the red Land Rover Defender with the Mickey Mouse sticker on the back window had been parked inside the barn. This was where she had found the women's underwear and haversack dumped in the refuse bin with all the other rubbish. This was where the sicko was holding the young woman he had kidnapped — if she was still alive.

Maybe he had already cut her throat or strangled her and buried her somewhere in the woods? Maybe there was no trace of her now? No matter, it was still worth taking a look. But it had to be done on foot. Silently, stealthily, unseen.

The writer opened the car door as quietly as possible, and stopped dead. The glow of headlights lighting up a bend in the road perhaps a quarter of a mile away, and the clatter of a rough diesel engine were unmistakable and growing louder by the second. The vehicle appeared suddenly, bearing down on the parked car at speed. It was a Land Rover, that was immediately obvious, and, as she ducked down in the seat to avoid being picked out by those powerful twin beams, the engine note slowed dramatically, and a groaning squeal indicated fiercely applied brakes. She risked a quick glance and saw the Land Rover abruptly swing left to enter the driveway to the target house. The sicko had just come home then, had he? The luminous dial on her slender wrist gave the time as just on eleven fifty pm. Where had he been at this late hour? The pubs and restaurants would be closed by now and Somerset's nearest nightclubs were miles away in Taunton or Bristol.

She opened the car door again just as the moon re-emerged, closed it gently but left it unlocked. The last thing she needed now was for the alarm to go off.

It was just a brisk hundred-yard walk to the entrance to the property. She paused to stare into what looked like the black mouth of a tunnel formed by tightly packed undergrowth and overhanging trees. It shut out all but the faintest trickles of moonlight and looked singularly uninviting, and she was tempted to abandon the whole adventure there and then. But to turn back could mean losing a once-in-a-lifetime opportunity. Out of the question.

Moisture from recent rainfall dripped from the trees as she advanced cautiously along the muddy track, her partially masked torch gripped tightly in one hand.

The woodland was alive with its foraging, nocturnal inhabitants. Things moved with agitated rustlings in the gloom, little furry things that ran across the track in panic. Winged phantoms swooped silently from one tree to another, issuing mournful, warning cries as they vanished into the night, and the not too distant call of the marauding vixen was repeated several times with a shriek like a child in agony. Even the trees provided their own muted accompaniment to nature's discordant symphony, groaning and creaking under the slight breeze as if conversing in some alien tongue.

She jumped several times as she negotiated the track, but pressed on with grim determination, until it veered sharply to the left, blossoming out into a wide hardstanding in front of an old dismal-looking house — without a doubt, the psycho house of earlier acquaintance.

The empty Land Rover was parked in the full light of the moon by the double doors of a familiar black barn with a corrugated iron roof and, though lights glowed dimly in several of the windows of the house, there was no movement or any other sign of life.

Cautiously, she approached the barn and the Land Rover, switching off the torch and skirting around the edge of the hardstanding, partially hidden in the shadows thrown by the encircling woodland.

The vehicle was empty, and a quick glance revealed no Mickey Mouse sticker. Surely this *was* the right house? She couldn't have made a mistake, could she? Risking detection, she flicked the torch back on to study the rear window more closely. At first, nothing, but then at the bottom, close to the corner of the rubber seal where the sticker should have been, she saw a tiny piece of coloured plastic still attached to the glass. Further examination revealed an even more minute and slightly proud strip of what looked like dried glue a short distance from the left-hand edge of the window running upwards in a two to three-inch vertical line. Bingo! The bastard had obviously read the newspaper story and removed the evidence — but he hadn't removed enough of it.

But she had no time to gloat over her discovery, for at that precise moment a frenzied scream arose from somewhere deep inside the house.

The writer froze. It was definitely a woman's voice, and the chilling sound carried with it the sheer, mind-numbing terror and total despair of someone close to the end of all physical and mental endurance.

She knew that the sensible thing to do was beat a rapid retreat to much safer quarters, then call the police on her mobile. It would have been so easy to do and yet she made no attempt to turn back. The adrenalin was already surging through her veins. This business was turning out to be more thrilling than she could ever have anticipated. It had to be investigated to the full before she decided on her next move. She darted across the hardstanding to the front door of the house.

She found to her disappointment that the door was securely locked, as were the three front windows, but there turned out to be a wooden door at the side and a quick test of the handle proved it to be unlocked. Ace!

Inside, was a study/library, and a further door which opened onto a long hallway. This ended a few feet to the right before a stout, wooden door with a brass letterbox — obviously the front door. To the left, several other doors opened off on each side and at the far end a staircase was plainly visible, providing access to the upper floor.

Treading warily along the hallway towards the staircase, she found that all the other doors stood half open, with the rooms inside unlit. A brief flash of the torch into each revealed that two were living rooms and a third a kitchen, with a sink piled high with dirty dishes. All were unoccupied.

So, where had the scream come from, and where was the woman being held? Upstairs seemed the most likely place

— one of the bedrooms perhaps. But, on the point of checking this out, she made another discovery — an open door under the stairs, with more steps leading down to some sort of lighted basement. More importantly, what sounded like water splashing, and someone choking and hyperventilating could clearly be heard from below, coupled with a man's voice raised in anger.

Returning the torch to her pocket, she began her descent, wincing at every creak of the wooden risers. The basement was lit by a strip light and seemed to contain nothing more interesting than tea chests and rolled-up carpet. Then she noticed a crack of light in the deep shadows at the far end of the room, revealing the presence of another door. The sound of the woman hyperventilating was still audible, but there was no more splashing of water and the man's voice had now dropped to an unintelligible, soothing murmur.

For some reason, this triggered alarm bells in the writer's brain, and she turned back towards the stairs. But she was too late. The partially concealed door was suddenly thrown open, framing a heavy-set figure in a blaze of oblong light.

There was no time for flight. All she could do was shrink into a gap between some tea chests stacked against the wall, trusting in the shadows to conceal her. Clenching her teeth until she thought they might shatter, she stayed perfectly still while the man closed and locked the door behind him and stomped back across the room towards the stairs. To her relief, he appeared totally unaware of her presence and, looking neither left, nor right, carried on up the stairs, whistling softly. Seconds later she heard the door at the top slam shut.

Releasing her breath in a long, heavy gasp, she eased herself out of her hiding place and stood for a moment, heart thumping, legs trembling in the shock of her near discovery. It was time to get out while she could, but first she had to be sure of the identity of the woman he seemed to be holding. Approaching the locked door, she shook the handle several times to attract attention and waited for a moment before pressing her mouth against the gap.

‘I’m a friend,’ she said as loudly as she dared. ‘Who are you?’

There was a scuffling sound on the other side of the door and shortly afterwards a tremulous voice responded, ‘Tammy — Tammy Logan. He — he’s shut me in here. I think he’s crazy. I’m frightened he’ll kill me.’

‘Stay calm,’ the writer called back. ‘I am going to get help.’

‘Please don’t leave me here,’ the other sobbed, but her would-be rescuer was no longer listening. She was already making her way up the stairs to the hall door, her excitement at fever pitch, thinking about the importance of the discovery she had made and how best she could make use of that information to her own advantage.

The hallway still seemed to be deserted, and she headed for the study through which she had entered the house with a sense of relief. All she had to do now was get back down the driveway to her car, and then she was in the clear. But her relief turned out to be premature.

What had made him suspect he had an intruder was a mystery, but that he had became immediately apparent when he launched himself at her from behind the door of the study, pinning her against the wall and trapping her neck in the crook of one muscular arm.

‘Well, well, well,’ he sneered over her shoulder. ‘Look who it is. Sent anymore nasty letters, have you? I would never have guessed it was you.’

She was given no opportunity to reply. The grip on her neck tightened, compressing the carotid arteries, and within seconds she had blacked out.

CHAPTER 18

The telephone rang in the little thatched cottage at precisely five am, jerking Kate into instant wakefulness. It was the police control room.

'Sorry, skipper,' the operator said without a hint of an apology in his tone, 'but you are down as "on call" tonight.'

Kate scowled at the humped shape of Hayden lying beside her and snoring heavily, blissfully unaware of the strident ring of the phone.

Dragging herself up into a sitting position, she wiped the sleep from her eyes. 'So, what's up?' she asked, sounding so befuddled that she feared the operator must think she was drunk.

'We've had a call from the ambulance service to say they're dealing with a death by drowning incident. Young girl apparently found in a private swimming pool. Uniform are there now and have asked for CID backup.'

Kate switched on the bedside light and had the malicious satisfaction of feeling Hayden stir. 'Okay, you'd better give me the address.'

There was a brief pause as the operator checked. 'Place called Winston House,' he said. 'At—'

'What?' she exclaimed, cutting him off. 'Colonel Winston's home?'

'Oh, you know it, do you?'

Kate took a deep, trembling breath. 'Yes, I know it. Any idea who the deceased is?'

'Apparently, some guy who lives there — an Elton Jones — says it's a Gabriella Winston.'

* * *

Even in the now strengthening dawn light, the pulsing blue strobes and beacons of the emergency services were clearly visible on the horizon well before Kate drove through the main entrance of Winston House. Beside her, Hayden was still grumbling about having been dragged unnecessarily from his warm bed.

An ambulance and two marked police patrol cars were drawn up at the front of the house, which was ablaze with light. Typically, Roscoe's battered Honda Civic was badly parked, with its headlights still blazing, half on and half off a strip of lawn separating the shingle forecourt from the encircling shrubbery. Gabriella Winston's red Jaguar E-Type was parked by the front door but there was no sign of any other vehicle, suggesting that Colonel Winston was not yet back from his business trip abroad.

'DI's round the back, skipper,' a young constable said, stepping forward to meet them.

'We know where to go,' Kate replied tersely. 'Where's Elton Jones?'

'Inside, skip. State of shock.'

'Not surprised. Make sure he stays there until I can speak to him.'

The ambulance crew were already on the way back to their vehicle — their job obviously done — as Kate and Hayden tramped down the path at the side of the house, and she recognised the chunky figure of the DI in his knee-length coat and pork-pie hat standing with a uniformed inspector and sergeant close to the swimming pool. Something lay, covered by a tarpaulin, on a patch of grass between the pool and the changing-room hut. Kate did not need to be told what it was.

Roscoe turned towards the two detectives, eyeing them in his usual critical fashion.

'Take a look,' he invited, waving a hand towards the tarpaulin. 'At least you've seen her before and can confirm her ID.'

Kate nodded and, bending down beside the tarpaulin, gently pulled it back a fraction. The face of the young woman beneath was the colour of ivory, the sightless eyes, no longer mischievous or seductive, stared back at her, almost wistful. Kate shuddered and forced herself to raise the tarpaulin a little more to confirm something else she had already suspected. Gabriella was completely naked, which suggested she had been in for one of her skinny dips at the time of her death.

She replaced the tarpaulin and rejoined the group by the pool.

'It's Gabriella all right,' she confirmed. 'Did Elton pull her out?'

Roscoe nodded. 'Apparently he found her in the pool when he came back around half an hour ago.'

'Came *back*. In the early hours of the morning?'

The DI shrugged. 'Out all night at a friend's apparently. Says he tried resuscitation but she was already dead. He'll need to be interviewed but I'll leave that with you.'

He jerked his head towards the changing-room hut, indicating that she should follow him, and moved a short distance away from the other officers until he was sure they were out of earshot.

'I gather Colonel Winston is out of the country at present,' he said.

She picked up on the agitation in his tone. 'On business, I'm told.'

'When is he back?'

'No idea. Maybe Elton knows?'

'He claims he doesn't, but he has a contact number and said he will let him know what's happened here — which means he could be back anytime.'

He chewed rapidly for a few seconds, studying her. 'The shit is really going to hit the fan over this, and we need to make sure we do everything that's required — and I mean everything. Got that? Police surgeon is on his way and should be here shortly, but that's all. We don't need SOCO or the forensic pathologist for an accidental drowning, and calling them out would only suggest to the press that we think there's something fishy about the death.'

'And you don't think there is?'

He spat his gum into the adjacent shrubbery.

'No, I bloody don't.' He turned slightly to nod towards the pool. 'There's an empty bottle of vodka on the grass by the steps leading into the water. Stupid little bitch was obviously on a bender before she went for her skinny dip and suffered the consequences. End of.'

'A tad convenient for that bottle to be there, though, don't you think, guv?' she commented drily.

'Not if she'd just been swilling from it, I don't. What was she supposed to do with it — find a dustbin before diving into the pool, just to prove she's eco-friendly?'

Kate shook her head stubbornly. 'I just can't understand how she drowned like this. She told me she regularly used the pool and it was obvious from the look of her that she was pretty fit.'

He glared at her. 'Don't you go trying to make something out of this, Lewis, like you did with Maisie Taylor and the stiff in the fire. It's a straightforward death by drowning. Coroner will probably record a verdict of misadventure. There's no suggestion of anything else here.'

Kate made a grimace. 'But you have to admit that it's a bit unprecedented to have three so-called accidents in one village within days of each other.'

He snorted. 'Unusual, I'll give you that, but that's not a basis for a criminal investigation. Taylor was an old woman who simply tripped and fell down the stairs. No suspicious marks on her body to suggest she may have been attacked and no signs of a break-in. Southerby lived alone in an old cottage heated by butane gas and even the fire chief reckoned that the place went up due to a loose connection or a damaged hose on the gas cooker—'

'You're forgetting that we have photo evidence of the sus Land Rover outside Taylor's cottage the night she died, while Southerby rang the nick, allegedly with information on the sus motor, just before the fire. The two deaths have to be one hell of a coincidence.'

'Yeah, but a coincidence is what they are and I'd be very interested to see how you link their deaths with that of a young girl who goes for a moonlit swim with a belly full of vodka and ends up drowning herself. Even your imagination cannot be that fertile.'

He thrust his head forward belligerently. 'And what about Jackson? Are you going to claim someone topped him too? Rigged up his shotgun to make his death look like suicide? We must be up against a bloody clever and very versatile serial killer if that's the case.' He straightened. 'Get real, Sergeant,' he rapped, 'and get this thing put to bed asap — preferably before the colonel comes home.'

Then he turned on his heel and headed back towards the front of the house, leaving Kate staring after him in a mood of angry frustration.

'More words of wisdom from the guv'nor?' Hayden asked, wandering over to her.

'More shit, you mean,' she replied. 'Now, let's go have a nice chat with our friend Elton and see what further crap he comes out with.'

* * *

Elton was in the Winstons' drawing room, sitting on the edge of the same chaise longue Gabriella had draped herself across on her last meeting with the two detectives. He was white-faced, wearing just a dressing gown, and his hair still looked wet. He was clutching an amber coloured drink in one trembling hand. A half-full decanter stood on a coffee table beside him and Kate couldn't help wondering how the colonel would have reacted to the sight of his manservant knocking back what was no doubt an expensive single malt whisky.

Elton glanced up quickly when Kate and Hayden appeared through the open doorway and gave them a cursory nod. His eyes were a little too bright and his tongue constantly flicked along his bottom lip between gulps from the glittering crystal glass in his hand, suggesting that he was in a considerable state of shock. No trace of supercilious arrogance now, Kate thought vindictively, as she and Hayden sat down in armchairs opposite him.

'The colonel will kill me when he gets back,' Elton blurted out suddenly, and it was significant to Kate that his first thought was for his own skin rather than the death of his employer's beautiful daughter. 'Is — is she definitely—?'

'Dead?' Kate finished for him. 'Oh yes, she's dead all right, but you must know that if you pulled her out of the pool.'

His Adam's apple seemed to go into a series of spasms, and he took another gulp from his glass.

'Would you put the drink down, please,' Kate said sternly. 'We want to talk to you, and we need you to be sober.'

He hesitated, then nodded and put the glass down on the coffee table beside the decanter.

'I was out at a friend's all night and came home to find — find her lying there,' he suddenly blurted. 'I — I jumped in, pulled her out and tried to — to resuscitate her, but—'

'What made you check the pool?'

He swallowed several times. 'I park my — my car round the back of the house and, as the back door is invariably locked, I — I go in through the — the front door with my own key. That means using the path running alongside the pool. That — that's when I saw her.'

'So, when did she last use the pool?'

He cleared his throat and seemed to make a determined effort to take control of his nerves. 'The day before, I think. Though I didn't actually see her swimming, I did see her go down there in — in the early afternoon, dressed in her towelling robe.'

'Did she often use the pool at night?'

'Never, as far as I know.' He made a face, adding bitterly, 'No one to — to see her in the buff then, was there? She liked to shock and to show herself off. Postmen, delivery men, anyone who happened to come by.'

'When did you last see her alive?'

'Just after I made her dinner, around seven-thirty, before I went out.'

'So, when you left, she was in the house on her own?'

He looked away, unable to meet her gaze. 'Yes — though I suspect she went out at some stage.'

'Oh? Why do you say that?'

'She was a bit of a night owl — sometimes didn't get back until the early hours. Loved to party when she got the chance. We all have our own remote-control key fobs for the electronic gates, you see, so she could come and go as she pleased.'

'I presume her father wasn't too happy about her behaviour. He seemed to be something of a stickler.'

'I — I think he was past caring. There was not much love lost between the two of them since Gabriella's mother died, and he just let her go her own way. Trouble was, she had never grown up and was perpetually bored. She — she needed to be constantly stimulated. Hated living in what she saw as the back of beyond and despised the people in the village. Called them dead — deadbeats. Once told me the whole place needed shaking up.'

'That didn't stop her visiting the village pub and mixing with the locals, though, it seems.'

There was the trace of a cynical smile and his voice strengthened. 'That's true enough. She spent most of her time at the Soldier's Arms. Once she told me she felt superior among all those yokels and she really loved baiting the men. Drank too much there too.'

'But you can't be sure she went out last night? She could have had an evening in and gone for a swim just before you got back?'

He shook his head. 'Her — her car had been moved — parked in a funny place actually. When I went out, it was by the front door, where she usually left it. When I got back, it was parked some yards away by the path which runs down the side of the house.'

'You mean the path leading to the pool?'

'Yes. Struck me as odd, because she idolised that car and insisted it was always parked in full view of her bedroom window at the front of the house.'

'You're saying someone else may have driven her home?'

An even firmer shake of the head. 'She would never have let anyone else drive that car — not even her father.'

'Or you?' Hayden added meaningly. 'Maybe she was drunk and got you to pick her up and bring her home in case she was stopped by the police. Then she decided to go for a moonlit dip with her father's loyal retainer.'

There was a look of panic on Elton's face now and he shook his head several times. 'No, no, no,' he protested. 'I've told you I was out all night and she would never have let me behind the wheel anyway. You — you must believe me, I found her drowned in the pool when I got back—'

He broke off, as something else occurred to him, and a self-satisfied sneer crept into his voice. 'Anyway, if I had gone to pick her up from somewhere, I would have to have driven there in my car, wouldn't I? If you care to look, you will find it is still parked at the back of the house behind the swimming pool.'

'You could have used a taxi.'

Now imbued with a new confidence, Elton's sneer was even more pronounced. 'Then check with the local taxi firms. There are only two of them, so it shouldn't be that difficult for you.'

Kate's mouth tightened. She deliberately changed tack. 'Okay, so if, as you claim, you were out all night, where exactly were you?'

Elton threw her a quick guilty glance, his bravado evaporating in an instant. 'As I've already said, with — with a friend.' He paused briefly. 'I was with a friend.'

'And who might that friend be?'

'I'd rather not say.'

Kate sighed heavily. 'Elton,' she said firmly, leaning forward in her chair, 'we are dealing with the unexplained death of a young woman here. On your own admission, you were the one who recovered her body from the pool. That makes you central to our inquiries and it could put you in an awkward position if you are not prepared to cooperate.'

His eyes widened as, despite the amount of alcohol he had drunk, it dawned on him what she was getting at.

'I didn't do anything to her,' he exclaimed, panic back in his voice. 'I — I left here at eight-thirty and didn't get back until after four. Bloody hell, I tried to save her and—'

'So, I repeat, where were you? We need to be able to check this out. If you were sleeping with someone, we have to know who she is, however embarrassing that might be for you.'

To the surprise of both detectives, he emitted a high-pitched, almost hysterical laugh. 'She? She? Why should it have to be a she?' Then he added, 'I'm gay, for frig's sake — I was sleeping with another man. Are you satisfied now?'

Then he covered his face with his hands and burst into tears, sobbing like a child.

Neither she nor Hayden made any immediate response, which he seemed to take as a form of silent condemnation. Slowly raising his head and wiping his eyes on the back of one hand, he stared at each of them in turn.

'Shock you both, does it?' he accused them bitterly. 'Think it's obscene, do you? See me as some kind of dirty pervert?'

Kate stopped his outburst with a dismissive cut of her hand. 'You've misread the signals, Elton. We think nothing of the sort. Your relationships are your own private business and we are not interested in whether you are sleeping with a man or a woman.' She took a deep breath. 'But what *is* of interest to us is the fact that Gabriella told us she was having an affair with you, and that she had once had sex with you in the hut by the pool—'

His jaw dropped. 'Gabriella told you that?' He emitted an incredulous laugh. 'That's impossible. I have no interest in women. I have been seeing my current boyfriend for close on eighteen months. I've only kept it quiet because of the colonel's prejudices — if he finds out, he'll sack me on the spot.'

'So why would someone send her an anonymous letter suggesting you *were* having sex with her?'

'A letter? What letter? She said nothing to me about that.'

'She said she didn't want you or the colonel to know,' Hayden explained.

He shook his head again, plainly confused. 'Why would someone write a pack of lies like that? It never happened — never could happen—'

He broke off, frowning as something else seemed to occur to him. 'If someone actually wrote such a letter at all. The thing is, Gabrielle was a fantasist and an exhibitionist, always wanting to be noticed. I wouldn't have put it past her to invent the whole thing just for the sheer hell of it. She knew about the poison pen writer in the village — her own father had received one of the letters — so it wouldn't surprise me if she hadn't decided to send one to herself to attract attention.'

Kate glanced quickly at Hayden and saw from the look on his face that he was thinking exactly what she was thinking.

'We'll come back to the name and address of your boyfriend later,' she said, getting to her feet. 'For now, we'd like to see Gabriella's room. Then my colleague here will take a statement from you.'

'Her room? Whatever for?'

'Just a hunch, nothing more, but it can't do any harm since she is dead anyway.'

'But the colonel—'

'Is not here right now,' Hayden cut in.

Elton stared at him for a moment, then shrugged and picked up his whisky glass again. 'Suit yourselves,' he muttered. 'Upstairs. First on the left.'

* * *

All the rooms upstairs seemed to have white painted doors with gilt embellishments and handles. Gabriella's wasn't difficult to find. It had her name on it, also in gilt lettering, and carried a large poster of a red E-Type Jaguar.

'Well, she certainly had taste,' Hayden commented.

'Bit juvenile, though, don't you think?' Kate said. 'After all, she wasn't a teenager anymore. She must have been in her mid-twenties at least.'

She pulled on a pair of protective nylon gloves, reached into her pocket and handed him a second pair. 'Better put these on, just in case.'

'In case of what?'

'In case we find anything worth finding,' she retorted. 'Don't be so obtuse. You know the drill.'

The room itself was thickly carpeted and furnished with the latest design in furniture, including a desk accommodating a stand-alone computer and colour printer in one corner. Large posters of sports cars, half-naked muscular men and heavy rock bands plastered the barely visible, pale blue walls and an assortment of dresses, tops and trousers had been dumped on the floor by the unmade bed, as if it had been too much trouble to put the stuff away.

'This is a typical teenager's room too,' Kate remarked, glancing critically around her. 'Like the poster on the door, it suggests that Gabriella was rather immature.'

'A fantasist and exhibitionist, as Elton succinctly put it,' Hayden drawled from across the room by the window. 'A bored little rich girl who had too much time on her hands and not enough to occupy herself with — which is probably why she wrote all those letters.'

'What?' In the process of inspecting the computer, Kate spun round.

Hayden was standing by another larger, old-fashioned desk under the window, with a newspaper in his hands.

'*Voila*!' he said, inclining his head towards the ancient-looking manual typewriter on the desktop. 'There was a copy of the local newspaper spread over it, so I didn't see it at first.'

'It's an old Imperial,' Kate breathed, joining him beside the desk. 'The same as Maisie Taylor's.'

'But in much better nick,' Hayden went on, opening one of the desk drawers. 'And there's more.'

Even before he slipped his hand into the drawer to lift something out, Kate guessed what he had found. She stood for several seconds after he had placed it beside the typewriter, staring at the loose sheets of familiar coarse grey paper. It was identical to the pad she had purchased from the shop.

'Let's see what other treasure we can find,' he went on and opened the deeper drawer underneath, immediately issuing a low whistle. 'The icing on the cake,' he said, producing a sizeable black camera bag.

She waited while he placed it on the desktop and unzipped it. Inside was an expensive-looking Nikon SLR digital camera, complete with an additional 200mm telephoto lens.

'It would seem we've identified our poison pen at last,' he remarked unnecessarily.

'As well as the person who set up poor Maisie Taylor.'

He nodded. 'And no doubt when we check the memory stick, we will find some choice photos of Peter Jackson and his friend — *in flagrante delicto*. There's a nice colour printer over there too, which would have been quite capable of producing some excellent pictures to post to someone.'

Kate glanced across the room. 'Everything a poison pen writer would need,' she said. 'So, the letter Gabriella claimed to have received was just crap. As Elton suggested, she must have sent it to herself — though not simply to attract attention, but to avoid any possibility of suspicion falling on her.'

'And it would appear that she sent one to her own father too,' he added, 'maybe to punish him for being such a pompous, self-righteous hypocrite. I sensed when we first visited the house that they didn't get on too well — bit of an atmosphere in the room — and Elton confirmed the fact.'

He picked up the newspaper he had dumped on the windowsill and opened it out again, stiffening almost immediately. 'Look at this,' he said.

A thick black ring had been drawn around the paragraph of Debbie Moreton's front-page story which mentioned the Land Rover Defender, and Kate saw a further black line extending from the circle to a handwritten comment in the margin. The comment read, '*Psycho house.*'

'Psycho house?' she echoed. 'Bloody Nora! She knew where our kidnapper was living — had probably visited the place on one of her foraging expeditions.' She snapped her fingers. 'Quick. Check the camera. There might be a pic on that memory stick, if it's still in there.'

'Bravo, old girl,' he said enthusiastically and, opening the camera up, grunted in satisfaction. The memory stick was intact.

'Time for a film show, eh?' he continued and, switching the monitor facility on, he pressed "replay" and held the camera up in front of them so that they could both see the screen.

Immediately, pictures of Peter Jackson and Julian Brookes in Jackson's barn appeared. Kate nodded her head irritably and looked away. Hayden took the hint and scrolled through until another picture appeared. At first sight, it seemed to be just a shot of some women's clothes, neatly spread out on a black dustbin lid, which had been placed upside down on the bin itself. He carried on to the next picture, which turned out to be one of a number of selfies and photos of the E-Type Jaguar. There were no other pictures at all on the stick.

'Sorry. Nothing,' he said, switching the camera off.

She shook her head thoughtfully. 'Go back to those clothes,' she instructed.

Mystified, he shrugged and turned the camera back on.

'Now, why would you take photos of a pair of sandals, shorts, a crop top, a bra and a pair of knickers?' she said, studying the screen with a frown. 'They don't look particularly new. It doesn't make sense.'

'The photo seems to have been taken in a garage or barn,' he said. 'You can see a concrete floor there and, behind the dustbin, what looks like a slatted wooden wall.'

She looked closer. 'And attached to the wall, there appears to be half of a poster with the pic of a car on it—'

'A Morgan,' he said smugly. 'You can see part of the front grill and a headlight — quite distinctive. The owner of the place is obviously keen on classic cars.'

'But what's that pile of stuff right down in the bottom corner of the photo?'

He lowered the camera and peered at the screen again. 'Looks like just a pile of rubbish — maybe taken out of the bin. There's an oil can, I think, a tin of brake fluid, bottles and other bits — oh yes, and what looks like the top of a rucksack.'

'A rucksack? Can you zoom in?'

He fumbled for a moment and the picture went out of focus, then steadied with a close-up of the rubbish.

Kate released her breath in a sharp hiss. 'Look at that.'

He squinted at the screen. 'What? It's just a pile of rubbish.'

'Look at the rucksack. There are initials on the flap, painted on it in white letters.'

She studied it again, then read slowly out loud. 'It looks like *TI* — no, it's *TL*. See? *TL*.'

She stared at his puzzled expression impatiently. 'Think, man! Tammy Logan. This is too much of a coincidence. The rucksack and the clothes, it's all Tammy Logan's gear, I'd stake my reputation on it. Gabriella must have accidentally stumbled on the stuff while rummaging through the dustbin.

The little bitch then spread it out on the lid to capture a photograph so she could use it to taunt Tammy's kidnapper later on, either to pursue another of her juvenile games or to try a bit of blackmail.'

'Which means she must have guessed the stuff belonged to Tammy.'

Kate pondered that conclusion for a few seconds, then shook her head. 'I sense not. Maybe she didn't know about our misper then. Maybe she just thought it strange that such skimpy fripperies were in the dustbin of the particular person who lived in the house. Could be he's very elderly or a bachelor—'

'Or was someone she already suspected of being a pervert?'

This time she nodded several times. '*And* perhaps someone in a respected social position who had a lot to lose if all this got out.'

'Like a vicar?'

'Let's not get ahead of ourselves, but yes, like a vicar, though I can't really see the Rev Salter as a candidate.'

His eyes widened. 'Gordon Bennett, I do believe you're right — and, if only she had known what she'd got, she could have led us straight to him — and to Tammy.'

Her face was grim. 'If Tammy is still alive, that is. If these *are* her clothes, the mere fact that they are in the bin suggests she no longer needed them because he had already stiffed her.'

He frowned. 'But in that case, why didn't he just bury her body? He might as well have left the clothes on her. After all, what difference would it have made if her corpse were to be discovered by someone later on?'

'Good point, so why do you think he decided to strip her?'

He shrugged. 'No idea. I'm not a psychopath or a sexual pervert.'

She raised both eyebrows. 'That, my dear Hayden, is a matter of opinion.'

CHAPTER 19

The police surgeon was just about to leave when Kate returned to the scene of the tragedy, leaving Hayden to take Elton's statement.

Standing in the morning sunlight, Raymond Makepiece smiled frostily when he saw them. 'My favourite sleuth,' he sniped. 'I'm telling you, this village is beginning to look a bit like that TV drama, *Midsomer Murders*. Corpses have started popping up everywhere since you embarked on your inquiries.'

'Sorry, Doc,' Kate said with a brief smile.

'No, no,' he replied in a tone laced with sarcasm, 'please don't apologise. At least you have given me a bit of variety. A shotgun blast, a broken neck, an incineration and now a drowning. I wonder what I will have to test my skills on next?' He emitted a mock sigh. 'Just let me get a decent night's sleep before you present me with another one, will you?'

'So,' Kate said, walking back with him to her car, 'what's the verdict on this one? Anything I should be concerned about?'

He turned to face her. 'Death definitely due to drowning. Rigor mortis just starting and, going by body temperature and the present ambient temperature, I would say death occurred probably within the last three hours at the most. No defensive marks, as far as I can see, and no signs of other external injury, apart from a noticeable abrasion on the outside of one wrist and some curious scratch marks on her neck, which could have been caused by accidental contact with something prior to her death—'

'Or?'

The frosty smile was back. 'Could also have been made by someone's fingernails, though I'm not really qualified to say. We'll have to wait to see what the PM tells us.'

Kate's eyes had narrowed appreciably now. 'The indications are that she had been drinking heavily prior to her death. Any thoughts on that? You obviously saw the empty bottle of vodka on the grass at the side of the pool.'

Makepiece frowned. 'Yes, very convenient. Of course, if our deceased had that lot inside her, no wonder she wasn't capable of staying on top of the water—'

'But?'

Another more genuine sigh. 'No buts. Just curiosity and a certain amount of professional uneasiness about the circumstances of the young woman's death, that's all.'

'You're not happy that this death was accidental then?'

'As a doctor, I don't make judgements without hard facts. But I've been in this game a long time and every so often I get the feeling that something's not quite right. Call it a tickle, if you like.'

'A tickle?'

'Something like that, yes, but nothing I can put my finger on and certainly nothing I'm prepared to officially hypothesise about at this stage — though you might want to take things a little further to be sure.'

'What, forensically, you mean?'

He snapped his briefcase shut. 'It's your shout, I'm afraid,' he said unhelpfully.

'What's new?' Kate muttered to herself as she watched him walk away in the direction of his car. 'It's always my bloody shout.'

'So, what now?' Hayden said, rejoining her. 'Seems to me that Winston's death is looking more and more sus by the minute.'

Kate nodded. Seems very much like it. Now, before I see Roscoe, I'd like you to run off a hard copy of that pic of the clothing we found on the memory stick. It's a long shot, but maybe at some stage we'll be able to match it up with the garage or barn in which she took it.'

He stared at her. 'But that's evidence. You know the procedures. If this becomes a crime scene, the stick could be an exhibit in any future court case and should be logged in as such with the exhibits officer, in accordance with the official protocols.'

She shrugged. 'It isn't a crime scene at present, it is only a potential suspicious death — so there *is* no exhibits officer. Once we have the hard copy of the photograph, we can do the necessary and hand the memory stick in, together with the appropriate documentation to ensure there's a proper paper trail. All right?'

He sighed heavily. 'You really are sailing close to the wind on this one, Kate. They could throw the book at us if this goes pear-shaped — especially if it costs the force a future prosecution.'

Her expression was bleak. 'I am more concerned about saving the life of an innocent young woman than adhering to bureaucratic protocols, and I can feel it in my waters that time is fast running out for Tammy Logan — if it hasn't already.'

* * *

Job done! Everything had worked out well in the end, but what a night. Now back home again, he stared at his drawn, white face in the mirror and shivered.

Forcing the vodka down the girl's throat as she began to come to had not been easy. She'd struggled quite violently but luckily, he'd already anticipated this by wrapping a handkerchief around the neck of the bottle to reduce the risk of injury to the inside of her mouth or damage to her teeth, which a pathologist might spot later. She was totally out of it when he dumped her in the bath and held her head under the water, and her struggles had been much too feeble to present any real problem for him.

In any other circumstances, he would have found driving the E-Type Jaguar exhilarating but, conscious of what he was carrying in the boot, it had only been stressful. At any moment headlights could have come racing up behind him, the pulsing blue light of a police strobe flooding the car, followed by a curious patrol officer carrying out a so-called "routine check." It never happened. In fact, he'd seen very few vehicles on the road between his place and the big, walled house and he reached his objective without incident. The iron gates were closed, but he had sussed the purpose of the little gadget attached to the car's ignition keyring and breathed a sigh of relief when they slowly swung open at the press of the button.

The house was in darkness, but with no way of knowing who, apart from Gabriella and her father, lived there, he had extinguished the car's lights and driven cautiously up the driveway, parking to one side of the house and shutting down the throaty engine.

Getting her out of the tiny boot had presented a further problem. Somehow, she'd become wedged in the confined space. Then the blanket wrapped around her caught on something and she'd sagged against him while he was disentangling it, one arm coming free of the blanket folds and draping itself around his neck.

It temporarily spooked him and, in shaking her arm clear in a fit of revulsion, he almost dropped her. It felt as if the limb was some leprous thing that had crept up on him from the woodland. Abruptly regaining control of himself with a shuddering gulp, he'd rested her behind on his knee and shut the boot as quietly as he could. Then he'd hoisted her body, still wrapped in the blanket, over one shoulder, grateful for the fact that, despite the water that probably remained inside her, she was still light enough to carry. A waning moon had provided sufficient light to enable him to pick his way along the path down the side of the house, but he'd known the way anyway. He had been to this place before — some weeks ago, in fact.

She'd been swimming in the pool on the afternoon he had gone there, wearing nothing but a seductive smile. He remembered his embarrassment as she'd deliberately climbed out of the water to pick up a towel lying on the grass, enjoying every minute of his discomfort, and, to his shame he also remembered the stirring in his loins at the sight of her blatant nudity. He had prayed really hard that night, but it was a long time before he'd been able to get that lithe tanned body out of his mind.

'Dirty little bitch!' he muttered as he finally laid her corpse on the grass at the side of the pool. But despite his newly awakened outrage at the memory, he was still acutely conscious of the same shameful and uncontrollable feelings he'd experienced after he had killed and then stripped her. His gaze had once again lingered a little longer on her nakedness than was necessary before he'd picked her up, carried her to the edge of the pool and very carefully slipped her into the strongly smelling, chlorinated water, watching her slowly sink with morbid fascination.

He had been tempted to say a prayer for her soul before leaving — after all, her licentious behaviour had been an unforgivable affront to the Almighty and all his works — but he knew he couldn't risk further delay and there was a long walk home ahead of him.

So, after returning to the car to collect the clothes she was wearing and dumping them in the adjacent hut, which he knew served as a changing room, he'd carefully placed the empty vodka bottle on the grass, close to the pool. Then, retrieving the blanket, he'd walked swiftly across the wide expanse of lawn to the encircling woodland and the security of the trees, heading for the gap in the perimeter wall he knew was there.

It was a real pity he'd had to kill such a pretty girl, but it was her own fault. She shouldn't have poked her nose into his business to start with. Furthermore, if she was, as he suspected, the poison pen writer, then she hadn't been a very nice person anyway, had she? It was also due to her shenanigans that he had made the mistake of killing poor old Maisie Taylor, so perhaps she'd deserved her fate after all.

He never enjoyed killing — and heaven knows, he had done enough of it during his years in the army — but sometimes it was unavoidable — a thing that had to be done for all sorts of reasons. Deep down, he knew he wasn't well in the head. For some time now he had been experiencing frequent bouts of confusion and irrationality, his thoughts all mixed up, along with an inability to separate past from present. Most of the time these episodes had been triggered by a specific event or date that had the effect of dragging him back into a past from which he found it difficult to extricate himself and he was terrified that one day his irrational behaviour would attract the wrong sort of attention. So far, though, he had been lucky and, on those occasions when he'd felt he might actually be about to give himself away, he had been able to drop out of sight, excusing himself by feigning a severe attack of the migraine from which he was known to suffer.

He laid the blame for the way he was on the terrorist scum in Afghanistan. Two tours over there, including many months in the rat-infested hell-hole of Helmand Province, had turned him into an efficient killing machine — but one plagued with guilt, traumatic memories and an inner conflict that had degenerated into a form of deep-seated psychosis. If they had been consulted, the medics would have called it PTSD — they had a word for everything nowadays, didn't they? But whatever it was, the final screw had been turned by that other horrendous, personal tragedy which haunted him still and made him do what he did.

The girl he had snatched was a stage on his path to redemption — like all the others before her. In his rational moments he knew she wasn't Janice, any more than the others had been, but she was the spitting image of his daughter, and this time he was determined that what had happened to her wouldn't happen again. It was the only way he could stop the nightmares, those whispering, accusing voices in his head.

* * *

'What the devil are you stopping for?' Hayden protested. 'We need some breakfast and all the best bits of bacon will be gone if we don't get a move on.'

'Something just occurred to me,' Kate said grimly.

She spun the wheel and did a tight U-turn.

'You're not going back?'

'Oh yes I am. There's something we should have checked while we were at the scene.'

'What?'

'You'll see when we get there.'

It took just ten minutes to return to Winston House, where a uniformed presence was still waiting patiently for the undertaker. Kate pulled up beside a marked patrol car and made her way across the forecourt to the E-Type, still parked by the path leading to the pool. After a moment's hesitation, Hayden stumbled awkwardly after her.

'What on earth are you up to, old girl?' he panted. He joined her by the sports car, where she was again pulling on her protective gloves.

For reply, she carefully opened the passenger door, holding it with the tips of her fingers, and peered inside. The keys were still in the ignition.

'I wonder whether the boot is wet?' she said. 'After all, it's the only place you could fit a corpse in an E-Type, isn't it?'

'Pardon?'

'Well, it's a two-seater, idiot. There's no back seat.'

Realisation dawned and he threw her an admiring glance. 'You think she was drowned somewhere else, driven back here in her own car and then dumped in the swimming pool for someone to find?'

She nodded. 'Well, Elton did say that the car was parked in an unusual place when he came back to the house. He also indicated that it was her pride and joy which she jealously guarded. In which case, she would hardly have left the keys in the ignition and then gone off for a swim, would she?'

He snapped his fingers, his eyes gleaming. 'Yes, and where is the towelling robe she usually wore to the pool? We know she liked to show herself off, but I doubt whether even she would have walked across to it completely naked.'

She moved to the back of the car and opened the boot hatch. He followed her round. 'Smell the damp?' she breathed.

He bent forward and sniffed. 'It smells a bit musty, I'll give you that.' He waved an arm towards the encircling woodland. 'But it could be coming from the undergrowth.'

She bent forward and tested the floor of the boot with her hand. 'Still wet,' she declared. 'Not much, but you can feel it nevertheless.'

She straightened up and swung the boot hatch shut. 'The bastard obviously didn't bother to dry her. Probably had her wrapped in a sheet or blanket and the wet seeped through it when he put her in there.'

He nodded. 'I have to admit, your hypothesis sounds about right to me and it would explain why he reversed the car in here, so he was as close as possible to the pool to avoid having to carry her body too far. Er — can we get back to the nick now?'

She shook her head. 'Couple of other things I want to check first.'

Groaning, he reluctantly followed her down the path that led to the pool.

Roscoe was long gone, but the uniformed policeman was still standing by the tarpaulin-draped body.

'Undertakers en route yet, skip?' he asked, no doubt bored stiff.

Kate smiled grimly. 'There's likely to be a hold on that,' she said, 'so you could be standing here a while yet, I'm afraid.'

Crossing the lawn to the wooden changing-room hut, she poked her head inside. A pile of clothes lay on one of the slatted benches and she picked up a blouse and a pair of jeans. She squeezed them, pressing her nose against them and sniffing, before dropping them back on the pile and turning to face Hayden standing in the doorway.

'Still soaking wet,' she said grimly. 'He drowned her with her clothes on, then stripped her, brought her here and dumped her in the pool.'

Pushing past him, she strode back towards the pool, but instead of stopping by the corpse as he had expected, she walked around the edge, onto the adjoining wider expanse of lawn.

'Good job they hadn't cut the lawn,' she commented as he came up behind her. She bent down to peer at the grass. 'Good for us at least.'

Mystified, he stooped to see what she was looking at.

'See?' she said, pointing. 'Marks still just visible.'

'Marks?'

'Yes, my dear Watson, footprints. Ground's soft after recent rain and our man had very heavy feet, which sunk into the soil underneath.'

'Good lord, I see what you mean.'

'If I'm not mistaken, he left the premises through the woodland over there and walked home.'

Kate's theory gained even more credence when the pair entered the trees. The ground was still muddy and a trail of footprints led up to the perimeter wall and along it for a short distance to the gap in the wall Gabriella had told them about. There, Kate stopped and bent down again. 'See that?' she said, pointing at a jumble of collapsed brickwork, but Hayden didn't need her to point it out. The traces of earth clinging to the edges of two bricks were clear to see.

'So he went through here then,' he summarised unnecessarily.

‘Exactly. As I said, he drove Gabriella here, dumped her in the pool, then walked home — and there’s the last bit of proof.’

There was a small patch of earth on the road on the other side of the wall and a couple of further patches towards the centre where it had obviously fallen off the killer’s shoes or boots.

Kate straightened. ‘No decent shoe prints back there for us to capture, just indistinct marks in the mud, but they tell us all we need to know.’

She stared at him, her eyes gleaming. ‘Hayden, old son,’ she breathed, ‘for the first time since this business started, I do believe we have enough circumstantial evidence to justify launching a criminal investigation that even our beloved leader can’t argue with.’

He sighed. ‘Does that mean we can go back now then?’

She slapped him on the arm. ‘Breakfast!’

He grinned. ‘Bring it on, sister,’ he said in a bad *Humphrey Bogart* accent. ‘Just bring it on.’

* * *

Roscoe took some convincing, but in the end, with the police surgeon’s reservations, the material Kate and Hayden had found which incriminated Gabriella Winston as the poison pen writer — giving someone a clear motive for killing her — and the number of inconsistencies with a supposed accidental drowning incident that had now been uncovered, he finally buckled and agreed to treat the incident as a suspicious death. This led to the call-out of the forensic pathologist and scenes of crime team, and the cordoning off of the swimming pool and its immediate environs, enforced by a uniformed presence.

Despite his capitulation, Roscoe was still not a happy bunny. He would have been even less happy if he had known about the camera Hayden had found and what Kate was doing with the memory stick. And his woes were destined to increase. On the point of paying a return visit to Winston

House to set things in motion and to liaise with the SOCO team, he received a long-distance call from Colonel Herbert Winston asking him "what the hell" was going on and what had happened to his daughter.

It turned out that Elton had been too terrified to give the colonel the full story when he'd contacted him by mobile text message and had only told him that his daughter had met with a nasty accident, which required his immediate return. When the DI put the record straight, he heard no obvious shock or shedding of tears. Instead, the ex-army man's verbal response caused the telephone to practically melt. This was followed by the dire threat that Winston would be returning immediately to "sort you buggers out" — something Roscoe was clearly not looking forward to.

Kate and Hayden didn't stay around to provide their boss with any reassurance or moral support but left in the middle of the phone call. Barely suppressing their smiles, they signalled that they were well overdue for something to eat, and they left him to it, almost feeling the heat from Roscoe's scowl as they left.

* * *

Even though his body was crying out for rest, and the return of his headache had forced him to take more pain-killers, Tammy's captor decided to check on her again. He had no choice — he had to finish what he had started.

Tammy had heard him coming and was lying in bed with her eyes closed and a sheet drawn up over her nose when he unlocked the door.

'Don't try that one on me,' he said harshly. 'I know you're awake.'

She opened her eyes and stared at him. 'What happened to that woman?' she said, the tremble back in her voice.

'What woman?'

'The one who came down here tonight. You murdered her, didn't you? I heard her scream.'

The cold accusation cut through him like a knife, triggering something inside his head. 'She ran off,' he lied. 'She won't be back.'

He saw the sheet quiver and heard her sobs as she buried her face under it again.

Then suddenly the headache was back. He felt his balance start to go, forcing him to lean against the doorframe, while his senses swam and his thoughts became a hopeless, confused jumble. For a few moments he couldn't think where he was and he was conscious only of the whisperings inside his head — spiteful, hissing snakes.

'You need help,' he heard the girl say. 'You're not well. Why are you doing this to me?'

She was sitting up in the bed, one bare foot over the edge, readying herself to try and escape again. Her mouth was still moving, but no sound was coming out.

Why was she so keen to leave him? What had he done? He'd always been a good father, hadn't he? It wasn't his fault that that awful thing had happened — or was it? He couldn't remember.

'*What did you do to her?*' the voices whispered in his brain. '*How could you do that? Repent or face eternal damnation!*'

He shook his head to clear it.

Other different, louder whispers joined in. '*It must not happen this time. She must repent her sins before it is too late. You must drive out the devil in her.*'

Then the girl's voice intruded again, drowning the whispers. 'Let me go. Please don't hurt me anymore.'

What did she mean? He wasn't going to hurt her. He would never hurt Janice. She was his daughter. He loved his daughter. But she had done wrong, hadn't she? Glastonbury, that was where it had happened — the festival. She'd taken cocaine. He'd found her. But what had happened afterwards?

He stood upright again, his hands clenched into fists. Temptress, that's what she was. The cocaine, it had done that to her. She was dirty but oh, so sexy. She had made him want her. Bad girl. Needed to be punished. Needed the devil driven out. God demanded it. But not now — he was too tired. Later . . . Sleep, that's what he had to do now. Just a few hours.

He stepped back, let the door slam shut and stood there looking at it. The whisperings had died away but he was still confused. What was he doing? What had he come here to do?

The fog in his brain started to clear, and he remembered. Lock the door, that's it, make sure she can't escape again. He turned the key in the lock, then rested his head against the wood for a few moments. Recollections of the past few hours came flooding back — the bath upstairs filled with water as he had held the girl down, the nightmare drive, the body slipping into the pool . . . He felt weak, giddy and sick. He needed to lie down.

Ignoring the sobbing cries of the girl held in the room, he stumbled back across the cellar, colliding with the banister post. He grabbed the rail and hauled himself up the stairs towards the open door. Fragile sunlight greeted him as he made his way unsteadily along the hallway and he could hear the scrabbling of birds in the eaves of the old house. A bright new day was dawning, but in the dim recesses of his mind, he knew that his own private nightmare would remain with him forever.

CHAPTER 20

It was after midday by the time Kate and Hayden made it to the canteen at Highbridge police station, the memory stick from Gabriella Winston's camera back in Kate's pocket with the hard copy Hayden had just run off. Hayden was virtually salivating as he picked up the mixture of aromas wafting along the corridor.

By then, tiredness had left Kate with hardly any appetite at all and she picked at the near cold lasagne on her plate with little enthusiasm. Hayden, on the other hand, wasn't about to let lack of sleep interfere with his digestive capabilities, and he tucked into a massive plate of fish and chips while Kate watched his maniacal assault with a mixture of disgust and disbelief.

Only when he had demolished the lot, plus a large apple pie and custard, and had admitted defeat with a final burp, wiping his hands down his trousers, did she shake herself out of her lethargy and make an attempt at conversation.

'So, where do we go from here?' she said.

He hiccupped several times and beamed at her. 'Home for a kip might be a good idea. After all, we've been on duty since the early hours for the second time this week.'

She ignored the suggestion. 'I've been thinking about the comment Gabriella made on Debbie Moreton's story in the local rag. I wonder when she scribbled "*psycho house*" if she was describing the house where our perp lives or the perp himself. It was a funny thing to write.'

He sighed heavily. 'Maybe both. Our man is almost certainly psychotic in some way if, as we suspect, he's kidnapped and is holding an innocent young girl and has also murdered three other people in cold blood. And it's also possible he lives in a similar sort of old, derelict pile like Norman Bates did in that Hitchcock film, *Psycho.'*

'Why?'

'Why what?'

'Why would he necessarily be living in an old derelict?'

He shrugged. 'The words "*psycho house*" were hers, not mine.'

'So, what does a psycho house look like?'

'Who knows? Some creepy, gloomy place with rattling shutters and mist rising among the trees—'

'Now you're being stupid.'

He emitted a short, derisory laugh. 'Well, what do you want me to say? I don't know. It could be any house. It all depends on an individual's perception and maybe what they know about the place.'

'But the same would go for the person living there then?'

'Of course. Which brings us back to square one. There's no way you or I could tell by looking at a place or a person whether they fitted the bill or not — we would have to know that some dastardly doings had taken place on the premises first. I hardly think that if Gabriella Winston had been aware of such a thing, she would have simply chosen to walk away and keep it all to herself.'

'Yet she used the word.'

Another shrug. 'I rest my case. But you can always ask Des Percival how the house to house inquiries went when he gets back, and whether any of the plods spotted any psychos or psycho houses on their travels.'

'So, what's with the psycho house?' a familiar voice asked, and the detectives glanced at the uniformed figure who had pulled up a chair and sat down at one end of their table, setting a coffee cup in front of him. 'Don't mind if I join you two "secret squirrels," do you?'

Kate treated Reeves to a weary smile. 'More like shagged out squirrels after the night we've had.'

'Oh?' he said, his policeman's nose twitching. 'So what's going on? Most of the early turn and day shift seem to be causing havoc knocking on doors in my village, and control room just told me SOCO are attending an incident at Winston House.'

'Gabriella Winston was found drowned in her swimming pool this morning,' Kate said grimly.

Reeves froze in the act of taking a sip of his coffee. 'Gabriella Winston? How the hell did that happen? She was a strong swimmer by all accounts.'

'On the face of it, she appeared to have been on a mammoth drinking binge before taking her dip. There was an empty bottle of liquor lying by the pool.'

He frowned. 'On the face of it? What are you saying?'

Kate nodded. 'We think it is likely she was drowned elsewhere and was dumped in the pool afterwards.'

He emitted a low whistle. 'Poor little Gabby.'

Kate studied him for a minute. 'Did you know her then?'

He shrugged. 'Knew *of* her more like. My house is not too far from Winston House on the other side of the village. I only met her once.'

'What, officially or socially?'

He snorted. 'Hardly socially. I don't move in the same circles as the Winstons. No, I had to execute an arrest warrant on her for non-payment of a fine for speeding, but she then paid up. You know, the usual sort of job us plods have to do, but you probably don't remember your time as a wooden top.'

She smiled at the dig. 'What did you make of her?'

'Well, I don't like to speak ill of the dead and all that, but a bit spoilt, I thought — and definitely a man-eater. Frequented the Soldier's Arms pub a lot and raced around the village in that flashy E-Type of hers, showing her bits off and looking for anything in trousers, so they say. Any leads?'

Kate didn't answer straight away, the inbuilt reluctance of the detective to part with any information unless absolutely necessary making her hesitate.

'Oh, come on, Kate, what's the big secret? I'll find out soon enough anyway when word gets out. I did help you with Ted Southerby, didn't I?'

She acquiesced with a flick of her eyebrows, but still remained guarded. Eventually she said, 'Gabriella was our poison pen.'

'Gabriella?' He emitted another soft whistle. 'Well, that really is a surprise. I'd never have thought she would have been into something like that.'

'It just goes to show, you never can tell.'

'So, you suspect that someone she sent one of her anonymous letters to forced, the vodka down her throat before deliberately drowning her?'

'It's a logical scenario.'

'So, what's all this about a psycho house? How does that fit into all this?'

'Ah, maybe you can help us there,' Kate said, finally capitulating and telling him about the scribbled note on the newspaper, the photo on the camera's memory stick and the possible link with the missing person inquiry and Tammy Logan's kidnapping. 'Maybe Gabriella went to this house in the course of her nocturnal wanderings and saw the Land Rover we're looking for,' she explained. 'There's just a chance that we can match up the interior wall of the actual barn with what we have on this.' She produced the memory stick and twirled it briefly between her fingers.

He raised a critical eyebrow. 'If this is going to become a crime inquiry, shouldn't that be with the exhibits officer?'

She made a face. 'It will be shortly, when we've finished with it. We found it in the camera before that decision was made and it's not strictly relevant to Gabriella Winston's death anyway, but to her activities as a poison pen.'

He looked doubtful. 'That's rubbish and you know it. They might be linked, and that stick would then be material evidence. You could be in a lot of trouble over this, especially if Roscoe finds out about it.'

'He won't if you don't tell him.'

He snorted. 'Well, I'm not likely to, and it's your funeral. But what do you want from me?'

'Local knowledge, Tom — any suggestions re Gabriella's reference to a person or property as a psycho.'

He scratched his nose. 'Well, I have to say, I don't know any local psychos, except maybe poor old Roscoe. As for psycho houses . . .' he frowned and rubbed his chin, 'I suppose Ted Southerby's place might have fitted that description but, as it's just ashes now, that's no good to you, is it? There *is* a derelict farm, though, a couple of miles out of the village towards Cheddar — Bob Dale's old place—'

'Dale?' Hayden glanced across the table at Kate. 'Wasn't he the chap mentioned in the anonymous letter sent to Colonel Winston?'

'He got one as well, did he?' Reeves said. 'From his own daughter too? Serves the pompous old devil right.'

Before Kate could say that this was confidential, Reeves was off again. 'Poor old Bob died not too long ago, and his place has been bought up by a London property firm.'

'Cardin Developments?' Kate suggested.

Reeves nodded. 'Sounds like the name of the firm, but, as far as I know, no one is living there now. Going by the state of the place, not even the most desperate dosser would want to sleep there.'

'We can check it out this afternoon,' Kate said. 'Anywhere else, Tom?'

He made a face. 'Not that I can think of — 'cept maybe the James's pile on the edge of the village, though it's pretty unlikely. Bob and Miriam James are long dead now and the house is a bit of a ruin, but I think their son Graham is in the process of doing it up.'

'What, Beverley James's husband?'

'Yeah, quite a dab hand at DIY is our Graham, I gather, and, as he and Bev are going through a few marital problems right now, I think he spends most of his free time there.'

'So, even that is common knowledge?'

He laughed again. 'There isn't much that escapes the village gossips, and my occasional visits to the Soldier's Arms, off duty, can be very informative.'

'Don't we know it,' Kate replied wryly. 'The crowd in there struck me as a bit like a witches' coven.'

'Good description.' Reeves drained his coffee cup and glanced at his watch. 'Well, better get going. On again at two for another twelve-hour shift. Did you want me to take you out later to either of the two places I mentioned?'

Kate hesitated. 'That would be very helpful, but only if your shift inspector is agreeable.'

He nodded. 'No problem. Dave Sharp is as good as gold. Let me get the briefing and duty rosters for the troops out of the way and then I'll give you a bell.'

Following his heavy-set figure with her eyes as he pushed through the exit door of the canteen, Kate did not actually see him leave. Her thoughts were on other matters. Noting the distant expression on her face, Hayden bent forward and waved a spoon in front of her eyes.

'Penny for them?' he said.

She gave a little smile. 'You don't want to know.'

'Try me.'

'It's just that I think we've missed something important.'

'At the scene, you mean?'

'Not necessarily *at* the scene, but certainly something connected to it, though I can't quite put my finger on what it is.'

He grunted. Not one of your woman's intuition things, is it?'

'You sound like Roscoe.'

'Heaven help me. Just for that, I think I'm going to have another apple pie and custard.'

CHAPTER 21

Tom Reeves was as good as his word and poked his head round the door of the CID office at just after two thirty. A misty rain had just started to fall, and the afternoon had appreciably darkened by the time Kate and Hayden left the station, tailing Reeves's police patrol car in the spare CID car.

They reached the near-deserted village within fifteen minutes, passed through and took a minor road, heading out in the general direction of Cheddar. Reeves slowed just after a sharp bend and turned up a rutted track between tall hedges. The derelict house, with its large barn and other outhouses, soon loomed into view through the rain. Both vehicles pulled up outside the house and Kate scanned the buildings dubiously. The front door seemed to be closed, most of the windows were boarded up and a big sign attached to the wall read, "Cardin Developments. Danger. Keep Out." It didn't look as though anyone had been there for a very long time, though Kate knew that appearances could sometimes be deceptive.

'When poor old Bob lost his wife, he let the place go, I'm afraid,' Reeves said when Kate joined him by the barn. 'He became more or less a recluse in the years that followed. Then, when the development company bought him out and he went into an old people's home and died, all his stuff went for auction. All very sad. The place has been empty a while now and Cardin Developments don't seem to be doing much with their proposed development. Probably waiting for the value of the land to rise.'

Kate grunted. 'Doesn't look like the sort of place Gabriella would have visited,' she said, joining Reeves by the barn. 'Why would she even bother to come here?'

He shrugged. 'Just a thought. After all, your kidnapper wouldn't necessarily hold her at his own home, would he? This would be an ideal place to use. Maybe she followed him when he was carting the Logan girl here.'

Kate sighed, still not convinced. 'Well, we've come now, so we might as well take a look around.'

He nodded. 'You and Hayden check the barn and I'll give the house the once-over. Okay?'

The double doors of the barn were open slightly but jammed in position and immovable. Fortunately, there was just enough of a gap between then to enable the detectives to force their way through, but there was little to see inside. Nothing but waist-high nettles and other weeds, no doubt nurtured by the elements over the years, due to the almost total absence of a roof. The whole place smelled of damp and decay and Hayden jumped back in alarm when his passage through the "undergrowth" was brought to an abrupt halt by the rotting carcass of what looked like a fox.

It was patently obvious that this could not have been the barn in Gabriella's photograph.

'I don't know why we came in here in the first place,' she called out to Hayden. 'Come on, back to the car.'

There was no sign of Reeves when they emerged and, after checking a couple of outhouses, Kate called out his name. There was no response.

She sighed. 'Better make sure he's okay. He must be somewhere inside the house.'

The front door had been wrenched back, almost certainly by Reeves, its rusted padlock broken and hanging on the hasp. Once inside, they were confronted by a gloomy, windowless hallway.

'Torches,' Kate threw back over her shoulder at Hayden. 'Get the torches from the car. I think we're going to need them.'

'Don't go in there on your own,' Hayden said. 'The place is falling down.'

'Don't bloody argue,' she grated. 'Get the torches.'

As Hayden reluctantly headed back to the CID car, she moved slowly forward into the gloom. The dark slashes of two open doorways emerged on both sides. Then, a few feet further on, another doorway appeared to her left. She pressed on, carefully feeling her way along the left-hand wall.

'Tom?' she shouted again, cupping her hands around her mouth. When there was still no response, she felt a sudden stab of real anxiety. Where the hell had he got to? He must have heard her.

Then the staircase was there, rising to the upper floor. She paused to listen. Rain rattled on a pipe outside the house and there was a sharp crack from somewhere deep in the heart of the old building as the timbers expanded or contracted.

'Kate! Wait for me!' The beam of Hayden's torch lanced down the hallway, picking her out as his heavy feet thumped towards her.

'Tom?' she shouted a third time. 'Where are you?'

There was still no reply.

Hayden was by her side now, thrusting another torch into her hand.

She moved it slowly to her left and picked out another open door in front of her, which appeared to be closed. Probably a kitchen, she thought.

'Upstairs,' she snapped at Hayden. 'You check upstairs. I'll do down here.'

'Do you think that's wise?' he protested. 'We should stay together. You don't know what's down here.'

She gave a derisory snort. 'I'm not afraid of ghosts, Hayd. Just do it, will you? We're wasting time.'

She headed away from him towards the closed door and tested the handle. It was unlocked. She opened it and peered inside, her torch unnecessary in the vandalised kitchen, which lay beyond. There was a doorless opening at the far end, admitting a grey light through a curtain of driving rain and revealing part of an overgrown garden beyond.

She turned back into the hall. Hayden had gone and she could hear what she thought were his heavy footsteps crunching through broken glass above her head, apparently moving from room to room. She shivered. Maybe it was old Bob Dale's ghost. But ghosts didn't make a noise and break glass, did they?

At that moment she saw the door under the stairs and wondered how she had missed it on her way to the kitchen. It was pushed right back against the wall and hanging by one hinge. At first, she thought it simply accessed a broom cupboard and was about to move on, when she thought she glimpsed a light flash briefly in the gloom, as if another torch had been switched on and off deep inside. Bending down slightly to probe the interior with her own torch, she was surprised to see another opening to her left, and stairs dropping away to a lower level. There was obviously a cellar under the house. How curious.

Ducking down further, she eased herself through the doorway and directed her torch into the stairwell, but could see only the first few stairs marching down a steep incline in front of her before they were cut off by the base of the main staircase above.

'Tom?' she called again, thinking he might have gone down into the cellar to check it out. Nothing answered her but the rattle of the rain on the boarded-up windows above.

She hesitated, her police training urging caution. She was on the point of turning back out into the hallway to call Hayden, when she heard the strange sound. It was a brief but unmistakable groan, followed by a thud, like a door closing on tired hinges, and it seemed to have come from somewhere in the blackness below.

That was enough for her. Without further hesitation, she responded in the only way an impetuous soul like Kate Lewis could possibly respond.

The stairs cracked like pistol shots as she began her slow descent, persuading her to take extra care with every step. Most likely they were none too secure after all this time. There was a stout wooden door at the bottom, with an iron ring handle. Though very stiff, it opened with a despairing groan — the sound she had just heard. Someone was down here.

'Kate? You there?' Hayden's voice called faintly, but she didn't answer. She had detected a faint sound somewhere in the gloom close by.

'Tom?' she called again, her heart making peculiar squishing noises as she slowly swung the torch to her left. The beam travelled along a bare stone wall, past what looked like an old boiler with thick pipes protruding from the side of it disappearing through twin holes in the roof. Otherwise, nothing.

She swung the torch to the right. And there — something moving rapidly across the beam and vanishing as quickly as it had appeared. A dark figure, impossible to distinguish. More furtive sounds, this time in front of her, and the brief flash of a torch, as if it had been turned on by accident. She lurched across the room in the direction of an ornate archway she had spotted at the far end, her torch picking out the stone columns on each side.

'Stay right where you are,' she blustered, knowing full well that in this near impenetrable darkness she had no way of telling where they were anyway.

The torch flashed once in front of her again, like a will-o'-the-wisp. They were playing games with her, but she now knew where they must have gone. Through the archway into another room on the other side. She stumbled towards it.

It was the tell-tale draught of cool, dank air that saved her life, but only just. One foot was already into the void when her hand instinctively shot out to grab whatever there was to hang on to. By sheer luck, her fingers closed on what turned out to be the remains of some ironwork attached to the left-hand column of the archway. It brought her to an abrupt stop, leaving her swinging crazily in space from one arm, until her scrabbling boots managed to secure a proper foothold.

At the same moment, the torch flew from her other hand. She watched in horrified fascination as the beam plunged away from her into the gaping mouth of the well she had almost stepped into, becoming just a rapidly diminishing spot of light. Several seconds later, she heard the faint echo of a splash rising from the depths like a goblin's cackle.

Staggering back from the archway, her legs gave way and she sank onto the concrete floor, shaking uncontrollably at the thought of how close she had come to a hideous death. And, as she lay there, unashamedly hyperventilating, she couldn't have been more relieved to hear the familiar voice calling her name, 'Kate? Are you down there?'

Seconds after she had marshalled sufficient strength to shout back, there was the sound of heavy footsteps and the beam of Hayden's torch blazed in her face.

'What on earth are you doing down there, old girl?' he said. 'You okay?'

'Watch your back,' she gasped as he helped her to her feet. 'He's hiding down here somewhere.'

Hayden circled, shining his torch slowly around the room, lighting up each corner in turn. 'No one here. You must have let your imagination run away with you.' He chuckled. 'Unless it was old Bob Dale's ghost.'

'This is not funny, Hayd,' she retorted, her hand to her chest as she tried to will her heart back to a steady rhythm. 'The bastard tried to kill me.'

But he'd already wandered away to the nearby archway, apparently having not heard a word she had said. 'Good lord. Do you know there's a well down here?'

Kate closed her eyes in resignation. 'Unbelievable,' she breathed. 'Absolutely unbelievable.'

They found Tom Reeves shortly after returning to their car. He was sitting on the edge of the front passenger seat of his patrol car, looking shaken. There were dirty marks on one side of his face and traces of mud on one arm of his uniform tunic and both of his trouser legs.

He smiled ruefully at them. 'Checking the back of the house. Saw this hooded character come flying out the kitchen door. Chased after him and fell down a bank in the copse over there. He just kept going. I feel such a fool. Getting too old for this kind of thing.'

'You and me both,' Kate said ruefully. 'But at least you didn't injure yourself.'

She related what had happened to her, noting with satisfaction Hayden's horrified gape when it dawned on him how close she had come to a nasty end.

'The bastard deliberately lured me,' she said. 'Like a bloody will-o-the-wisp, he led me on with quick flashes of his torch, right in the direction of that well.'

Hayden closed his mouth and frowned. 'That's going a bit far, old girl, isn't it? You obviously disturbed him when you went down into the cellar, but he couldn't have known you would go there. He was probably as scared as you and simply ran off. He may not even have known himself that the well was there.'

'I'm telling you it was deliberate,' Kate persisted angrily, 'and, as to how he could have known I would go down there, I've just told you, he flashed his torch to light up the cupboard under the stairs and attract my attention in the first place. He knew I would follow those stairs down to investigate.'

Hayden held up his hands, grinning. 'Okay, okay. No need to bite my head off.'

Kate glowered at him, then turned back to Reeves. 'You must have spotted him right after he bolted from the cellar, though how he got out without running into Hayd here, I haven't the foggiest.'

'Funny,' Hayden said suddenly, 'I thought I heard something when I first went down there — a sort of scuffling sound — but I was too concerned about you lying on the floor to take much notice.'

Kate nodded grimly. 'He must have been hiding in the corner, most likely crept out behind you in the dark.'

'Then shot out the back door like a startled rabbit,' Reeves added. 'He's certainly taken us for idiots.'

'Did you get much of a look at him?' Kate asked.

Reeves made a face. 'Wearing a hooded coat. Probably a dosser.'

Kate smiled slightly. 'Which certainly explodes your theory that no dosser would want to spend the night here.'

'I can't understand why a dosser would want to entice you to fall down a well, though,' Hayden commented, chancing his arm again. 'It wasn't like you were a threat to him.'

Kate gave him a cold look. 'Maybe he sussed I was Old Bill. Our twilight friends can smell a copper a mile off.'

'Bit drastic though, don't you think? He could have just hidden until you'd gone.'

She didn't answer and, seeming to sense the tension in the air, Reeves said quickly, 'Unless, of course, your kidnapper *was* using or thinking of using the place and got caught by us in the process.'

Kate shook her head. 'No evidence of that, though, is there? No signs of any bedding, blankets, food or any of the other stuff you'd expect to find. And it would have been taking one hell of a risk to leave Tammy Logan banged up here on her own for adventurous kids, a dosser, or a representative of Cardin Developments to find on a chance visit.'

'Well, there's nothing more we can do here now,' Reeves went on, 'and it's not worth calling for backup. Our homicidal friend will be long gone.'

'Are you fit to drive yourself back?' Kate said doubtfully. 'You look a bit shaken. I can take you, and Hayden can drive the patrol car back for you.'

Reeves shook his head with a weak grin. 'I'll be fine. Nothing that a clothes brush and a wet face-cloth can't fix. I'll take the thing back myself.'

Kate nodded. 'If you're sure. We'll crack on and check out Graham James's place. You never know, maybe we'll get lucky there.'

But they didn't. They found James up a ladder in the rain at the front of the house, trying to fix a broken gutter, and it was obvious that he wasn't best pleased to see them.'

'Can we have a chat inside, Mr James?' Kate asked, after introducing Hayden and herself and giving him her best smile.

He glanced at the rain clouds and nodded towards the open garage. 'In there. I hope this won't take long. I've got work to do.'

The garage was piled high with more guttering, boxes of tiles, bags of cement and a whole variety of building materials, and it smelled strongly of a mixture of turpentine and paint. She could see at a glance that the garage wall was nothing like the wall in Gabriella's photograph. The doors of the large barn to the right of the house were closed, denying her any cursory inspection.

James leaned against a workbench, his arms folded across his chest, studying them. Not a good omen.

'We're carrying out a number of inquiries in the area,' Kate began, 'and we're seeking to eliminate certain properties from those inquiries in relation to a missing person.'

'So?'

'You are not under any suspicion, of course, but we would like to have a quick look around the property, if you don't mind.'

'What for?'

'It is possible that the young girl may have taken refuge in an outbuilding,' she said, 'and we are checking all possible places.'

'Is it that girl who's been in the local paper — Tammy something or other?'

'Yes.'

'Well, I can tell you straight, she's not here. Anyway, I thought she'd been kidnapped? Some feller in a red Land Rover Defender, according to the newspaper.'

'Er — that's just one avenue of inquiry we're pursuing. The fact is, we don't know for certain what's happened to her.'

'Well, I don't own a Defender and never have, so you're wasting your time bothering me.'

'We'd still like to check around.'

'Got a warrant, have you?'

For a moment Kate was taken aback. 'Well, no. It shouldn't be necessary in these circumstances.'

He grunted and straightened up. 'Well, you'd better get one, Sergeant,' he snapped. 'You're not looking around otherwise. Now, as I've just said, I've got work to do.'

'Can we at least have a look in your barn over there?' Hayden put in. 'Just a quick glance.'

James seemed to bristle. 'You hard of hearing, mate? I've just told you — no.'

He watched the detectives walk reluctantly back to their car, and then shouted to Kate as she climbed behind the wheel, 'And next time, Sergeant, if you want to interrogate my wife about anonymous letters, speak to me first.'

'Ouch!' Hayden remarked as they drove off. 'He's obviously found out about what his wife did. But do you reckon he's a possible suspect? After all, he wasn't exactly welcoming, right from the start.'

She shook her head. 'Very unlikely, in my opinion. A man who has a kidnapped girl hidden away in his house or a sus motor in his barn would hardly want to antagonise the police. He would be more likely to act cooperative to allay suspicion — you know, make some excuse as to why it would not be convenient for us to have a look around. No, I think he was arsey simply because his wife told me her guilty secret before she told him.'

'So, are we just going to leave it there then?'

'Well, we'd never get a search warrant on what we've got.'

'We could always sneak back after dark and have a look at the barn unofficially?' he suggested helpfully.

'That's an unusual thing for *you* to suggest, Hayd,' she exclaimed, clearly taken aback, then added drily, 'but if we were to be banged up for burglary, I don't think prison food would agree with you at all.'

CHAPTER 22

Kate and Hayden were pretty downbeat when they returned to Highbridge police station, but, unbeknown to them, their potential "cheerleader" was already waiting for them, and he materialised the moment they pushed through the foyer's security door.

'Just the guys I want to see,' Dave Gort said with a grin. 'I think I might have something that will brighten up your day.'

Kate cast him a cynical glance. 'Something certainly needs brightening. So, what have you got?'

'A moment of your time,' Gort said, and led them along the corridor to his office.

'I got to thinking after you left last time,' he said when they were seated. 'That maybe, just maybe, Tammy Logan was not your kidnapper's first victim. Maybe he'd done the same sort of thing before.'

'Go on,' Kate said, immediately interested.

'So, I did a misper check on PNC, covering the past five years.'

'And?'

He tapped a collection of computer printouts sitting on the corner of his desk.

'Obviously quite a few missing person reports during that period,' he continued, 'most of them not relevant to your current inquiry. But I did manage to turn up two reported cases in which the victims seemed to share similar profiles to Tammy Logan and where the circumstances of their disappearances also appeared very similar.'

Hayden leaned forward and, scooping up the printouts, began scanning the contents while Gort continued. 'Both of these women were in their mid-twenties, dark-haired and very petite, going by their photographs, and both vanished without trace after attending the Glastonbury Festival. In 2015, a Brenda Gain from Salisbury, went missing and in 2016, a Madelaine Cross from Chelmsford, also disappeared. Neither of them was ever found.'

'What about 2017 and 2018?' Hayden queried, looking up briefly.

Gort held up one hand. 'Ah, now this is where it gets interesting. It seems that there wasn't a festival at all in 2018. Apparently, it was decided to make it what they called a "fallow year" to give the heavily trampled site a chance to recover. During that year no females with similar profiles were reported missing in that general area.

'But back in 2017, I found a report of an *attempted* snatch just outside Pilton — where, as you know, the festival is actually held — of another young woman with a similar profile to the other two. The target was a Jennifer Roberts, a local girl from not too far away, at Wells, who had also been hitching a lift home. She fought off her attacker and he fled the scene when she activated a personal rape alarm she was carrying. He got more than he bargained for on that occasion, but it seems to have been a pretty near thing.'

'Any description of her attacker or the vehicle?'

'Not her attacker, no, apart from the fact that he was a big, heavy man. But she described the vehicle as a VW Camper van, though she couldn't come up with the number. Along with the other two reported mispers, her case is still open and there are no leads or suspects.'

Kate tried to control her rising excitement. 'Excellent work, Dave. Pity we can't tie this incident to our sus Land Rover, but at least it gives us one avenue of further inquiry.'

Gort looked less than optimistic. 'Not sure it will get you anywhere, though. I would think that Bridgwater CID, who are dealing with all three cases, will have got all they could out of Roberts at the time.'

'I'm sure they thought that then,' she agreed, 'but, now we have a bit more info on the likely attacker, maybe there is still one little snippet Roberts could provide that will join up some of the dots.'

'Talking of joining up the dots,' Hayden put in, 'there certainly seems to be a bit of a pattern here. As Dave said, all the mispers were of a similar age, build and hair colour and all had been attending the festival. Furthermore, according to what it says in these printouts, all of them were known to have left the festival ground on their own in the late morning to early afternoon and were spotted trying to hitch lifts along the same stretch of road — between Pilton and Glastonbury — when they disappeared.'

'Tammy Logan wasn't actually hitching,' Kate pointed out. 'She was intending to catch a train home to Birmingham.'

Hayden nodded. 'That's true, but she started out as a hitcher anyway and, though she did then change her mind and state her intention of catching a train, if our hypothesis is right, she never caught it, but is still around here somewhere.

'But she actually went missing after leaving the rave near Mark, not Glastonbury.'

'Still on her way home from the festival, though, wasn't she, old girl? And the significant thing is that all three of the previous cases, like that of Tammy Logan, occurred straight after the festival ended in the latter days of June. Yet in 2018 when there *wasn't* a festival, there were no reported mispers fitting the same physical profile either. For me, that suggests there is a link somehow between the disappearances of those young women and the festival itself.'

Kate frowned. 'What? Are you saying you think our man was — is — a festivalgoer?'

Hayden shook his head. 'Not at all. Personally, I don't think he has anything to do with Glastonbury. I still firmly believe he is local to the village where we've been concentrating our inquiries. But maybe he hangs around the festival when it is on and selects his victims as they are leaving. I agree that Tammy Logan's case is different in that she went missing in Highbridge, as far as we know, but it could be that our man stumbled on her by accident and seized the moment.'

'So why would he be hanging around the festival in the first place? What's been motivating him?'

'Well,' Hayden said, 'like the full moon is supposed to trigger madness in certain people, maybe the festival is actually triggering the kidnapper's desire to snatch young girls of a particular type. Perhaps something happened to him at an earlier festival and his conduct is being influenced by that?'

Kate stared at him narrowly. 'That's a bit off the wall, don't you think? Just because in the one year out of five when there was no festival we didn't receive a report of a misper fitting the same profile doesn't mean the perp wasn't at it somewhere else or in a different month.'

He held up both hands. 'Again, true, but it's something to bear in mind, isn't it?'

'Maybe it is if you're a shrink,' she retorted.

He was beginning to sound exasperated. 'But think about it. If we could come up with the motive, there's every chance we could ID the perp. It's a basic criminal investigation technique.'

She emitted a low whistle. 'Well, get you. I can see you've been reading those funny books again. I shall have to watch that in future.' Then, seeing the irritation on his face, she grinned. 'Okay, Hayd, only joking. I do see you've got a point, but it's something to think about after we've seen this Jennifer Roberts — perhaps in consultation with a criminal psychologist or profiler. Is she still at the same address, Dave?'

Gort shook his head. 'According to the file, shortly afterwards she moved to Lower Godney, out on the Levels. She's unmarried and lives with her brother near the village. If you're intending to pay them a visit, you may want to clear it with Bridgwater CID first. You'll see that there's a note on the file to say that before any further approaches are made to Roberts, the OIC should be contacted.'

'Advice noted. Who *is* the officer in the case?'

'Charlie Woo,' Hayden said after checking the relevant print-out.

Kate smiled faintly, remembering the Bridgwater detective, recently promoted to sergeant, who had joined the force from the Hong Kong police and had previously helped her with the nightmare hunt for the twisted psychopathic killer nick-named "Twister."

'Right then, Hayd,' she said and, jumping to her feet, scooped up the printouts and headed for the door, 'let's go see a Chinaman about a misper.'

* * *

Luckily, Charlie Woo was on duty when Kate rang to fix up a meeting. He was waiting for them at his desk when they arrived, but, though he was as helpful as he could be, there was not a lot more he was able to tell them, other than what was already on the print-out or in the file, which he had managed to get hold of and now had to hand.

'By all means go and see her, if Roscoe lets you,' he said with a grin, 'and don't worry about treading on toes here. But I'd be very surprised if Jennifer Roberts is able or willing to remember anything more about the attack than she told us at the time. And you might have a problem tying your perp into this job anyway, as it seems our man was using a completely different sort of vehicle to the one you're looking for.'

He thumbed through the file and paused briefly to scan the appropriate document. 'Says in her statement here that it was a light coloured VW Camper van with a sliding door, but she didn't get the number.'

Kate shrugged. 'The motor isn't that significant actually. The attack on Roberts was all of two years ago, so the perp could easily have changed it in that time — or may even be using more than one vehicle.'

Woo carried on reading. 'Apparently the offender was stopped on the side of the road with the side door of the van open. As Roberts walked past, he grabbed her from behind and tried to drag her into the vehicle. She screamed and struggled, then slammed the heel of her boot into his shin. He let go and she ran off.'

'And he didn't pursue her?'

'No. Apparently, another group of festival-goers appeared around a curve in the road at that point and he drove off.'

'Yet we didn't manage to trace any witnesses — after a violent incident like this, on a main road, in broad daylight.'

'A press appeal was put out, but there were no responses and there were no properties close to the scene that we could check.' He grinned again. 'Cows don't make very good witnesses.'

Kate shot him an old-fashioned look. 'Well, we'll pop over and see Miss Roberts anyway. Nothing ventured, nothing gained, as they say.'

Woo nodded again. 'I would suggest you tread carefully, though. She was badly traumatised after the attack and her brother, Ed, who is a bit of an oddball himself, accused the police of not doing enough to nail her attacker.'

'Situation normal then?' Kate said drily.

'Yeah, but on top of that, some dick of a press reporter found out where she lived and tried to force an interview on her. Her brother sent him packing quite aggressively, I gather, and in response, against all the protocols, the newspaper chose to publish her name and address with their story. She suffered loads of harassment after that. As a result, she and her brother moved to the village of Lower Godney, where she's become a semi-recluse, and neither she nor her brother has welcomed visitors of any kind since. Even I got a verbal rough ride when I went back to do a follow-up. So, you might well get quite a hostile reception.'

'Great. Can I borrow the file?'

Woo hesitated.

'I won't bloody lose it, Charlie, but I need to go through her statement and everything else so as to be completely *au fait* with all that happened before I go and see her. Also, I want to study the press cuttings I see you've got stapled inside.'

'You could do that here.'

'Not if I then want to go through particular issues with her.'

He sighed and pushed the file across the desk. 'If you do lose it, I'm going to have to catch the next flight back to Hong Kong,' he said with another grin. 'And Hong Kong's no fun at the moment, with all the rioting that's going on.'

* * *

Kate and Hayden got back to Highbridge police station to find the CID office deserted save for Ronnie Crouch, the civilian office manager, who was sitting at his desk with his back to them.

'Before you ask,' he said without turning around, 'The DI, Danny Ferris and Jamie Foster are all still down at the Winston drowning scene, but Mr Roscoe did ring to ask where you were.' He chuckled, and this time half-turned. 'He didn't seem too impressed to hear you'd gone out. I think he wants you down at the scene to hold his hand.'

'Some chance of that,' Kate muttered, dumping the misper file she had borrowed from Charlie Woo on her desk. 'You haven't seen us, right?'

Crouch threw his hands up in the air, presenting his back to her again. 'Your funeral. I'm off home in a minute anyway. Oh, by the way, you have another visitor downstairs. Been waiting a while, so I don't know if she's still there.'

'Who is she?'

The business card appeared in his hand as if by magic, and Kate quickly relieved him of it, her curiosity aroused. The card read, "Jane Lucas, Investment Strategist," and gave a London address.

'What does she want?' Kate snapped, anxious to get on the road to Lower Godney before Roscoe got back and scotched her plans.

He shrugged, still with his back to her. 'Haven't a clue, I'm only the office manager. But I did get the impression it was something important.'

Cursing under her breath, Kate descended the stairs to the front desk two at a time, leaving Hayden slurping coffee at his desk while he studied his emails.

'Lady's in there,' the SDO said to her, pointing at the waiting room. 'I've given her coffee and biscuits.'

The attractive blonde woman was sitting in one corner, thumbing through the local newspaper. When Kate entered the room, she stood up, one hand extended, a tight smile on her face and her blue eyes tired and dull.

'Kate Lewis?' she asked in a soft, slightly weary voice.

Kate confirmed the fact and, waving her back to her chair, sat down opposite.

'I'm Jane Lucas,' she said. 'I'm on my way back to London and I wanted to speak to you before I left. It's about my uncle, Ted Southerby.'

Kate's interest immediately sharpened. 'A bad business,' she said, 'and I'm sorry for your loss.'

Lucas nodded. 'Yes, it was awful,' she said. 'I gather from the fire service that a gas cooker is suspected, but I can't see how it could have happened. He was old but very switched on and usually extremely careful. I haven't seen my uncle for a while, but I make periodic visits when I'm down this way to make sure he's all right — I travel around a lot with my job, you understand, and happened to be in Bridgwater when I read the news in the local paper. I only saw Uncle two months ago and he seemed quite with it then and I had intended visiting him this morning.'

Kate tried to control her impatience. *Get to the point, love. I have to get to Lower Godney this afternoon.*

'The thing is,' Lucas continued. 'It's not actually the fire or Uncle's death that I called to see you about.' She tapped the newspaper on her lap. 'It's about another story in here that attracted my attention. I understand the police are looking for a red Land Rover Defender with a Mickey Mouse sticker on the back window?'

Kate felt her heart jump. 'Yes, it's in connection with a possible kidnapping — or worse.'

'So I believe, which is where I may be able to help you. You see, Uncle owned a Land Rover exactly like that up until around a couple of years ago when on one of my visits I noticed it was missing. In its place was an old Renault van. I asked him if he had bought the Renault to express solidarity with the Remainers in Brexit, since it was French. He laughed and said he had sold it to someone else in the village—'

Kate could not contain herself. 'In the village, you say? Did he tell you who?'

She shook her head. 'I'm afraid not. 'But he was cock-a-hoop because it was a wreck and he'd got a good price for it — a shrewd businessman was my uncle.'

'You don't happen to know the registration number, do you?'

She shook her head again. 'Sorry, but seeing the story in the paper about that sticker on the window, I felt I should let you know about it.'

'But how come you noticed that sticker on the motor in the first place?' Kate asked.

'Because I put it there, Sergeant. He must have had that Land Rover quite a number of years. I was in my early teens — I am twenty-five now, so I must have been fifteen or sixteen then — and visiting him with my late mother. I got the sticker with a load of others in one of those teen mags and stuck it on the window as a good-luck charm.' She made a rueful face. 'Maybe his luck deserted him when he sold the vehicle.'

'And you have no idea who he sold it to?' she asked again.

Lucas shrugged. 'I just thought you should know that he once owned a vehicle of that description.' She looked at her watch. 'Now I really must be going. I have a date tonight in London.'

Kate watched the woman leave with mounting frustration. So near and yet so far. It was a real bummer.

Returning to the CID office, her ill-tempered mood was not much improved when she saw Tom Reeves sitting on a corner of her desk and Hayden conspicuous by his absence — no doubt grabbing a last bite in the canteen before it closed, she thought.

'Hi, Kate,' Reeves said, scrambling hastily to his feet under her critical gaze.

'Don't you ever go home?' she said uncharitably, knowing full well that he had told her he was on until two in the morning.

He grinned. 'Can't do enough for a good guv'nor,' he said. 'Back on nights tomorrow. The trials and tribulations of being in uniform.'

'My heart bleeds for you.'

He chuckled. 'I'm sure it does. So, how goes it otherwise?'

'*It* isn't going at all,' she replied tartly. 'In fact, *it* is a real pain in the arse.'

He grinned. 'Well, maybe I can help you there. Got a bit of news for you.'

She slumped behind her desk, pulling Charlie Woo's missing persons file towards her and frowning at the creases Reeves' backside had left on the cover.

'Okay, what?' she said.

'Tony Samuel is on the wanted list again. He was in the Soldier's Arms this afternoon. Had too many bevvies and got aggressive. When the landlord asked him to leave, he got a bunch of fives for his trouble — broke his nose. Samuel then proceeded to smash the place up.'

'ABH then.'

'At the very least, and when the lads and lassies find him this time, he won't be going anywhere except to a nice warm cell. Thing is, it seems Samuel went to the village after following you there. He was boasting in the pub that he's been keeping tabs on you ever since he was released.'

'Cheeky bastard. At least it suggests he's loyal and is determined to find Tammy Logan.'

He frowned. 'There may be another reason.'

'Oh?'

'What if the Land Rover had nothing to do with Logan's disappearance, or if it had, it was actually being used by him and he dumped it somewhere afterwards? What if Samuel killed her and is trying to make things look good by staying around? He's violent enough, and I wouldn't put anything past him.'

Kate shook her head. 'See your point, Tom, but that's already been considered. Why would he kill Maisie Taylor, Ted Southerby, and Gabriella Winston? What would be his motive? No, I can't buy that, Tom. But thanks for the info anyway.'

She looked at her watch. 'Anyway, one thing is certain. I won't be able to do what I had intended to do this afternoon. It's after six now, so it will have to wait until the morning.'

'What will have to wait?'

Kate hadn't heard the office door open and that familiar growling tone was the last thing she wanted to hear. Reeves winked at her and beat a hasty retreat. She closed her eyes.

Looking as if he was set to explode, Ted Roscoe stood for several long seconds, glaring at her, his hands clenching and unclenching by his sides.

'My office — now!' he snarled, storming off.

Kate rose wearily from her desk and followed him like a lamb to the slaughter.

For the next ten to fifteen minutes the walls of the inner office practically reverberated to the sound of Roscoe's voice as he tore into Kate. Among other things, he reminded her, with accompanying expletives, that he was the DI and she was just a DS, which meant, in case she hadn't realised it, that she was subordinate to him and didn't have *carte blanche* to "abandon a potential crime scene" and "go swanning around the countryside" just when the mood took her.

When Hayden chose that inopportune moment to return from the canteen, closely followed by Jamie Foster and Danny Ferris, he was not slow to enact a smart about-wheel in the doorway and lead the way smartly to another part of the police station, where all three remained until a later recce told them that it was safe to return to the department.

By then Roscoe had exhausted his energy and colourful repertoire enough for Kate to respond. In an icy but controlled tone, she explained in detail everything she and Hayden had been doing while they had been "swanning around the countryside," as he had put it, even down to the discovery of the memory stick, which had exposed Gabriella Winston as the poison pen writer and had established a possible link between her death and the kidnapping of Tammy Logan.

He listened with his jaws working overtime. His boot-button eyes darted around the room, resting anywhere but on her. By the time Kate had finished, his voice was back to its normal growl, his tone grudgingly conciliatory.

'Seems there's no doubt about Gabriella Winston being the poison pen then?' he said, without making the slightest effort to apologise for his unwarranted outburst, or to congratulate her on what she had achieved. 'But the circumstantial evidence you've put together to say she was not only stiffed, but stiffed by the same perp who snatched Tammy Logan, strikes me as a bit of a leap in the dark.'

'So, what about the photo of the women's clothes, bearing Tammy Logan's initials, on Winston's camera?' she snapped, chancing a come-back from him over her breach of investigative procedures regarding the memory stick. 'That can hardly be coincidence.'

He grimaced, fortunately not appearing to have picked up on the issue. 'It was just a load of women's clothes that could have belonged to anyone with similar initials, but I accept you might be onto something there. It doesn't really get us anywhere unless we can find out where that photo was taken, though, does it?'

She released an exasperated hiss. 'Which is exactly what Hayden and I have been trying to do in the past few hours. As a result of which, I almost ended up at the bottom of a bloody well.'

She proceeded to tell him about her close call at the derelict, but instead of commiserations, she was treated to an indifferent shrug.

'Maybe that will teach you not to go off at half-cock in future,' he said. 'After all, it wouldn't be the first time you've done something like that, would it? That's why you've earned the nickname "Maverick Kate."'

She ignored his sneering remark, but, on the basis of his continued obstreperous attitude, decided not to mention the possible link between Tammy Logan's disappearance and both the Jennifer Roberts inquiry and the other two outstanding missing person cases, just in case he opposed her planned visit to Roberts. As she told Hayden later, where Detective Inspector Ted Roscoe was concerned, perhaps the old "mushroom" management strategy — of keeping someone in the dark and feeding them on bullshit — was the most appropriate course of action to take.

So, instead, she ended the briefing there and then, rising to her feet and turning for the door. 'Thanks for your concern, guv,' she said as her parting shot. 'At least I'll know not to expect a wreath from you at my funeral!'

CHAPTER 23

Kate was relieved that Roscoe was nowhere to be seen when she and Hayden walked into the CID general office the following morning. 'He's out,' Ronnie Crouch said without offering any further explanation, so, with a shrug, Kate retrieved the Jennifer Roberts file from her desk, grabbed the keys of a CID car and headed for the door, with Hayden close behind.

'Where will you be, in case anyone asks?' Crouch called after them.

'Out,' Kate replied, without offering an explanation either.

The two detectives had good cause to remember Woo's warning about the sort of reception they were likely to receive when they arrived at Green Marsh Farm, just outside Lower Godney, around half an hour later. The property was set back from the approach lane at the end of a rutted driveway which had to be at least a quarter of a mile long. It comprised an unattractive stone house with an adjacent brick barn and a number of dilapidated-looking outbuildings and caravans scattered across a large, marshy field. On both sides of the field, more fields, dotted with patches of woodland and scrub, stretched away across the flat countryside. There were perhaps half a dozen cows in one of the adjacent fields, and chickens and ducks roamed across the bare, undernourished grass in front of the house in what seemed like an incessant hunt for food.

It wasn't the look of the place that put both Kate and Hayden off, but the double-barrelled shotgun levelled at Hayden's stomach from a few feet away. Where the thin, rat-faced man in the blue dungarees and peaked baseball cap had come from was a mystery — he seemed to have emerged from nowhere — but the shotgun in his hands carried absolute conviction.

'Who are you and what you doin' 'ere?' he demanded in a thick voice, swaying slightly as if he had a balance problem. 'Private, this be.'

'Police,' Kate said, meeting his hard gaze. 'Detective Sergeant Kate Lewis and Detective Constable Hayden Lewis, Highbridge CID.'

There was no sneering comment about the fact that they shared the same surname and instead, the man with the gun, took the hand steadying the weapon off the barrel and made a beckoning motion. 'Show me — like carefully,' he said.

Kate pulled her wallet out of her pocket and flipped it open at arm's length to show her badge and warrant card.

'Bring it over,' he ordered, and she walked slowly towards him, conscious of the fact that the weapon was now pointing at her.

The sharp blue eyes gave her the once-over as the hand reached out for her wallet. He studied it, then handed it back.

'What do you want?'

'Well, first, I'd like you to put down the shotgun,' Kate said, conscious that her voice was wavering slightly.

He hesitated and then reluctantly lowered the weapon. 'I asked what you wanted,' he said again. 'We don't like trespassers here.'

'We are not trespassers,' Hayden put in. 'We're here on police business.'

'What sort of business that be?'

'Your sister — Jennifer, isn't it? We need to have a chat with her.'

'She ain't here.' He looked away, suddenly shifty.

'Then, where is she?' Kate asked.

He shrugged. 'How should I know?'

She took a deep breath. Mr — er — Can I call you Ed? We have a missing woman and we think she was snatched by the same man who tried to take Jennifer.'

She saw him tense, but carried on speaking. 'We think she is in great danger and we need to find her before it's too late.'

'That's her look out,' he almost spat. 'You coppers didn't help Jennifer none. Never caught t'feller what tried to grab her, so why should she help you now?'

'Because it's her one chance of seeing him put behind bars.'

He stared at them both, biting his lip. 'She ain't well. Draggin' all this up again could put her back.'

'We'll be gentle.'

He hesitated again. 'Ten minutes an' no more. An' if she says she be done, you goes. Agreed?'

Kate nodded. 'Absolutely,' she said, throwing a quick, relieved glance at Hayden.

'Okay, then come in an' I'll ask 'er if she'll see you.'

Moments later they were shown into a small kitchen furnished with a plain wooden table and four chairs. An old-fashioned cast-iron cooker stood in one corner. Crockery and saucepans filled the Belfast sink under the single window and a cat lay sleeping on a shabby armchair just inside the door. Beside the chair a bottle of Bells Whisky and a half-filled glass stood on a little table, and it didn't take much to work out what Ed Roberts had been doing prior to their arrival.

'Stay 'ere,' Roberts said. 'I'll see where she be.'

He disappeared through an internal door. The two detectives stood waiting patiently, listening to his heavy boots stomp up some stairs and into a room above. They heard him call his sister's name loudly several times, then mutter something angrily before tramping on, presumably to another room. It was a good few minutes, and the sound of much toing and froing, before his boots clattered back down the stairs. When he came back into the kitchen his face was flushed and there was panicky glint in his eyes.

'She ain't there,' he said unnecessarily. 'I gotta find 'er. She never been right since the attack. She 'ad a breakdown, see, and is on tablets.'

He strode across the kitchen and jerked the back door wide. 'She be somewhere nearby. Might 'ave gone to check the 'orses.'

Following him outside, they saw him run diagonally across the patchy expanse of grass to what looked like a newly built stable and fling the doors wide. They heard him shouting his sister's name again, but she was obviously not inside. Kate cast Hayden an anxious glance. He reappeared and stood for a moment, panting heavily and throwing quick, worried glances around him, seemingly trying to make up his mind which of the various outbuildings to check first.

Then abruptly he headed for a ramshackle corrugated-roofed shed a short distance from the stable, disappearing inside for some seconds before re-emerging and running straight across the open space to a large barn, which stood with one of the double doors half open.

Again, he wasn't gone long, but when he reappeared, it was in a different state of mind. He was staggering like a drunk, waving his arms frantically and shouting for help. Even as they got to him, he collapsed on to his knees, beating the ground with both fists and sobbing hysterically.

Seized with an awful premonition, Kate left Hayden trying to restrain him and took off towards the barn at a run, scattering chickens in every direction and slamming through the half-open door without stopping — only to be confronted by the full horror of what the building concealed.

The barn was piled high with bales of what Kate in her ignorance assumed to be hay. Daylight filtered in through several high-level slits and the young woman could clearly be seen. She was hanging from a beam, the noose around her neck biting cruelly into the flesh. A wooden ladder lay on the floor underneath her and one of her wellington boots had fallen off so that a bare foot poked out grotesquely from the leg of her jeans.

Jennifer Roberts had at last found peace, but it was not the sort of peace that anyone would have wished for her.

* * *

'Roscoe's going to love us,' Hayden declared. 'Yet another stiff — he'll think we're jinxed.'

A search of the immediate area had found no trace of an intruder, just acres of flat, marshy countryside, sparse woodland, populated solely by curious, mud-spattered cattle with staring, unblinking eyes.

Kate nodded gloomily. Hayden sat on a hay bale, looking pale and pretty shaken, and she guessed she didn't look any better.

The young woman appeared anything but peaceful in death. Her white face was contorted and the haemorrhaging that often accompanies a hanging or a strangulation was horribly present in her wide-open, bulging eyes.

Hayden had guided Ed Roberts firmly away from the scene and settled him into the armchair in the kitchen beside the whisky bottle while they waited for the police surgeon and the local police team to arrive. He was in an advanced state of shock, completely shot away, shaking fitfully and incoherent. Hayden had lit a cigarette for him from a packet on the table and tried to calm him down, with only partial success. He had got little sense out of the man apart from a garbled expression of remorse at leaving his sister on her own, and a stumbling diatribe on her mental state.

'He thinks she took her own life,' Hayden said on returning to Kate. 'Apparently, after the attack on her, she suffered a breakdown and has been plagued by recurring nightmares and the obsessive belief that her attacker would come for her again. She's needed psychiatric help ever since and was on tablets after a previous attempt at suicide.'

'So, what do *you* think?' Kate asked, staring at him fixedly, 'Do you reckon this is a suicide?'

He grimaced. 'Hardly. And if it is, it's a mighty convenient outcome for someone.'

The young fresh-faced DI from Bridgwater, who materialised shortly afterwards with Charlie Woo in tow, seemed to be of a similar mind and, following the attendance and departure of Raymond Makepiece, the police surgeon — whose official pronouncement of death was accompanied by grave reservations as to the cause of it — he made the decision to call for the necessary forensic assistance, including a photographer and the SOCO team and to secure the potential crime scene.

'Bit of a clumsy job, this, in my opinion,' forensic pathologist, Lydia Summers declared after her own arrival several hours later. She straightened up from her examination of the body, shaking her head critically. 'I think the deceased would have found it rather challenging to climb up that narrow wooden ladder in wellington boots, slip the noose around her own neck and somehow manage to kick the ladder away again with the heels of her boots still on the rungs.'

'So, we *are* talking murder then?' Kate said sharply and she saw the young DI stiffen beside her.

The pathologist sighed. 'Now then, Kate, don't go putting words into my mouth. You know you can never be positive about anything until the PM has been completed.'

Kate knew Summers only too well from previous crime investigations, and it was obvious that the pathologist was up to her old baiting tricks. There was a mischievous glint in her eyes, and in the next breath she delivered the goods. 'Taking all things into account, though, it would seem to me that your victim was probably manually strangled, then hung from the beam afterwards to make the thing look like suicide.'

Summers waited for her words to sink in, then continued in a more sober tone. 'There are a number of indicators pointing to that fact. First, there's the impracticability of the ladder being used to facilitate the suicide. Second, pronounced petechiae — or bloodspots — tend to appear at some stage following a strangulation, due to ruptured capillaries — some of which are already present on her face now — and plainly, there has also been a substantial subconjunctival haemorrhage, which suggests to me the likelihood of a violent struggle before her death.

'Furthermore, with a straightforward hanging, by now you would expect to see at least some sign of ecchymoses — redness around the neck, where the ligature, rope or whatever else is used has ruptured the blood vessels and left a discernible mark. But there is not even the faintest sign of it here. This suggests to me that the lady was already dead when she was hung from the beam, since blood vessels do not rupture after death. Finally, the tongue and neck are plainly very swollen and erythema, and tell-tale bruising around the eyes is starting to emerge too, as well as around the throat — below the Adam's apple, which in itself is significant, suggesting forcefully applied thumb pressure, which has constricted the carotid arteries and jugular. I suspect that during the PM we will also find that the hyoid bone at least has been fractured and the trachea ruptured.'

'And that's it, is it, Doc?' the DI asked mildly.

Summers smiled, as she always did when she had her police investigators dangling on the end of a string. 'Not quite. The most telling evidence is in, or rather on, her hands. See?'

She bent down and, with a little effort, was able to partially lift the left arm of the corpse, which seemed already to have appreciably stiffened up. Even from where she was standing, Kate could see the deep red scratches on the back of the hand. 'It's the same with both hands,' Summers went on. 'Very recent injuries, which I would guess were caused when her assailant knelt on her hands while she was lying on her back, to stop her struggling, and she scraped them on this rather rough, gritty floor. This is also why two of her fingers appear to have been broken and twisted at an unnatural angle, probably because she had them bent into her palm when your perpetrator, perhaps unwittingly, knelt on them.'

Kate smiled her thanks. For once, she had been given a clear-cut professional assessment of the situation, which, unlike the other incidents she had been investigating, brooked little room for argument from anyone — Roscoe in particular.

'And time of death, Doc?' she asked.

Summers considered the question for a second, staring hard at the corpse, as if seeking an answer from the dead woman herself. 'Difficult to say in view of the long delay before I was called, but going by the present body temperature, the degree of lividity and the ambient temperature in the barn, together with the present state of rigor mortis — which normally begins within thirty minutes to an hour of death — I would say six to seven hours, though at this stage that can only be a reasonable guesstimate on my part.'

Kate nodded. 'When we cut her down at about ten fifteen, I noticed that her muscles had already begun to stiffen up. So, going by what you say, the onset of rigor mortis must have already started. Taking into account that you have just finished your examination,' she glanced at her watch, 'at sixteen hundred hours, then it is likely she was murdered at least an hour before we arrived ourselves, possibly at around nine?'

Summers also glanced at her watch, then shrugged. 'If you say so, Sergeant, but I can only tell you what my examination suggested when I completed it. I'll leave you to work out the rest.'

'Looks like we've hit the nail right on the head this time,' Hayden commented after Summers had left.

Kate nodded, drawing him away from the immediate scene. 'I couldn't agree with you more, and even Roscoe has no pull on this job. But there's something else we need to discuss — in private.'

Hayden followed her to their car and stood leaning against it. 'I'm all ears.'

She made a brief grimace. 'If this was, as we suspect, the work of our elusive perp, how the hell did he find out this poor woman's address and know we were coming to see her?'

He thought about that for a second. 'Well, the only way he could have done that was by following us, like you told me Tony Samuel did. We weren't thinking of a tail, so we have no idea who was behind us on the way here.'

She shivered. 'That really *is* creepy.'

'It's the only feasible answer, though, isn't it? After all, your name has been splashed all over the local rag. We've also been carrying out inquiries in the village and, if our man stiffed Maisie Taylor, Ted Southerby and Gabriella Winston, he would know you had attended all three scenes. All he had to do was watch and wait for you to make your next move.'

She bit her lip, frowning. 'True, and we mustn't forget the incident at that derelict. He must have been there ahead of us and was just waiting to catch me on my own in the cellar to stage his little accident. It all adds up.' She stared at him, incredulous. 'We're under bloody surveillance, Hayd — can you credit it? We're being spied on by the perp instead of the other way around.'

He gave her a weak, humourless smile. 'As they say, there's a first time for everything.'

'Maybe there is, but what lacks satisfactory explanation is how he was able to get ahead of us to stiff Jennifer Roberts in the short time we were delayed by her brother.'

Hayden glanced at his watch. 'It was probably a good half hour after we arrived that Ed Roberts discovered she was missing. Don't forget, we were outside talking for what must have been around ten minutes, and that was before he went looking for her.'

Kate shook her head. 'Sorry, but that theory just doesn't hold water. The killer would have had to act pretty damned quick, even so.'

'So, you are suggesting what?' he said.

'That somehow our man knew in advance that we were coming here — the pathologist's assessment of time of death seems to bear that out — and he came on ahead and laid in wait. We don't know when Ed Roberts last saw his sister. Plainly, she has the run of the farm and regularly feeds the chickens and tends to the horses as part of her everyday routine, so in normal circumstances, he probably wouldn't have gone looking for her.'

She paused.

'Furthermore, the whisky bottle and half-filled glass beside it in the kitchen suggest he was on the juice, so maybe he had no idea when she'd even left the house, let alone where she'd gone. He was noticeably swaying when he confronted us, no doubt already under the influence. Not exactly a reliable witness, I would say, so we don't know how long his sister was out of his sight. I reckon the killer saw her go into the barn well before we got here, did the job and left without her brother being any the wiser.'

'And the rope? What about that?' Hayden asked.

'There was a load of it hanging on pegs and lying in corners. I suspect that he strangled her, then simply strung her up.'

'So, the burning question — two, in fact. First, if you're saying the killer knew in advance that we were coming here, how so? And, second, how did he know where Jennifer Roberts lived?'

'I don't have a crystal ball with me,' she said, 'but I still think that the perp knew where we were going before we left the nick and, as I've said, got here before us.'

'You realise what that means?' he said.

She nodded. 'Only too well. Either someone at the nick is passing on information to the perp or they are the perp themselves.'

Hayden said nothing for a moment, staring at her as the full implication of what she was alleging sank in. 'And the only people who knew we were coming here were Charlie Woo and our own very helpful LIO, Dave Gort.'

She returned his stare with a fixed one of her own. 'And that's what's bothering me.'

* * *

Charlie Woo materialised as Kate and Hayden hurried back towards their car. 'Not quitting on us now, are you, Kate?' he said with a grin.

'Not at all, Charlie,' she said. 'Just didn't want to cramp your style.'

He glanced quickly across at the DI, who was talking to the SOCO manager, and lowered his voice. 'Still got my misper file, I hope?'

Kate nodded. 'In the car.'

He breathed a sigh of relief. 'Now this has happened, I will need it back before his nibs asks for it. He'll be wondering why you were over here to start with, as it's well out of your own area.'

Kate shrugged. 'No problem. If he asks, I'll tell him.'

She walked with him to the car and handed the file over. 'There's no room for parochial sentiments here,' she said. 'As we have now almost certainly established a link between the attack on Jennifer Roberts and the disappearance of Tammy Logan, we are looking at one major crime investigation, instead of two separate incidents, so I don't think there will be any reason for anyone to feel that their nose has been put out of joint — not even your DI.'

'I hope Roscoe is equally magnanimous when a senior investigating officer is appointed over his head to lead the inquiry,' Hayden murmured as Charlie Woo walked back to the scene and they climbed into their CID car. 'Glad I'm only a humble DC and don't have to break the news to him as to where this business is now going.'

'I don't think I'll have to break any news to him,' Kate said drily. 'If I'm not mistaken, the wires will be humming long before we get back to Highbridge.'

CHAPTER 24

Clumsy! Inexcusably clumsy, the whole thing. He'd found out where the woman was living easily enough and got there well before the police. She'd also handed herself to him on a plate when she'd walked out of the house and gone to the barn, where he was already waiting. But from there it had all gone wrong. When he'd left home, he'd been a bit undecided as to how he was going to do the job and had considered using the headlock method he had learned in the army — wrenching her head to one side and breaking her neck. But when he'd got to the barn and seen all that rope hanging from hooks inside, he'd hit on the idea of making the whole thing look like a suicide.

But she had heard him coming up behind her, turning on him with that bloody pitchfork in her hands and catching him on the neck and drawing blood. He remembered the panic in her eyes and the look of fear on the white, mask-like face before he'd wrenched the pitchfork from her grasp and tossed it into the corner. She'd opened her mouth to scream then, but he'd slammed into her at the same moment, knocking all the breath out of her and sending her sprawling into a pile of loose hay. His hands had been around her throat even as she'd opened her mouth again, his knees on her hands to prevent her struggling. He'd felt the life go out of her very quickly — just like a little bird — convulsing twice and then lying still.

There was a wooden ladder leaning against one wall and, placing it against one of the roof beams, he had climbed up and secured a length of rope to the beam, fashioning a noose at the other end. She was heavier than he'd expected and lifting her up had proved to be more taxing than he'd thought possible, so that at one stage he'd almost dropped her. But then it was done and, pushing the ladder away so that it fell on to the floor underneath her, he had left her hanging there like a pathetic *Aunt Sally* doll.

At that moment he'd noticed the scratch marks on the backs of her hands and had inwardly cursed his clumsiness, knowing full well that the police surgeon would spot them and was likely to draw the worst possible conclusion from them. But by then it was too late to do anything about the situation. At least he'd had the good sense to clean the blades of the pitchfork to remove any traces of his blood and toss it to the other side of the barn, so they'd find no DNA there.

He also took comfort from the fact that, if the woman had remembered anything about the man who had attacked her after the Glastonbury Festival all that time ago, she was no longer in any position to tell anyone about it — except, he'd mused with a cynical smile, through a séance.

Sitting in his study at home a couple of hours later, a double brandy in his trembling hands, he thought about the girl in his cellar. She had become a potential liability now. Detective Sergeant Kate Lewis was too damned persistent by half, and she was getting closer all the time. It would only take one slip-up or stroke of bad luck for her to be on his back, and he couldn't afford that to happen. Get rid of the girl — that was the only answer, bury her in the woods alongside the others and he could rest easy. But not just yet. God had given him a task he had to fulfil if he was to achieve his own redemption, and he couldn't afford to fail yet again and be cast into eternal damnation. So he had no choice but to wait a little longer and try just one more time to force her to repent. So, draining his glass, he headed out into the hall in the direction of the basement.

* * *

Kate was certainly right about the wires humming, and it was apparent from Roscoe's smouldering gaze when she joined him in his office later that afternoon, that he already knew about the Jennifer Roberts murder.

'So, we've been at it again, Sergeant, have we?' he grated. 'Swanning off on an inquiry without telling me beforehand?'

'Sorry, guv,' she replied without meaning it, and sat down awkwardly on a chair facing his desk, 'but you weren't in a very receptive mood when we last spoke, so I didn't say anything.'

'Didn't say anything, eh?' he echoed. 'Now there's an admission. So, what else haven't you bothered to tell me?'

She laid the computer printouts Dave Gort had run off the PNC on his desk in front of him and told him about the suspected link between the three reports and the disappearance of Tammy Logan.

He sat there throughout her briefing, making no comment, emitting only the occasional grunt, and showing none of his usual aggression or scepticism. It was certainly a marked contrast to the raging bull he had been just the day before. When she had finished, he continued to sit for a long moment, staring into space as if his mind was elsewhere.

'A major crime inquiry is being set up following the murder of Jennifer Roberts,' he said finally, 'and it will almost certainly investigate all matters that appear to be linked to it, including those earlier mispers, the disappearance of Tammy Logan and the suspicious death of Gabriella Winston.' He smiled sardonically. 'So, you got what you wanted in the end, didn't you?'

Kate felt like saying, 'not before time,' but decided against it, instead asking, 'When will it be operational?'

He shrugged. 'Couple of days to be fully up and running, but the major crime unit is already being assembled, in view of the complexity of this business, and a major incident room is being set up at Bridgwater nick. There'll be a conference at Bridgwater within twenty-four hours, once an SIO has been appointed to lead the investigation, and you'll be required to attend, to brief the senior managers on your inquiries to date.'

She watched him narrowly as he reached into the right-hand drawer of his desk and produced a half-full glass of what looked suspiciously like whisky, which he had obviously poured earlier and was hiding away in there.

'Colonel bloody Winston's back,' he said heavily, completely changing the subject, and took a gulp from the glass. 'Flew back today by private jet from wherever he was. I wish I was on one going the other way.'

Kate frowned, puzzled and not a little irritated by the fact that he seemed to think that Winston's return was even worth mentioning under the present circumstances.

'Bastard has already been on to headquarters,' he went on. 'Apparently got through to ACC Ops. As a result, Super is having kittens, DCI has thrown every one of his toys out of the pram and guess who has become the fall-guy and is getting all the flak? Yes, you've guessed it, Yours Truly! Amazing what money and position can do, isn't it?'

Kate stared critically at the glass he was holding. 'That help you to deal with the flak, does it, guv?' she commented drily.

He glanced at the glass, and then stared back at her, a familiar sneer on his face. 'Ever the moralist, aren't you, Kate? But in answer to your question, yes, it does — especially when you get a personal invitation from the DCI to consider taking early retirement because he thinks you are past your sell-by date.'

Kate raised an eyebrow. 'So, what are you going to do?'

He responded with another of his wolfish grins. 'What would you like me to do?'

She shrugged. 'Not up to me, is it?'

'No, it bloody isn't,' he grated, his usual belligerence once more surfacing, 'and for your information and the information of anyone else who wants to know, I'm going nowhere, okay?'

Kate nodded. 'Fine with me, but in view of the fact that it looks like the major crime unit will be taking over the Tammy Logan investigation, what do you want Hayden and myself to do now?'

He drained his glass and, reaching down, lifted a bottle of Bell's whisky from under his desk.

'Do?' he echoed, refilling his glass. 'I don't give a shit what you do. And seeing as I'm unlikely to be part of the investigation, I don't care what they do either.'

'And Tammy Logan?' she persisted. 'Don't you care what happens to her?'

He paused with the glass halfway to his lips, his boot-button eyes boring into her. 'Don't push it, Sergeant. Just piss off, will you?'

And Kate did just that, leaving him to enjoy his misery — and his bottle.

* * *

'Well, what did the boss have to say?' Hayden asked as she led him, unsurprisingly without opposition, down the stairs to the canteen to make up for the lunch they hadn't had.

'Not a lot,' Kate said tightly. 'He was on a whisky infusion.'

Selecting a now rather congealed lasagne and salad from the residue of meals on offer, she followed him and his plate, overflowing with pie and chips, to a quiet corner and told him about her conversation with the DI.

'So, what happens now?' Hayden queried through a mouthful of pie. 'Do we shelve everything and leave it to the major crime unit, or what?'

Kate shook her head. 'We need to finish what we started before it's taken out of our hands altogether. And we haven't much time left in which to do it.'

He looked puzzled. 'But I thought you've actually been pushing for a major crime investigation ever since Maisie Taylor ended up at the bottom of the stairs?'

She nodded grimly. 'That's because I didn't want things cuffed, as per Roscoe's usual style. I am delighted that the decision has been taken out of his hands, but I sense we are now so close to nailing the perp and finding out what has happened to Tammy Logan that I am keen to finish what we started before we are swallowed up in all the bureaucracy of a major crime inquiry.'

He paused with a large wodge of pie on the end of his fork. 'Roscoe won't like it if we go it alone again, not after all that has happened.'

She snorted. 'The way Roscoe is at the moment, and the hurt he is feeling over how he's been treated, I can't see him giving a damn — even when he does finally emerge from his self-induced alcoholic fug.'

He shrugged. 'You're the sergeant, old girl. So what's our next move then? Frankly, despite our earlier discussions, I really don't see either Dave Gort or Charlie Woo as being the person we are looking for.'

'Neither do I. I've known Charlie Woo for several years and have always considered him to be a hundred percent straight. Furthermore, in the statement Jennifer Roberts provided after she was attacked at Glastonbury, she described her assailant as a big, heavy man and extremely strong. Not by any stretch of the imagination would that description fit Charlie — he's built more like a ballet dancer.'

He nodded. 'And, as for Dave Gort, though I don't know him that well, his physique doesn't fit either and anyway, I can't see him being involved in anything like this. After all, he has gone out of his way to help us with our inquiries — with the surveillance tape of the sus Land Rover, as well as establishing a possible link between Tammy Logan's disappearance, the disappearance of the previous two mispers and the attempted abduction of Jennifer Roberts. The last thing the perp would want is to put information our way which could result in his own arrest.'

She sighed. 'Which means that we have to put our thinking caps on and try and work out who else could have had information on our movements.'

He brightened. 'Best way of doing that is a brainstorm over a nice bottle of red wine at home.'

She glanced at her watch, then at one of the canteen staff swabbing down the tables in the near empty canteen.

'Okay, Hayd, I give in,' she said. 'It's practically six o'clock and the canteen is obviously closing. There's nothing more we can do here tonight, so if you're prepared to forego the last of those greasy bread puddings on display, which I know you've got your eye on, we'll call it a day.'

He agonised for several seconds, glancing back at the counter several times. Then, finally, with a sigh of regret, he nodded. 'Okay, deal. I'll see you there in a tick.'

* * *

A bottle of red wine was already warming by a newly lit log fire when she got back to the thatched, two-bed cottage they shared in the tiny village of Burtle. She kicked off her boots and dropped onto the settee suddenly realising how tired she was, while Hayden poured her a large glass. Whether it was the wine, the heat of the room or a combination of both, she soon drifted off and immediately found herself in the grip of a nightmare of flashing lights and sinister, smoky figures flitting through crumbling ruins, while a multitude of strange, nasal voices muttered to her in an incessant, incoherent chant.

She awoke what turned out to be two and a half hours later, to find Hayden asleep and snoring fitfully in the armchair opposite and the fire just a mass of smoking, white ash.

Leaving him to snore away, she went out to her car to collect her briefcase in which she kept all the confidential papers, notebooks and personal case observations that she didn't want others to see. She was restless after her disturbing dreams and felt that an hour going through everything on the Tammy Logan case over a strong cup of coffee might produce some new revelation or pointer that hadn't occurred to her before.

The stab of stomach acid hit her immediately. The briefcase was not in the boot, and a check of the passenger compartment revealed that it was not there either. It was obviously still on the floor by her desk at the nick. She had forgotten the damned thing. Now she felt really sick. One of the notebooks in the briefcase was a log of all her run-ins with Roscoe, which she had kept as an "insurance policy" in the event that he attempted to make her the scapegoat for one of his own *faux pas*.

Deep down, she knew it was unlikely that anyone in the department would bother to go into her briefcase, but she couldn't afford the risk — particularly if that person happened to be Roscoe himself.

Scribbling a note and placing it on the coffee table in front of her still snoring other half, she slipped on her boots, grabbed a coat and her ignition keys and ran to her car.

It was past nine when she swung into the car park at the rear of Highbridge police station and slipped her warrant card into the card reader by the back door. As she entered, she heard raucous laughter coming from the briefing room where the night shift crew were obviously assembling for the night turn at ten, but otherwise the place seemed completely deserted.

The CID office was virtually unlit, with most of the strip lights already switched off, leaving much of the place in deep shadow. The main light in Roscoe's office was also off, but his desk lamp was still on and it was apparent that he had also left for the night — no doubt at that moment ensconced in the Black Cock, diluting his whisky infusion with Best Bitter.

She had only just entered the room, letting the door swing to behind her as she headed for her desk on the other side, when she sensed stealthy movement a little to her left and paused briefly to peer into the gloom in front of her. At the same moment she caught a glimpse of a shadow passing through the edge of the pool of light cast by one of the strip lights that was still lit. Someone was creeping about in the office.

CHAPTER 25

Tammy Logan heard his heavy footsteps approaching long before he turned the key in the lock, and she shrank back in the single bed until she was pressed right up against the wall.

She flinched under his hard gaze as he took in the untouched food on the bedside table and the Bible open at the end of the bed.

She waited for him to snarl at her and then stride towards the bathroom to turn on the taps again, but he didn't. Instead, he came over to the bed, pulled a chair after him and sat down beside her. She flinched as he reached out to take one of her bare feet in his hands and began to stroke it.

'You know you've been a bad girl, don't you?' he said in an unusually soft, conciliatory tone, as if talking to a child. 'That's why I've had to punish you. You don't want me to punish you again, do you?'

She shook her head vigorously, without taking her eyes off him.

'I have learned the Lord's prayer,' she blurted suddenly. 'It — it was on a piece of paper in the Bible.'

He raised his eyebrows in surprise and nodded slowly.

'Recite it to me,' he said.

In a halting, shaky voice she did as he asked, missing out one line in the process, but then stopping to go back to repeat the whole passage.

His dark eyes seemed to come alive. He was obviously delighted.

'At last we begin to get somewhere,' he breathed. 'You have done well. I have to go now, but while I'm gone, I want you to read *Genesis*, Chapter 3 in the Holy Book. It is about the temptation of the serpent. When I come back, you can read it to me and tell me what you have learned from it. Then in a little while, it may be time for you to make your confession before the Almighty, and to receive his forgiveness for your sins.'

'Will — will you let me go after that?' she whispered. 'I promise not to say anything to anyone.'

He smiled indulgently and stood up. 'Your sins will soon be cast from you, after which, you will find the eternal peace with our Lord that awaits all true believers.'

Then he left her, almost overcome with elation. He was nearly there. He could hardly believe it. After all his hard work and despite his previous failures with the other two girls, he was finally close to receiving the absolution for his sins that he craved. All he had to do now was fulfil his promise to the Lord to save a wayward soul from hell's fire in exchange for his own redemption.

Yes, this one would make a worthy offering and, in return for shaking off the shackles of this decadent world, she would be rewarded by the Almighty with eternal life in paradise. He decided that he would not reveal to her what her destiny was to be until he was satisfied that she had truly repented, and when the crucial moment of her passing came, he would ensure that it was as painless as possible. After all, he still had a small quantity of the sedative he had used before to subdue the girls he had selected, so she would not suffer in her final moments. Her death would be a small price to pay for the glory that would ultimately be hers . . .

* * *

Kate stood stock still, her heart racing.

'Hello? Who's there?' she demanded.

Silence, but she thought she could detect heavy breathing close by.

'I asked who was there?' she said again, but there was still no answer.

Frowning, she turned and strode back towards the light switch by the main doors, but even as she reached it, feeling for the row of switches on the panel, there was a sharp crack, then another door slammed at the far end of the room and she heard the sound of heavy feet on metal stairs.

A second later, the room was flooded with fizzing, flickering light, but as it adjusted to a pale, yellow glow, she knew she would find the place empty. There was no mystery as to where the intruder had gone. The bar on the fire escape door in the far corner was down and the door itself not properly closed.

Crossing the room at a run, she pushed the door wide and stepped out onto the landing beyond to peer down into the car park. There was no moon and the light from the security lamps gleamed on rain-washed tarmac and the roofs of several parked police cars. Nothing moved. The car park appeared to be deserted.

Feeling goose-pimples on her arms and a stirring of the hair at the back of her neck, she descended the fire escape and strode quickly to the car park exit. The street beyond was empty. Turning back, she checked around the parked police cars. She got down on her hands and knees to peer underneath each vehicle, her heart pounding in her ears. At any moment she expected to be confronted by a prone figure staring back at her. But there was nothing, just grit and oily dirt on the palms of her hands and damp patches on the knees of her trousers.

The chuckle just feet away while she was levering herself up from the last car made her jump and, straightening, she stared a little ruefully at the uniformed figure standing there.

'Tom,' she acknowledged, feeling more than a little embarrassed.

Another chuckle. 'Whatever were you doing down there?' Reeves said. 'I can think of better places to do press-ups.'

'Very funny,' she retorted, rubbing her hands together to get rid of the grit attached to her palms. 'I disturbed someone up to something in the CID office. He fled down the fire escape and I thought he might be hiding down here.'

He turned to look around him. 'How did he get into the office?' he exclaimed. 'Wasn't the fire escape door shut?'

She shrugged. 'I would have thought so, but I don't know. Even if it was, it's not a door you could get through from the outside.'

He stared at the ground floor rear door of the police station. 'Well, he couldn't have got into the building any other way. He would have needed a security card to gain access from the car park.'

'Maybe he had one,' she replied, almost immediately regretting her words.

His smiling, good-natured face crumpled into a frown. 'What on earth are you suggesting?'

She sighed. 'I don't really know. Maybe I'm just het up, that's all.'

'Could have imagined it then?'

'Possibly, yes.'

'Well, that's a relief. I wouldn't want to think one of our own was snooping around your office. Raises all sorts of questions. And anyway, I've only just come out the back door to get my sarnies from my car, so your intruder would have had to pass me on his way in.' He hesitated. 'Do you want me to come upstairs and check the office for you?'

She stiffened. 'No thanks,' she retorted more sharply than she had intended, 'I think I can just about do that myself.'

He stepped back, raising his hands in front of him. 'Sorry, miss, didn't mean to offend,' he said in a comical voice. 'I won't do it again.'

She laughed. 'You're fine, Tom. Like I said, I'm just a bit edgy at the moment, that's all. Thanks for the offer. But I'll go back up and secure the door before I go. Must have been left ajar before.' She walked back towards the fire escape, adding over her shoulder. 'Don't forget your sarnies.'

The fire escape door locked in place as soon as she shut it and raised the bar, and she stood for a moment, studying it while she thought about what had happened a few minutes before. No, she hadn't imagined it, as Tom Reeves had suggested. There *had* been someone in the office and she was pretty sure the fire escape door would have been securely closed before they had fled. So, how had the intruder got in to start with?

She re-opened the door and stared upwards. The fire escape continued to the top floor, so it was possible whoever it was had gone up instead of down — she hadn't considered that when she had raced after them before. But it still didn't answer the question of how they had managed to get into the building in the first place, if they weren't someone who was already legitimately there.

Wedging the door open with a chair, she climbed the fire escape to the next level, which she knew gave access to the police club and bar, and was startled to find the fire escape door closed, but not secured on the other side, so that, with a little effort, she was able to pull it open.

The sparsely lit club room was empty, the metal shutters pulled down over the bar, the only sign of life the gaming machine winking at her from a few feet away.

'So, that's how you got in,' she muttered to herself, feeling slightly relieved that this seemed to indicate an outside intruder rather than one from inside the police station. Then, as further doubt crept in, she added, 'Or did you?'

She was on the point of returning to the CID office via the fire escape, when the partially lit clubroom blazed with light and a voice rapped out a challenge.

'Stay where you are!'

She stepped back into the room and confronted the uniformed civilian security man striding towards her, treating him to a grim smile. He stopped short.

'Oh, sorry, skipper,' he said. 'Didn't realise it was you. Sergeant Reeves asked me to check around the building again. Said you had an intruder in the CID office.'

Kate nodded. 'We did. They ran off down the fire escape when I challenged them.'

'Did you get a look at them?'

She shook her head. 'Sadly, no, but I found that open,' she said, nodding over her shoulder towards the fire escape door. 'I thought you regularly checked the building at night?'

He stepped past her to the door and peered at it. 'I do, and I'm sure this door was secure when I did my last tour at eight o'clock.'

She grunted. 'Well, it looks like he may have got in here and made his way downstairs.'

The elderly man frowned. 'Can't understand it. I'm positive this door was shut with the bar up when I checked the building on that last tour, and once these doors are shut and secured, you can't open them from the outside.'

She sighed. 'Big mystery then, eh?' She forced a smile. 'Anyway, I'll leave you to shut up shop. I'll secure the door in the CID office before I leave.'

Kate made a point of doing just that the moment she returned to the CID office, and she breathed a sigh of relief when she saw that her briefcase was where she had left it. But that relief was short-lived when she bent to pick it up and her eyes narrowed. The case was in the right spot, but facing the wrong way — with the lock towards the leg of the desk instead of the other way around. Lifting it onto her desk, she checked it out. It was fastened, as always, though unlocked because she had been working on the Tammy Logan misper file before going home. Everything appeared to be intact, but she fancied that other fingers had been through the papers inside. She was meticulous in her filing and always ensured that documents were inserted into their plastic sleeves the same way around and in the correct order, but it was apparent that some of the papers were out of sequence. So, her suspicions had been correct — someone had just finished going through her briefcase when she had disturbed them. But who? And had they got into the station via the insecure clubroom fire door or, more worryingly, was that just a blind and they had been in the station the whole time?

She was still pondering that point — wondering whether the night security officer had been correct in his contention that the clubroom door had been secure when he'd made his rounds at eight o'clock, or whether he had just been saying that to hide his own negligence — when the door to the department was thrown open and Tom Reeves appeared, looking worried and not a little embarrassed.

'Anything missing from your briefcase?' he asked.

Kate shook her head. 'Doesn't appear to be, thanks. I can't speak for any of my colleagues' stuff, though.'

He glanced around the room. 'What do you think they were after? I wouldn't have thought there was anything of value in here.'

She snapped her briefcase shut. 'Perhaps they just found the unsecured door upstairs and thought they'd try their luck.' she said, without really meaning it.

'What, in a police station?'

'It's happened elsewhere. I know of one nick some years ago where the perp nicked the petty cash box from Admin.'

He raised an eyebrow. 'That's a disturbing thought. I'll get our security bod to check their office out in a mo. Actually, I've just been talking to Dave Gort and he thinks someone's been in his office too—'

'Dave Gort — the LIO?' Kate exclaimed, cutting him off. 'What on earth was he doing here at this time? He works permanent days.'

He shrugged. 'Said he had some paperwork to catch up on and came in to clear up a bit of it. Apparently, his in-tray looked as though it had been disturbed by someone going through it, and his computer was on, even though he was sure it had been switched off when he went home earlier.' He made a face. 'Looks like someone has been wandering around the nick unchallenged. Bit worrying that, isn't it?'

Kate simply stared at him, unseeing, her mind elsewhere as it tried to process and evaluate the information she had just been given. Dave Gort — in the nick at this hour? That had to be unprecedented, whatever reason he had provided. LIOs never worked such late hours unless there was a very special reason — and she couldn't think of one right that minute, unless . . .

'There's one funny thing, though,' Reeves continued, interrupting her train of thought. 'After I spoke to Dave Gort, I went to check things out with the SDO and found him taking a report of a stolen bike from a feller in the front office. Apparently the clown rode in here earlier in the evening for a drink at one of the local pubs and left his bike outside. And, surprise, surprise, it was gone when he came out again.'

Kate tossed her head a little irritably. 'So, what has that to do with what we're discussing?'

He frowned and scratched his nose. 'Well, the feller was Ned Mason from my village, and I can't recall ever seeing him in Highbridge before. Struck me as strange that he came all the way out here for a drink when he usually drinks at his local.'

'You're saying he may have been the intruder?'

'Well, it's a bit of a coincidence that he was about at the same time, isn't it? And he could easily have doubled back after he had run off, then popped into the front office with a bogus story just in case he had been spotted and needed a reason to be here.'

Kate recalled the powerfully built villager she had seen in the shop and then in the Soldier's Arms. Her eyes narrowed and she remained silent for a few moments, thinking about what Reeves had just said.

'So, why would he want to snoop around the station?' she queried.

Reeves made a face. 'Dunno, unless he was trying to get the low down on your Jennifer Roberts case.'

'Which would mean he was the perp we're looking for, or was implicated in the snatch in some way?'

'As I say, I don't know. It just struck me as a bit funny, that's all — and he's not exactly one of our most upright citizens. He has previous for a bit of tea-leafing and poaching and was acquitted on a charge of indecently assaulting a barmaid at the Soldier's Arms six months ago.'

'Not exactly the sort of profile I'd expect to fit our kidnapper, though.'

'Maybe not, but it's worth mentioning that he lives alone in a darned great farmhouse on the edge of the village. Ideal place to hold your misper when you think about it,' he said.

Kate frowned. 'You didn't say anything about him the day we checked that derelict.'

'Well, no, but I didn't think of it then, it's just come to mind,' he said. 'I wouldn't exactly describe his place as a psycho type house anyway. 'Course, even if he had nothing to do with that job, he could have been in here just looking for any cash or other valuables left lying about.'

'Bit daft picking a nick for that, though, I would have thought, and it still wouldn't explain how he got in.'

He shrugged again. 'Yep, I know it sounds a bit far-fetched, but I felt I should mention it anyway.' He changed the subject. 'You off home now then?'

She nodded. 'I reckon so. Nothing more I can do here and there's a nice bottle of red waiting for me back there.' She forced a smile. 'That's if Hayd hasn't guzzled the lot already.'

He snorted. 'Wish I was on my way too. Nothing else lately but bloody nights, with not a whisper of anything happening — except for your mystery intruder tonight, of course. At least you had a bit of excitement today over at Lower Godney. I saw on the intranet that a woman was found murdered over there. Is that right?'

'So we believe, yes, a hanging. Nasty job.'

He gave a sympathetic nod. 'Hangings always are. No ideas as to who strung her up then?'

She shook her head. 'He got away.'

He sighed. 'That poor kid — and after all she'd been through with that attack on her a couple of years ago. Life can be really cruel sometimes . . .' His voice trailed off. 'Anyway,' he said more briskly, 'I'd better get downstairs to brief the shift, and I expect you'll be wanting to get stuck into that bottle of red wine.' He grinned suddenly. 'But don't you be worrying about me now, on duty here, out in the rain, while you're enjoying that nice warm bed.'

For a long moment, Kate stared through him, seeming to be unaware of his humorous parting shot. Something he had just said had breached the wall barricading her subconscious, finally releasing that critical fragment of information she'd been trying for so many days to seize hold of and joining with all the other hitherto disjointed elements floating around inside her head. Everything slotted into place like the pieces of a jigsaw, bringing with it an absolute, and unwelcome, clarity. The shock, as the picture revealed itself, chilled her to the marrow.

She left the office with her briefcase tucked under her arm, the bottle of red wine and nice warm bed Reeves had jokingly referred to gone from her mind.

CHAPTER 26

The Local Intelligence Officer's office was in darkness when Kate opened the door, just the computer's "power on" light glowing red in the gloom. Dave Gort had obviously gone home. She switched on his desk lamp and closed the door.

She knew she risked being caught with her knickers down if he returned unexpectedly, or one of the night-turn officers happened to walk in on her. After what she had just discovered, however, she felt she had no option but to follow up on her suspicions and, with her trust in her colleagues now shaken to its foundations, there was no one else she could take into her confidence.

Gort's in-tray was piled high with computer printouts and other documents, and she leafed through them quickly until she found what she was looking for. The intranet circular was marked "Not for Press" in bold, black letters. She checked the time it had been sent and the precise content of the short text message before returning it to the pile in exactly the same place, her mouth drying up as the full implication of what it had revealed dawned on her, along with the attendant action she must now take.

She realised that she wouldn't be able to gain access to Gort's computer — it would almost certainly be password protected. But she also knew the LIO kept other manual records that she felt sure would provide her with the address she needed, and she soon found the appropriate ring-binder stored between a street index file and a couple of old telephone directories on top of a locked metal cabinet in the corner.

But even as she thumbed through the alphabetical list, the binder resting on a corner of the desk, the risk attached to her clandestine search was rudely brought home to her. The bang of a door in the corridor outside alerted her first and she just had time to switch off the desk lamp and sneak behind the closed door before heavy footsteps approached from the direction of the stairs.

Holding the binder pressed against her chest, she closed her eyes tightly as the footsteps paused outside the office and someone coughed loudly. Then there was the metallic scrape of the door handle. The door swung open and a hand reached inside to switch on the main light. Kate held her breath, her heart thudding wildly in her throat as she visualised someone — probably the night security officer — scanning the room. If he discovered her in there, she could have some awkward explaining to do, especially with the ring-binder in her hands. She gritted her teeth and kept perfectly still.

Then, abruptly, after a long pause, the office light was extinguished and the door was shut again, plunging her into comforting darkness.

She waited several seconds after the footsteps had resumed their measured tread before making another move, which was to return to the desk and switch the lamp back on. She thumbed through the binder until she found what she was looking for and, mentally noting the address, returned the binder to its usual place, turned off the desk lamp and slipped out of the office.

She made it to the rear car park without running into anyone else and was in her car and heading out of the yard within minutes. Turning into the main road, she was presented with a dilemma — to race home to pick up her unsuspecting other half before following up on her suspicions or go it alone and risk the consequences of the whole thing going pear-shaped. In the end, fearing that the kidnapper might now suspect she was onto him and, if Tammy Logan *were* still alive, be panicked into silencing his victim for good, she made her decision.

Slamming her foot to the floor, she sent the wheel-spinning MX5 careering across the junction, onto the road out of Highbridge and into the inky blackness of the Somerset Levels.

* * *

He sat for a long time, thinking about what to do next. It had been stupid to poke around in the CID office the way he had. He might have known there was a high risk of being caught in the act and, as it was, he had got away by the skin of his teeth. That bloody woman! She was always turning up at the wrong time. He should have finished her in the cellar of that derelict, shoved her down the well when he'd had the chance. She might not yet be in a position to finger him, but he suspected she wasn't far off. Too damned clever by half, that one.

His instincts told him to get rid of the girl he was holding before it was too late. After all, the grave was already prepared, so it could easily be done before the night was out. But he was so close to fulfilling the task the good Lord had set him that to fail yet again at the final hurdle after his four previous unsuccessful attempts did not bear thinking about. The Good Book said that the Almighty had infinite patience, but it also intimated that He could be ruthless and vengeful in certain circumstances, and he suspected that the latter would apply to him if he failed to deliver on his promise. Damnation was forever.

Finishing his coffee, he straightened up. Time to finish what he had started. He was sure she was almost ready now.

* * *

A heavy shower greeted Kate as she pulled off the road into the very gateway in which, unbeknown to her, Gabriella Winston had parked her car on her last ill-fated foraging trip. She switched off the engine and sat for a few minutes listening to the deluge drumming on the roof of the Mazda. Then, when the shower had eased slightly, she climbed out of the car, turning up the collar of her leather coat and sprinting diagonally across the road to the grass verge opposite. She paused for a moment when she got to the driveway leading to the house and switched on her torch, grimacing as Gabriella Winston had done, when she peered along its beam into the tunnel formed by the overhanging trees and dense undergrowth.

Taking a deep breath, she headed as quickly as her torch would allow into the blackness, splashing through puddles and occasionally tripping on projecting stones or exposed tree roots as she went. The deluge had now subsided to a drizzle, but her hair was soaked and the upper part of the blouse she was wearing under her coat was also sodden from the tiny rivulets that dribbled down her neck and onto her shoulders. Shivering and inwardly cursing her stupidity for embarking on such a madcap enterprise on her own, she pressed on nevertheless, relieved when the track she was following came to an end and she was confronted across a concrete hardstanding by a dilapidated-looking house with a barn on one side. There were no cars parked outside or any light or sound within to indicate that someone might be at home. Apart from a light above the front door, which illuminated part of the hardstanding, and a faint, suffused glow emanating from two downstairs windows, the place was in darkness.

Grateful for the absence of moon, Kate darted across the hardstanding to the corner of the barn. The double doors at the front were both securely locked, but her torch revealed a path along the side to another single door at the end. She tried the handle, expecting this door to be locked as well, but it wasn't and, as she eased it open, her hand brushed against a key in the lock beneath. Someone had been a mite careless. She slipped inside and shone her torch around the interior.

She saw the red Land Rover Defender first. Her heart skipped a beat, even though she had been half-expecting to find the vehicle there. A check of the vehicle's rear window revealed that, although there was no Mickey Mouse sticker in evidence, there was, as Gabriella Winston had found before her, a trace of dried gum on the glass and a tiny piece of coloured plastic still attached in one corner.

And if she had nursed any doubts as to whether this was the suspect vehicle, a check of the slatted wooden wall of the barn against the hard copy of the photograph run off from Gabriella Winston's memory stick revealed further evidence to suggest that she was on the right track. The beam of the torch picked out the dustbin first, its lid now in place, though completely empty. On the wall beside it, was a poster depicting a distinctive sports car, with the word "Morgan" emblazoned across the right-hand corner in large, fancy print.

For a second she simply stood there, her torch, slightly shaky, trained on the poster. The significance of what she had discovered gave rise to a grim satisfaction that was strangely mixed with other conflicting feelings.

'So it was you all the time,' she breathed, shaking her head. 'But what have you done with Tammy Logan, I wonder?'

The rain had stopped completely by the time she emerged from the barn. Strands from a newly arisen sickle moon touched the glistening broad leaves of the rhododendrons bordering the path with a spectral blue fire, and the nocturnal inhabitants of the surrounding woodland scurried about their business with a multitude of strange rustlings. Then, with a suddenness that made her jump, a colony of bats erupted from the eaves of the house, briefly blotting out the face of the moon as they soared heavenwards with a whirring of dozens of tiny wings, only to vanish into infinity almost as soon as they had appeared.

But Kate was in no mood to appreciate the magical beauty of the scene or the wonders of nature. She was acutely conscious of the risk she was putting herself in by even being in the grounds of the property, let alone — as she intended

— entering the house itself. No one knew she was here, not even Hayden, which meant there was no prospect of any backup and, were she to be discovered, she had no illusions as to what would happen to her.

Tammy Logan's kidnapper had almost certainly murdered Jennifer Roberts, as well as Gabriella Winston, Ted Southerby and Maisie Taylor — and probably the two other missing girls — and there was no guarantee that he had not put an end to Tammy Logan herself, so he was unlikely to be squeamish about killing one interfering detective sergeant. A familiar warning voice in Kate's head was urging her to get away while she could, for she was already on borrowed time.

The easiest thing to do would be to get on her mobile and call for assistance, but what if she was wrong? What if, despite all the so-called "evidence" she had uncovered, the perpetrator was actually someone else? She would not only look a fool, never to be trusted again, but could end up in very hot water over illegal entry and search without a warrant — the very thing she had criticised Hayden for suggesting two days before. No, she had to be sure of everything before she sent the balloon up and that meant getting the job she had come here to do over with as quickly as possible.

Decision made, she moved along the edge of the hardstanding, partially hidden in the shadow cast by the barn, and slipped down the side of the house. Trying to effect an entry from the front, in full view of the driveway and anyone who happened to be looking out of one of the windows, would have been stupid. She had to hope she'd be lucky enough to find an insecure door or window towards the back of the place.

The first door she came to — the one Gabriella Winston had actually used to access the house — was securely locked and every window beyond it also turned out to be tightly closed. Short of smashing the glass pane, which was obviously out of the question in the circumstances, she had no option but to press on. Within a few minutes, she found herself picking her way through denser shadow at the very back of the house, having to rely on her torch held in one hand, while the fingers of the other trailed the house wall to prevent her losing her balance on the uneven surface underfoot.

She passed two more windows and a further door, all infuriatingly secure, before she found what she was looking for. The short flight of steps dropped away into what appeared to be a paved, lower ground floor area and, investigating further, she was confronted at the bottom of the steps by another door, apparently accessing a basement of some sort. Though seemingly locked and/or bolted on the inside, the door shook when she tried the metal handle and it seemed none too secure. Closer inspection with the torch revealed that the door jamb accommodating the lock was badly split and the whole frame was rotten in places. It had obviously been neglected for a very long time.

She considered her options and then decided that, despite the noise this would involve, there was really only one. Tugging hard on the handle, she heard something crack and pulled again. The door seemed to open outwards slightly, but still held. Taking a deep breath, she slipped her torch into her pocket, gripped the door handle with both hands and, with teeth gritted, leaned back and yanked. Nothing. Then an even louder crack, a splintering sound and she crashed back into the wall behind her, still clutching the handle, and smashing her head on the rough brickwork in the process. For a few seconds, all she could see were coloured lights, and a stabbing pain sliced through her head. She also felt something wet dribble down the back of her neck, and she knew it wasn't rain.

Tossing the handle into a corner, she probed her scalp tenderly and found what felt like a nasty little wound which she dabbed at with a handkerchief. Then, retrieving her torch, she stared at her handiwork with a mixture of satisfaction and trepidation. She had managed to force the door open all right. Half of it hung from the hinge by a thread and the other half lay on the ground.

Kate took another deep, trembling breath, dabbing the wound at the back of her head with her handkerchief and trying to ignore the throbbing pain. How she was going to explain all this if her suspicions about the house turned out to be unfounded didn't bear thinking about. But what was done was done. There was one reassuring thing about it all — her suspect was obviously not at home. He would have had to be stone deaf not to hear her unorthodox mode of entry.

She grimaced. Yes, but that was not to say he wasn't already on his way.

Still holding her handkerchief to her head with one hand, she held the torch in the other and probed the darkness inside, picking out a table, a bed frame minus its mattress, rolls of carpet and a stack of plastic chairs in what was obviously quite a large basement area. She stepped into the room and saw a number of tea chests stacked, one on top of the other, against the wall on either side of the door and, to her right, a wooden staircase leading up to a closed door. The torch also picked out a switch on the wall beside the staircase, and she took a chance and crossed the room to turn it on. There was a crackling sound, a strip light flickered on and off, then steadied.

She blinked and looked around, disappointed. The harsh glare revealed no bedraggled figure of Tammy Logan chained to a wall. This was nothing but an empty storeroom.

Frustrated and demoralised, Kate decided she had no choice but to check the rest of the house. She already had her foot on the first stair when she heard it. Spinning round, she stared down the length of the basement and it was then that she saw the other door, from behind which came a soft whimpering. Forgetting the wound to her scalp and the pain still lancing through her head, she ran towards it, her heart thumping with excitement.

The door was securely locked and she could see that this was not one that would be opened by brute force.

'Tammy?' she called. 'Are you in there?'

'You're back?' the girl almost shrieked. 'Where have you been? You promised you would get me out.'

Puzzled, Kate shook her head. 'No, Tammy, I haven't been here before, but I *am* here now.'

'He killed her, didn't he?' she sobbed. 'I knew he would. He killed her — and he's going to kill me soon.'

Understanding came to her like an explosion of light. Gabriella Winston! She must have found Tammy, but the killer got to her before she could do anything about it. It all fitted, and was further evidence to support Kate's contention that the stupid young woman had been another of his victims.

'Tammy, listen to me,' she went on urgently. 'I am a police officer and my name is Kate Lewis. I am going to get you out, but you need to calm down. Where does he keep the key to the door? Do you know?'

She responded with another strangled sob.

'Tammy!' Kate's tone was harsh now, the warning voice clamouring in her head, telling her to run. 'The key. Where does he keep the key?'

'I don't know,' the girl wailed back. 'He always takes it with him.'

Muttering an oath, Kate glanced quickly around her, looking for a hook or a shelf with a key on it, but there was nothing.

'He's here!' The scream was a lot louder now and bubbling over with panic. 'I can hear his car. God help me, he's come back.'

Out of the corner of her eye, Kate glimpsed a flash of light high up on the wall on the other side of the basement, visible despite the illumination from the strip light. For the first time she noticed the two small, semi-circular windows close to the ceiling. Fanlights, which were probably visible outside at ground level. And burning through them, a pair of powerful headlights as a vehicle apparently manoeuvred in front of the house. Kate ran across the basement and snapped off the strip light, realising that it was probably too late. He would already have seen them.

She could feel the panic rising inside her. She couldn't just leave Tammy trapped in her room. Her abductor would certainly kill the girl now, just to shut her up, and then go looking for her. Where the hell was that sodding key?

She ran back to the door. She could hear the hysterical moaning of the terrified girl on the other side. She felt totally helpless and her brain was beginning to freeze up.

The sound of a car door slamming, and footsteps thudding on the hardstanding on the other side of the basement fanlights. In desperation, she ran her fingers along the head of the door frame, dislodging something, which fell with a loud "ding" on the solid floor. The key! She bent down, her torch flashing wildly around her as she scrabbled for it. Where was the damned thing?

A door flew open somewhere upstairs, hitting what sounded like a wall. Her fingers closed on the key and she jumped to her feet. She felt for the lock, found it, turned the key and jerked the door open.

She caught a glimpse of a small, square room, furnished with just a bed and a small table under a high, barred window, and then the girl practically hurled herself into her arms. But there was no time for anything except to run. Heedless of Tammy's bare feet, Kate dragged her across the basement. At the same moment the door at the top of the stairs was thrown wide and a heavy-set figure appeared on the landing, silhouetted against the light streaming down the staircase from behind him.

They made it to the door Kate had virtually demolished and up the short flight of steps, but instead of guiding Tammy back the way she herself had just come, Kate pulled her across the rough ground in front of them, ignoring her cries of pain from the gravel chips biting into the soles of her bare feet, and into the woodland beyond.

At almost the same moment, they heard the killer's feet pounding up the steps from the basement. Kate pulled Tammy down beside her in the sodden undergrowth, squeezing her arm to warn her to be quiet.

Silence. Their pursuer had paused for a second, undecided. Then, after a loud snarl of fury, he could be heard racing off in the direction from which Kate had previously come, no doubt reasoning that the fugitives would try to reach the lane at the end of the track.

Kate stayed perfectly still for a few moments, conscious of the fact that the moon had expanded from its crescent shape during her time in the basement and was now a brilliant yellow orb that blazed a cold, all-revealing trail along the strip of rough ground between the back of the house and the trees. Then, when she was satisfied that it was safe to do so, she cautiously stood up, peering through the bushes that had shielded them, while Tammy remained crouched beside her, shaking so badly that even the surrounding foliage shook.

'My — my feet,' the girl moaned softly. 'They really hurt.'

Kate bent down and, shielding the beam of her torch in her hand, took a brief look. Even in the poor light she could see the blood soaking into the leaves beneath and her mouth tightened at the sight.

'All we have to do is remain hidden until help arrives,' she said, and, feeling for her mobile phone, pulled it out of her pocket. 'I'm just going to call the station now.'

Tapping in her personal code, she swiped the screen, but instead of the usual row of icons appearing on the display, a brief message was displayed, reading, "Low Battery." A second later the screen went blank.

Trying hard not to show her panic, she felt in her pockets for the spare battery she usually had with her, but it wasn't there. She must have left it at home or in her car.

'Bad signal,' she lied, frightened that the girl might cave in altogether if she knew the truth.

'What do we do then?'

'Try to make it to the other side of the house. It might be a better signal there. We'll keep to the woodland, okay?'

Kate helped her to her feet, and, as quietly as possible, pushed through the bushes ahead of them, working her way round to the left towards the front of the house.

They reached a small, moonlit clearing among the trees and Kate paused for a moment to ensure that it was safe to cut across. It was then that she spotted the long mound of earth to one side of the open space. Frowning, she went over to it for a closer look and immediately wished she hadn't. The earth had obviously been taken from the deep trench on the other side of the mound. It didn't require too much imagination to see what it was.

The loud gasp behind her made her swing round. She hadn't realised Tammy had followed her and was now staring at the trench in horror.

'It's — it's a grave,' the terrified girl choked. 'He's dug it for me!'

Kate reached out to comfort her but she was too late. Tammy's legs suddenly folded under her. Then Kate saw the heavy-set figure emerge from the trees in front of them. The twin barrels of the shotgun pointing at Kate's chest seemed to bore into her very soul.

'I suppose I shall have to dig another one, now there's two of you,' said Tom Reeves.

CHAPTER 27

The mournful hoot of an owl floated on the still air from the depths of the woodland and a horse whinnied somewhere beyond the trees. Kate stared at the motionless figure of her colleague with a mixture of shock and disbelief. The tin numerals and sergeant's stripes on the epaulettes of his uniform glinted in the moonlight, frivolous adornments in stark contrast with the deadly weapon in his hands.

'Put the shotgun down, Tom,' she said in as level a tone as she could muster, casting a brief, concerned glance at the girl lying at her feet. 'This isn't you.'

Reeves shook his head. 'No can do, Kate. Everything's gone too far now.'

'For heaven's sake, man,' she blurted out, 'I'm your friend. Your colleague.'

He nodded. 'I know and I'm sorry it's had to come to this, but you shouldn't have interfered.'

'So, what about the oath you took to protect people?'

'Already broken, I'm afraid. What you see is just a man in a uniform. You know, when it comes down to it, the uniform doesn't mean a thing. It's the person inside that's relevant — good or bad.' He emitted a loud sigh. 'So, tell me, how did I give myself away? You might as well — while you still can.'

She swallowed hard. Fighting down her panic, she forced herself to stay calm and play along with him. She related, in a cracked, hesitant voice that didn't sound at all like her own, the conclusion she and Hayden had come to after the murder of Jennifer Roberts — that the perpetrator had to be one of their own colleagues.

'But why me?' he demanded.

'There — there were lots of pointers,' she said through the tremor in her voice, 'though they weren't obvious at first — not until I began to put two and two together.'

'So where exactly did I go wrong? I thought I'd covered my tracks pretty well.'

She swallowed again, conscious of the fact that what she told him now could well offend his ego and precipitate her execution. Nevertheless, she forced herself to carry on, every so often her gaze darting to the shotgun.

'You — you always seemed to be around asking questions while the investigation was going on,' she said at length, 'including being conveniently on hand when Maisie Taylor's body was found. Then you just happened to be on duty when the CID office was screwed tonight, though it isn't clear to me why you'd needed to snoop around in there again, as I assume you'd obviously already got what you wanted from Jennifer Roberts's file when I found you sitting on the edge of my desk the previous day with the thing under your backside—'

'Oh, I got the address from the file all right,' he interjected, seemingly unperturbed by the acid in her tone. His mouth twisted into a contemptuous sneer. 'But I wanted to see what else Somerset's "ace detective" may have found out. Not much, going by what I could glean from the notes I went through in your briefcase tonight. Most of it seemed to be just guesswork, stabs in the dark.'

'It was a lot more than bloody guesswork,' she snapped, riled in spite of her precarious situation. 'It was all the Freudian slips you made that really clinched things. Tonight, for instance, you asked me if anything was missing, not from the office generally, but specifically from my briefcase. How could you have known that that was what the so-called intruder was interested in unless you were that intruder? Before that, there was that slip of the tongue as you were quizzing me at the nick about the murder of Jennifer Roberts. You expressed sympathy for her and said "after all she'd been through with that attack on her a couple of years ago." I checked the intranet circulation in the LIO's office afterwards and it did not mention anything about her past history, so how could you have known about the attack unless it was you that had carried it out?'

'I could have read about it in some internal circulation the year before and remembered the details,' he pointed out.

'Maybe you could, but what your slip-ups did was to make me remember something even more significant, which had been bugging me ever since the murder of Gabriella Winston. In short, when I told you she had been found dead, you suggested someone must have "forced the vodka down her throat." But I never said what we thought was in the bottle we found by the pool, so how could you have known that it was vodka — unless you were the one who'd put it there?'

'Clever girl,' he sneered. 'I'd clap if I didn't have my hands full. It's clear to me now that when I lured you to that well in the derelict, I should have finished the job and made sure you actually fell. Big mistake.'

He gave another deep sigh. 'Still, it's all water under the bridge now, isn't it?'

She saw him tense and the shotgun rose a few more inches. She visualised, with a tight, watery feeling in her bowels, his finger tightening on one of the twin triggers.

'Why are you doing this, Tom?' she blurted out desperately. 'Are you really such a monster?' It was a touch and go remark, which she knew could go either way.

For a moment he just stared at her. 'Monster?' he echoed and shook his head several times, as if to clear his vision. 'I'm no monster,' he muttered defensively, more to himself than anyone. There was a heavy frown on his face now, which was plainly visible in the bright moonlight, and he seemed to be mentally wrestling with his thoughts, perhaps trying to rationalise what he had done or what he was about to do.

'It is the Lord's will,' he said in a puzzled, matter-of-fact tone, as if the answer to the question was patently obvious. 'The Lord has demanded it. I have sinned and I must seek redemption.'

This change in his demeanour was so abrupt it caught Kate by surprise. It was as though her words had triggered a chemical reaction in his brain and in a single moment, he had become another person — someone who had been hiding inside him, covertly looking out and waiting for an opportunity to engineer some kind of *Jekyll and Hyde* metamorphosis.

At first, she was thrown — not sure whether the change was genuine or whether he was simply playacting — and she didn't know how to respond.

The shotgun had dipped slightly and was now pointing at her stomach. But the downward movement gave her little comfort in the present circumstances. If he had genuinely flipped, he was just as likely to pull the trigger by accident as intentionally, and a blast in the stomach was as bad as one in the chest — probably a lot worse, as it would result in a more lingering, agonising death.

She considered her next question very carefully. 'And how can killing people be the will of the Lord, Tom?' she said, wincing inside as she asked it.

He snorted, the gun wavering unsteadily in his hands. 'They are heathens and would frustrate the Lord's purpose. They must be destroyed so that I may complete the work He has given me.'

'And how will you do that?'

'By saving the soul of the harlot, so that she may enter His glorious kingdom cleansed of her wickedness.'

'And which harlot is that?' she said.

She watched his face, waiting for him to revert back to his normal self, dropping the pretence as he tired of the game. But it didn't happen.

His face screwed itself up into an even tighter frown.

'She is like the rest,' he rasped, his tone savage now, 'every one of them depraved temptresses. Fuelled by drugs and alcohol they inveigle men into succumbing to their lustful ways. They walk around half-naked, brazenly showing off their bodies to all and sundry and inviting defilement. They must be made to repent in the eyes of the Lord. They must be cleansed.'

He was no longer looking at her directly, Kate noticed, but over her shoulder, as if at something only he could see. The shotgun dipped a little more and at the same time the girl stirred. Kate swallowed and her jaw tightened. The last thing she needed was for Tammy to suddenly jump up or dissolve into a fit of crying, shaking Reeves out of his trance-like state and precipitating a discharge from those twin barrels.

Taking a chance, she nudged the girl with her foot, hoping this got the message across.

'Janice would not repent,' Reeves went on. 'The devil had corrupted her and she had become his. I tried to resist her wicked wiles, but I was weak and she tempted me with her body into betraying the Lord through my lust. She had to be punished, you see?'

'Who is Janice, Tom?' Kate said. 'Where is she now?'

No response. He was now looking directly at her, but his gaze remained unfocused. She waited for the mocking grin, but it still did not materialise. He seemed to be lost in some kind of self-induced trance. It was weird, and left her at a loss. How should she play this?

'She — she went away,' he said distantly, 'but now she has come back to taunt me.'

The shotgun was now pointing at the ground. Should she tackle him or use her foot to try to surreptitiously encourage Tammy to crawl away into the relative safety of the woodland? It was an agonising dilemma. But as she thought about it, the decision was taken out of her hands.

The dark figure seemed to come from nowhere. One minute there was nothing and the next it was bearing down on Reeves from behind like a runaway train. The policeman must have sensed the movement behind him and he spun round. But he was already too late. The shotgun finally discharged with an ear-spitting bang, as the muscular figure of Tony Samuel crashed into him, sending the gun spinning into the adjoining undergrowth and bringing him to the ground. Tammy was on her feet now, waving her arms hysterically and screaming, and, as Kate recovered from the shock and lurched forward, she saw one of the two struggling bodies on the ground disentangle itself and scramble to its feet. It was Reeves and, as Samuel made a grab for his leg, he kicked him viciously in the head and charged off towards the far corner of the house. In seconds, he had vanished into the shadows.

Kate made no effort to give chase. It was pointless to even try. Her brain was numb, her whole body shook. She was even unaware of Tammy rushing across to where Tony Samuel lay, very still, on the ground.

After a few moments, Tammy's sobs cut through her paralysis and she stumbled unsteadily forward.

She pulled the girl off him. One side of Samuel's face was a bloody mess. Thinking that he may have caught part of the shotgun blast, she got down on her knees and bent over him to feel for a pulse in his throat. She was totally unprepared for his sudden movement, or the sudden gleam of his eyes as a broad grin practically split his face in half.

'Hiya, Sarge,' he said. 'Good 'ere, innit?'

* * *

It turned out that Reeves's kick had gashed Samuel's temple. Otherwise, he was bruised but miraculously uninjured.

His obvious joy and relief at rescuing Tammy from a horrible death was a lesson to anyone prone to judging a book by its cover.

Samuel may have given Tammy a "slap" from time to time, as he had admitted to Kate at the start of the whole business.

He may have beaten up Mickey Bishop in the mistaken belief that he was responsible for his girlfriend's disappearance. He may have broken the nose of the licensee of the Soldier's Arms, but Kate felt nothing but admiration for this inarticulate man and his unswerving devotion to the girl he loved.

'So how the hell did you know I was here?' Kate exclaimed, after retrieving the shotgun from the undergrowth and using Samuel's mobile to call for assistance.

'Been tailin' you for ages,' he said with another grin, pulling away from Tammy. 'Seen you leave the cop shop tonight and fought I'd clock where you was going.'

Kate nodded. 'Well, it's a bloody good job you did.'

It took the "assistance" twenty minutes to arrive at the front of the house, where Kate was waiting with both Tammy Logan and Tony Samuel. Roscoe turned up a further fifteen minutes later, smelling of beer.

'No trace of Reeves,' the DI growled, watching Samuel being led away in handcuffs, a sticking plaster covering the cut on his head. 'Bastard drove over here in that.' He waved a hand towards a marked police patrol car parked close to the house. 'His own Volvo V70 is still at the nick, so he must either be on foot or he has other wheels.'

'The Land Rover we were looking for was in the barn,' Kate said.

Roscoe shook his head. 'Well, it isn't there now and, as you can see, the doors are wide open.'

'Exactly, so he must have taken that then, mustn't he? He had hidden it away out of sight, probably when the balloon went up after he'd stiffed Maisie Taylor, for it was obviously the 'Drover that Denise Merchant heard drive up close to her place that night.'

She turned aside to shout at the two officers leading Samuel away. 'Go easy on him, lads. He saved our lives.'

Roscoe scowled. 'But if Reeves drove there in his 'Drover that night, how come he managed to turn up at the scene afterwards in a bloody job car? Bit difficult to drive two cars at the same time, I would have thought.'

'Easy,' she said. 'This place is only a couple of miles away from the village. All he had to do was leave the police motor here, pop out in the Defender to stiff Taylor, then drive back and collect the job car. His Volvo would have been waiting for him when he got back to Highbridge nick after the Taylor incident. And don't forget, he was a sergeant — a shift supervisor — so he had a roving commission. He could go anywhere he chose in the Highbridge area when he was out on patrol. No questions would be asked as to where he was, unless something came up — like Taylor's murder — and, from what Tammy Logan told me, he seems to have been back and forth at all times of the day and night, checking on her.'

'Funny that she never twigged he was a copper, though, if he was in uniform.'

Kate shrugged. 'Not really. Apparently, when he came to see her, he often had a long-sleeved pullover on and other times he would have been off duty anyway, in line with his shifts. Also, as I remember it, he had two rostered rest days in the middle of it all.'

Roscoe grunted, popping some gum in his mouth. 'Okay, points noted. But, getting back to the motor he's now driving, it seems we're looking for an old, red Land Rover Defender with a grey roof, driven by a uniformed copper. That should attract a bit of attention in daylight, don't you think? Which means he's not likely to get very far once we put out a circular. I'd put money on it.'

She frowned. 'If he intends bothering to try,' she said slowly, a disturbing thought beginning to take shape in her mind.

He stopped in mid-chew. 'What are you getting at?'

'Well, he's obviously suffering from some sort of deep-seated psychosis. That became apparent when I was talking to him. He was off with the fairies towards the end, just before Samuel turned up — apparently hung up on some sort of religious crusade.'

'Forget the bloody fairies. I asked you what you were getting at.'

'Well, he was talking a lot about the need for repentance before the Lord, and harlots being cleansed.'

'So, he flipped. How does that help us to find him?'

She stared at him levelly. 'He's a sidesman at the local church and is obviously very religious. I think that's what has motivated him all this time. And where would someone with those kinds of beliefs be likely to go to seek solace?'

But Roscoe was already making for his car. 'The church,' he shouted over his shoulder. 'The sodding village church.'

* * *

The church bell was tolling in a haphazard sort of way when Roscoe, Kate and a number of uniformed police officers turned up at the gates.

Lights burned eerily behind the stained-glass windows, and the porch doors stood wide open. Spirals of marsh mist curled around their feet as they pushed through into the nave. There seemed to be no one around, but then a large, overweight figure in a dressing gown appeared through a side door and beckoned to them. It was the Rev Salter, white-faced and grave.

'I — I heard the bells,' he croaked, 'and went to check . . .'

His voice trailed off. He sank onto a nearby pew and gestured towards the door through which he had just emerged.

Kate was through it first and way ahead of a panting, out of condition Roscoe on the narrow staircase leading to the belfry. She had an awful premonition of what she would find when she reached it, and those fears were immediately realised the moment she pushed open the wooden door and stepped inside.

Like Jennifer Roberts before him, Tom Reeves was not a pretty sight. His uniform tunic was lying in a bundle on the floor beside an overturned stool and he was swinging in a gentle side-to-side, up and down motion from one of the bell ropes. His final act of repentance before the Lord he knew he had betrayed.

* * *

Hayden had just woken up when Kate climbed into bed beside him.

'Sleep well?' he asked.

Not for the first time since she had married him, she stared at her husband in utter incredulity. 'Didn't you read the note I left?'

He wriggled up into a sitting position, puzzled for a second or two. 'Oh that. Er — yes. 'Course, I read it. Sorry I didn't wait up for you, but I was dog tired.' He beamed happily at her. 'Didn't even feel you come to bed, in fact. Any luck with the briefcase in the end?'

But she didn't answer his question. She couldn't, she was completely lost for words. When eventually she found her voice, she said briefly, 'Goodnight, Hayden,' turned over and promptly went to sleep.

AFTER THE FACT

The Rev John Salter sat for several minutes with his head in his hands while Kate waited patiently for him to speak. Finally, he raised his head, sat back in the swivel chair and sighed. With Roscoe and Kate both sitting opposite him — Roscoe in the only other chair and Kate on a pile of books in the corner — the little study seemed even smaller than usual. It was now just over a fortnight since Tom Reeves had committed suicide and, with an eye on the inevitable inquest, Roscoe had called for a meeting with the vicar to obtain some background information for the covering report he had to prepare for the coroner's benefit.

'Tom was a very troubled man,' Salter explained. 'We had many discussions here. It seemed to me that he had turned to religion for some kind of inner peace. You know his wife died suddenly?'

Kate nodded. 'Yes, I did know. A sudden brain haemorrhage, I heard.'

He nodded. 'It hit him really hard. They were a devoted couple. And that on top of his PTSD—'

'What PTSD?' Roscoe growled. 'I'm sure the force wasn't aware of that.'

Another nod. 'No, Inspector, it wouldn't have been. He refused to accept that he was suffering from it and was quite adept at concealing his problem. He used to come and see me on a fairly regular basis — I suppose because he needed to unload on someone and I *am* a pretty good listener. It was the army, you see. He served several terms in Afghanistan and saw things that no human being should ever have to witness. It obviously left an indelible mark on his mind.'

'Why didn't you report this to us?' Roscoe demanded. 'He was a serving police officer and we should have been told about it.'

Salter shook his head. 'It was not my place to do so, and anyway, he talked to me in strict confidence and, as a minister, I cannot break a confidence.'

'Did he tell you in *confidence* that he was also planning to murder half the village?' Roscoe added viciously.

Salter flinched and coloured up. 'No, he didn't,' he snapped, suddenly angry, 'and if I had known what was going on in that tortured mind of his I would obviously have told the authorities.'

Plainly embarrassed by her boss's blatant ignorance, Kate threw Roscoe a critical glance. 'I understand he had a daughter? I hadn't realised that before.'

Salter grimaced. 'Yes, Janice, and she was part of his problem. She was only about twenty-two or twenty-three when her mother died. They had been very close, and it had a bad impact on her. Following her mother's passing, Janice kicked over the traces and became something of a thorn in Tom's side. You know, getting into bad company, using cocaine, wearing skimpy, revealing hippy-type clothes — the sort of behaviours that are every parent's nightmare. I believe the modern term for it is "making a statement."'

'But surely she was entitled to do what she liked at her age?' Kate said.

Salter sighed again. 'Yes, but she was still living at home, and Tom was very strict. Also, by that time, he had become almost fanatically religious. Even after I had counselled him, he still could not accept that she was beyond his control. Things came to a head a few years ago when, against Tom's wishes, she went to Glastonbury Festival. Tom went after her and found her in a tent with a young man — er, naked. It seems the lad fled. Tom dragged her back to his car and took her home.' He shrugged. 'He never saw her again. She upped and left, informing him that she was going to travel the world—'

'And he told you all this?' Roscoe interjected.

'Yes. He came and saw me in a bit of a state, asking me for advice. I told him just to let her go, in the hope that she would come back home when she had got all the anger and resentment out of her system.'

'The thing is, Reverend,' Kate put in quickly, as Roscoe opened his mouth to say something else, 'we have checked, and Janice didn't hold a passport, so she couldn't have got very far. Furthermore, we have found three bodies buried in the woodland behind Tom Reeves's house. All the deceased are female. Two we believe to be missing persons — Brenda Gain and Madelaine Cross.' Her mouth tightened. 'The third was wearing a gold bracelet inscribed with the name "Janice."'

Salter's face now wore a look of absolute horror. 'He — he killed his own daughter? God have mercy on his soul.'

Roscoe nodded. 'We believe it could have been an accident, but it probably set him on the road he took.'

'According to a criminal psychologist we have consulted,' Kate said, 'it is likely that he was attempting to assuage the guilt that was eating away at him and secure his own redemption by kidnapping other young girls of about the same age and appearance as Janice and trying to change their behaviour through forcing them to repent — or, as he put it to me that last night, by "cleansing" them. This fits in with what Tammy Logan told us about how he treated her during the time she was held captive. Glastonbury Festival must have been the trigger because it happened every year it took place. Doubtless he would have continued with his unholy crusade if we had not intervened.'

'But . . . but to kill his own daughter,' Salter said, 'and . . . and all those other young girls . . .'

Kate stared at him for a moment, as if deliberating on whether or not to reveal what else he'd done, when Roscoe, with a characteristic lack of sensitivity, beat her to it.

'It appears that that wasn't all he did to her,' he said grimly. 'From what Tammy Roberts was able to tell us, it seems likely that Reeves developed an unhealthy interest in his own daughter. We think Reeves probably sexually assaulted Janice and murdered her to cover up his crime.'

It was plain that Salter was having great difficulty coming to terms with what he was hearing. 'But that would make him a . . . a monster,' he whispered.

Kate nodded. 'Yes, I'm afraid there was a monster lurking within him. The psychologist suggested that he was probably suffering from a multiple personality disorder. In effect, he was two people: the friendly, trustworthy copper on the one hand, but underneath lurked another person, who had a serious mental condition that could be triggered at any time. We can only think that his untreated PTSD, coupled with the traumatic death of his beloved wife, sent him over the edge, and that Janice was the last straw. Perversely, even though it was he who had sexually assaulted his own daughter, he blamed her and every other young woman for what he himself had done.'

'So, what happens now?' Salter said, still visibly shaken.

'We sort out the legal and procedural formalities,' Roscoe growled, standing up, 'arrange an inquest, then bury the bastard in the deepest hole we can find!'

'Was it really necessary to say that?' Kate said as they were on their way back to Roscoe's car.

He cast her a sidelong glance. 'Always believe in speaking my mind.'

'Then I'll speak mine,' Kate replied. 'With respect, *sir*, you are a prize arsehole!'

'At least they're useful,' he said with a wolfish grin. 'Oh, by the way, you can be the first to know — I've finally decided to retire.'

'Thank God for that,' she said.

THE END

AUTHOR'S NOTE

Although the action of this novel takes place in the real geographical area of Avon and Somerset, the story itself and all the characters therein are fictitious. At the time of writing, there is no police station in Highbridge. This entirely fictitious setting was created from the author's imagination and there is no connection between any existing police station or personnel in the force and the content of the novel. I would also point out that I have used some poetic licence in relation to the local police structure as well as the police procedures that are followed, in order to meet the requirements of the plot. The novel is intended to be primarily a crime thriller and does not profess to be a detailed police procedural, even though the policing background depicted in the novel is broadly in accord with the national picture. I trust that these small departures from fact will not spoil the reading enjoyment of serving or retired police officers, for whom I have the utmost respect.

David Hodges, 2020

ALSO BY DAVID HODGES

DETECTIVE KATE HAMBLIN MYSTERY SERIES

Book 1: MURDER ON THE LEVELS
Book 2: REVENGE ON THE LEVELS
Book 3: FEAR ON THE LEVELS
Book 4: KILLER ON THE LEVELS
Book 5: SECRETS ON THE LEVELS
Book 6: DEATH ON THE LEVELS
Book 7: POISON ON THE LEVELS

FREE KINDLE BOOKS

Please join our mailing list for free Kindle books and new releases, including crime thrillers, mysteries, romance and more.

www.joffebooks.com

Thank you for reading this book. If you enjoyed it please leave feedback on Amazon or Goodreads, and if there is anything we missed or you have a question about then please get in touch. The author and publishing team appreciate your feedback and time reading this book.

We're very grateful to eagle-eyed readers who take the time to contact us. Please send any errors you find to corrections@joffebooks.com

Printed in Great Britain
by Amazon

60914384R00168